EVEN THE DEAD WILL BLEED

PRAISE FOR EVEN THE DEAD WILL BLEED

"While the previous books were more couched in survival, zombie-smashing action, this gritty thriller is a classic revenge novel, and the hardness of the writing reflects that. Ramirez has delved deep into these characters to pull out relatable and inspiring elements of human nature. The body count and gory detail in this novel is no less impressive than in the others, but there is more savage realism here, as the enemies are not always the undead draggers and psychopathic cutters. The action-filled scenes crackle with electricity and the dialogue is sharp and believable."

— SELF-PUBLISHING REVIEW

"This action-packed zombie gore-fest is not for the faint of heart as carnage and rising body counts are described in stomach churning, gruesome detail, but at no point is character development sacrificed. There is a perfect balance of character growth and development, action, intrigue, and suspense that will keep the reader hooked from the first page to the ultimate conclusion. I've read my fair share of zombie style books, and this one certainly stands up there with the best. It's not your run-of-the-mill, mass-produced, zombie book; rather, it is intricately designed, well executed, imaginative, and plausible."

— READERS' FAVORITE

"Dave Pulaski is what makes this series so brilliant—a character Ramirez has drawn with great skill, who manages to be a sympathetic antihero, a troubled everyman, and an action lead all at once. His internal struggles and his interactions with other characters ensure that Ramirez keeps a rich seam of humanity running alongside the horrific events he depicts, making for a balanced read that has far more substance than one may initially expect from a zombie thriller. A conclusion that manages to excite as much as it does satisfy, *Even the Dead Will Bleed* brings the series to an epic conclusion, but also leaves enough untied that I'd be extremely keen for Ramirez to revisit this brilliantly built world at some point in the future."

— THE BOOKBAG

BOOKS BY STEVEN RAMIREZ

LITERARY FICTION

Let's Get Lost

HELLBORN SERIES

Tell Me When I'm Dead

Dead Is All You Get

Even The Dead Will Bleed

HARD TO KILL SERIES

Brandon's Last Words

Faithless

SARAH GREENE MYSTERIES

The Girl in the Mirror

House of the Shrieking Woman

The Blood She Wore

OTHER BOOKS

Chainsaw Honeymoon

Come As You Are: A Short Novel and Nine Stories

Come As You Are: A Novella

Glass Highway

Los Angeles, CA

stevenramirez.com

Publisher's Note: This is a work of fiction. Names, characters, places, and incidents are a product of the author's imagination. Any opinions expressed belong to the characters and should not be confused with those of the author. Locales and public names are sometimes used for atmospheric purposes. Any resemblance to actual people, living or dead, or businesses, companies, events, institutions, or locales is coincidental.

Even The Dead Will Bleed / Hellborn Series Book 3 / Steven Ramirez. 3rd ed.

Paperback: 978-1-949108-22-4

EPUB: 978-1-949108-23-1

Kindle: 978-1-949108-24-8

Audiobook: 978-1-949108-34-7

Library of Congress Control Number: 2023900375

Edited by Shannon A. Thompson

Cover design by Damonza

For David Latt and David Rimawi. Your kindness and generosity continue to inspire me.

EVEN THE DEAD WILL BLEED

HELLBORN SERIES BOOK 3

STEVEN RAMIREZ

glass highway

I had had enough. The blood was pounding in my head so hard that I felt about to explode. I aimed my gun at Cathcart and shot him four times in the face.

— JAMES ELLROY, *BROWN'S REQUIEM*

EVEN THE DEAD WILL BLEED

PART ONE

THE RUSSIAN GIRL

ONE

The dream is always the same. Holly trembling on the cave floor, her hands imploring me to prevent what we both know can't be stopped. And me unable to get to her because my feet are sawed off at the ankles. A gun fires. Someone screams as the bullet tears through my wife's head. But instead of blood, white light streams out of the hole, leaving the Holly I knew behind and taking her soul with it. After that, I'm alone at the bottom of a pit, calling her name. Unable to hear my own voice.

The angel woke me before dawn. I recognized the electric tickle down my spine and the whispering—like wind through a tiny forest. It always happened in the middle of a thin, hard sleep. I'd open my eyes, and she was there.

When I first saw her in the church, she was filthy. Ten years old, with blonde hair and hurt green eyes. Wearing shorts and a bloody T-shirt with the words *Li'l Princess* splashed across the front. She was identical to the little girl I'd put down at Shasta Lake when I was new to the whole undead-killing thing.

She was singing a hymn when I found her. And now, here she was again—clean, her hair luminous. She called herself Holly. I didn't know if God was being cruel on purpose since that was also my late wife's name. But I came to accept it.

My arm ached—I needed to change the bandage. I'd gotten into a fight in Quartzsite. It was early morning. Some tool thought I'd stolen his limonite cubes. As he stumbled out of a bar called The Lazy Eye, he noticed someone had broken into his truck. I had just come out of the mini-mart next door. Seeing me, he jumped to conclusions.

You piece of shit!" he said. "Where are they?"

This kind of thing was typical. Violence out of nowhere, like a flash fire in a weed lot. I seemed to attract it. Setting down my groceries, I scanned my surroundings. There were no security cameras, and the bar was closed. When I left the mini-mart, the clerk was busy stocking beer. No cars in either direction. The place was deserted except for a mangy yellow dog growling as it tore at a black garbage bag.

The soak didn't have a gun, but he carried a hunting knife. We decided to do it in the parking lot. He made the first move—tried to carve a hole in my face. I let him come at me and used his momentum to send him sailing past onto the dirty asphalt. It was a good plan, except the knife nicked me as he went by. Spitting out bloody, broken teeth, he got to his feet. His nose and forehead were scraped raw. He looked like he could use a puke.

"Gimme back the damn cubes!" he said.

Ignoring my injured arm, I watched and waited. "I didn't take them."

"Give 'em back."

This was going nowhere. I was supposed to be on the

road. My instincts told me to kill him and be done with it. I'd engaged in so much violence these past weeks and months. What was one more stupid drunk? But I wasn't in Tres Marias anymore. And despite the constant rage I carried inside, I was human—this person was human. Still, I needed it to end.

As he came at me with the knife, I shot him in the leg. His knee buckled, and he howled in pain. I waited for him to go down. Then, kicking away the blade, I dragged his mealy ass behind an abandoned Shell station and propped him up against the wall.

"Don't kill me, mister," he said, pissing himself. "You can have the limonite cubes—I don't even care…"

Back in the day, when I used to get drunk with my best friend Jim, I don't think I ever looked half as bad as this loser. Like me, he was in his twenties. Reeked of vinegar and urine. I wondered if he would make it to thirty. Something told me he wouldn't.

"Keep pressure on it." I took his hand and pressed it against the wound. "And for the record, I didn't take your limonite cubes."

"Don't matter." He was gibbering now. "They weren't even mine."

Just in case, I threw away the ball cap and jacket. I was pretty sure the mini-mart security camera hadn't caught my face. All the cops would have to go on was the clothes. I'd parked my truck on a different street, so no one could report a license plate. This was good practice for LA—a lesson in staying anonymous.

I left the sad idiot whimpering there and promised to call 911. Not that he deserved it. As I walked away, he told me to go to hell.

If only he knew.

TWO

Since arriving in LA, I'd slept poorly because of my nightmare. And also, well... I'll get to that in a minute. It seemed like I only ever dozed off in the early morning hours. The good news? I had a fat wallet thanks to my former employer, Black Dragon Security. Because Holly died while working for them, they paid out big.

I didn't want anyone to know where I was. So, instead of driving straight to Los Angeles as planned, I made a detour to Phoenix, where I withdrew all the cash. Then I ditched the vehicle my friend Guthrie Manson had lent me and bought a used Dodge truck. Knowing Warnick, he would've discovered the car rental in Redding. After that, the trail dead-ended.

When I arrived, I stashed the weapons and cash in a public storage facility. I rented a cheap apartment off First Street in Boyle Heights. The building was near the historic Evergreen Cemetery. If I died, which was likely, I'd end up in a potter's field. No name. No headstone. No one to pray for me.

I bet you're wondering why I chose this life. It wasn't that

I didn't value my friends. There were a lot of things I didn't care about. But Griffin, Fabian, and Warnick were everything to me, especially now that my wife was gone. Though we weren't related by blood, they were the only family I had.

After what happened in Tres Marias, I promised myself I would kill the people responsible. And I couldn't do that working for Black Dragon. I needed to settle things here and now, and I knew exactly what to do. Since leaving, I'd thought of little else.

Baseborn Identity Research. The name was bizarre and amorphous, like something out of *Resident Evil*. It was located in an industrial park in East Los Angeles, near Monterey Park. When I googled it, I didn't find much. I didn't even know what they did—officially. Whoever they were, they were deeply connected to Robbin-Sear, the secretive government-funded company behind the outbreak that wiped out my town.

How did I know all this? When our squad teamed up with the National Guard to raid a hidden lab in Mt. Shasta, we found people in hazmat suits loading test subjects onto semi-trailer trucks. Guess whose name was printed on the side. Yeah—Baseborn Identity Research. Presumably, the creatures were being transferred for further study.

This was Phase Two of the experiment from hell. Phase One consisted of infecting a local populace with a virus derived from rabies. As it spread, it killed its victims, transforming them into the slow-moving undead. *Draggers*. These unholy creatures existed for one purpose—to eat the flesh of the living. But something unexpected happened. They evolved.

The newly infected survived the transformation intact. And they got faster. Unlike the others, they were alive and could easily pass as regular people. Except they still craved long pig. And with the psychotic calmness of a surgeon, they carved up their prey and ate the warm, pulsating flesh as the victim screamed. It doesn't get any fresher than that.

I called this new breed *cutters*. Sooner or later, the dark forces behind the experiment would lose control of these high-functioning sociopaths. They'd get loose and begin feeding on an unsuspecting population. When that happened, it would be too late.

"They're coming," the angel said.

I looked into the eyes I knew so well. She reached out a small, soft hand with perfect nails and stroked my cheek. It was the first time she'd touched me since that awful night at St. Monica's when I knelt at the altar with Holly's body lying broken and bloody before me. I thought the angel's skin would be warm. But it was cool, like a shady spot under a willow in summer.

"Do not be afraid."

She'd said that earlier and tried not to show concern. But I could see she was worried. I used to believe in guardian angels thanks to my mother and Catholic school. Mine was Maurice, after the third-century Roman soldier who became a saint because he died for his faith. I never saw him, though— not once. The angel, I mean.

He didn't keep me out of trouble. Never helped me fight off the bullies. Never stopped me from taking my first drink. Free will's a loose-mouthed bitch, I guess. This one—the blonde angel—was different. She looked out for me. But for how long?

"When?" I said.

"Soon."

I climbed out of bed wearing only boxers and stood at the window facing west. The angel didn't seem to mind that I wasn't dressed. Cheap cream-colored curtains meant to resemble lace hung loosely from a flimsy rail. Ignoring the cockroach droppings on the sill, I peered down at the street.

Traffic was light in the still, gray morning. Short Latinas scurried up and down the sidewalks, late for something. Many pulled along young children in jeans and hoodies and wearing oversize backpacks. Everyone's movements were furtive.

Thunder rumbled in the distance. Soon, raindrops hit the glass, turning into rivulets that wept like Jesus at Gethsemane. The angel stood beside me, looking out the window and holding my hand. I would've been lost to evil forever if she hadn't stuck by me.

"I need more," I said.

She looked at me darkly. "You'll know them by the bodies they leave behind." Then she pointed a rosy finger. "Look!"

A black Escalade cruised past. Not bothering to slow for pedestrians, it turned at the corner and vanished. The graysuits didn't know where I lived—not yet. Otherwise, they would've stopped in front of my building. But they were getting closer. I didn't have much time.

"Don't do it, David," she said.

I felt her eyes imploring me and refused to meet her gaze. "I have to."

"But anyone who hates a brother or sister is in the darkness and walks around in the darkness. They do not know where they are going, because the darkness has blinded them."

"These devils *are* the darkness," I said. "I'm going to find them and kill them."

The rain became a steady patter, like chittering fairies at a cocktail party. The angel's hand evaporated in mine, and when I looked, she was gone. I knew she was mad at me, but it didn't matter. At least she'd warned me. Something—or someone—bad was coming. I had the feeling it wasn't the gray-suits. It was worse.

I thought about the thousands of innocents who'd died in Tres Marias and the hundreds of nightmare-plagued survivors. And there would be more bloodshed, more suffering. What was I supposed to do—let it happen again? The angel had warned me not to hate. Screw that. Hate implied action.

It was time to get moving.

THREE

When you're paranoid, everything looks like a threat. I'd picked this building because of its underground parking, and I got lucky. The space they had assigned me was on the alley side. Walking to my truck, I noticed movement in the shadows and froze.

I didn't live in the best neighborhood. Every once in a while, a junkie or a gangbanger would sneak in and wait till someone left for work. Then he'd pull out a weapon and rob the poor bastard. If the victim was a woman, he might do worse. Though I had plenty of guns, I didn't want to draw attention to myself. Inching closer, I gripped my VIPERTEK stun gun, ready to deliver nineteen million volts to the asswipe's neck.

It was Cuco, the maintenance man. In a twist of logic only a Mexican would understand, that was the nickname his family had blessed him with. His given name was Refugio. I'm not the smartest guy. But seriously, how do you get *Cuco* from that? I guessed he was in his mid-fifties. Lean and weathered, with straight black-brown hair and a missing molar you could see when he laughed. He never said much and worked hard—seven days a week. Fixing leaky pipes, rewiring light fixtures, and replacing apartment doors kicked in by the cops. And painting. He was always touching up this or that.

Today, he was on his way to the dumpsters, carrying two large garbage bags bursting with strips of wet Sheetrock. The bulging arm muscles and knife scars told me he'd had an interesting life. He was a good guy. Never questioned why a gringo decided to move into a building filled with immigrants from Mexico and Central America.

"¿Qué tal?" I said.

Grunting, he tossed the bags into the trash and slammed the lid shut. "Bien bien."

"So, anything?"

I liked slipping him twenty bucks now and then to keep an eye on my truck and alert me whenever he noticed anyone suspicious.

"The usual. Putas. Drug dealers. Magazine salesmen."

Even though he'd given me the all-clear, I wanted to make my own inspection. His crafty, sparkling brown eyes tracked me as I strode towards the street and peered out the small opening leading to the sidewalk. I did the same on the opposite side, facing the alley. As a final check, I returned to the garage entrance and looked out from behind the closed gate as sheets of rainwater slithered down the mottled driveway.

Something struck the bars. My right hand went for the stun gun tucked in my pocket. It was only a blue-green bouncy ball. A beat later, a kid in a short raincoat who looked to be around seven came running after it. His exasperated mother called to him in Spanish over the sound of the downpour. She was on the sidewalk, sheltering an infant under a large pink-and-purple umbrella.

"She sounds mad," I said.

Shrugging, he gave me a missing-teeth smile and, grabbing the ball, scurried up the driveway. When I got to my truck, I found the Mexican scratching his cheek. He was grinning.

"Want me to grab my machete and cut you a path?" he said.

"Only if *you* clean up the blood."

Laughing, he gave me a wave as I climbed in and headed out. Entering the street, I kept a lookout for black Escalades.

I thought about the angel's warning. For the first time since leaving Tres Marias, I questioned my mission. If this had been the old days and I lost Holly, I'd be lying dead drunk somewhere. Maybe on Skid Row, wasting away like those other damned souls. Though I still had the craving—and always would—my desire for revenge was stronger.

There was a Catholic church near the cemetery—Nuestra Señora del Rosario de Talpa. Inside were whitewashed walls and exposed wood beams on the ceiling. Morning Mass had ended, and the faithful were filing out. I sat in a pew in the back, gazing at Christ on the Cross. Wondering what He thought of my plan. Alone now, I knelt and clasped my hands together. My wife would've been proud.

"Tell me I'm wrong," I said.

A noise set me on edge. It was only some old woman coming out of the sacristy and carrying poinsettias. She placed them with the others in front of the altar. Maybe she had the answer I was looking for. She made the Sign of the Cross and disappeared. I stayed a while longer, waiting for a sign. None came. The angel told me not to continue down this path. But I wanted to hear it from the Man Himself.

When you pray, you're supposed to feel something, right? In that dark moment, I felt nothing—not even fear. I said a

Hail Mary for my dead wife and baby. Killing Holly had been the mayor's way of making things right. But that was Tres Marias—not LA.

Now, it was my turn.

FOUR

I drove through the wetness of an El Niño rain to Holy Grounds for an Ojo Rojo. Although the coffee with espresso was irresistible, I made it a point not to come every day. Instead, I varied my routine, mixing it up with Starbucks, Peet's, and whatever else I could find. Paranoid? Sure. But after what happened, can you blame me?

Tres Marias was an island cut off from the world during the outbreak. Like Las Vegas, what we did there stayed there. But LA was different. Lots of cops, CCTV cameras, and well-meaning do-gooders with smartphones. A single mistake would mean I was dead. And dead is fine—*after* you get revenge.

The place wasn't too far from where I lived. On Alhambra Avenue, I saw flashing lights. Fire trucks, police cruisers, and an ambulance were clustered around an alley entrance next to the coffeehouse. Chinese and Latino residents stood behind yellow tape, gawking. A middle-aged woman clung to a turquoise umbrella with yellow flowers painted on it. She looked like she might be praying. Slowing, I turned at the corner and parked down the street.

"What's going on?" I said, approaching the crowd.

A local gave me a shrug. "No se."

A young woman wearing stretchy jeans and a Holy Grounds T-shirt joined the conversation. "Somebody got attacked."

I recognized her as an employee, with piercings and colorful floral tats up and down her arms. Around twenty, she went by Amparo. She was Latina—possibly Mexican—with her dark brown hair cut short and eyes like black pools. If you stared into them too long, you could get sucked in.

"Cut up real bad," a man said. He had gold teeth, acne scars, and grease under his fingernails. "Prob'ly a hooker, homes."

This guy was straight out of a Cheech and Chong movie. People liked making up stories when they didn't have all the facts. Though my instinct was to investigate, I made it a rule never to get mixed up with cops. So, like a tourist, I waited with the others.

Across the street, an ABC7 Eyewitness News van screeched to a stop. The driver, a chunky dude with a beard, hopped out. He opened the sliding door and grabbed his camera equipment. Meanwhile, a Latina wearing a black suit and carrying an umbrella opened the passenger-side door. After giving her hair a quick brush, she walked towards us with her platform pumps clickety-clacking on the pavement. Risky considering it was slippery.

She was around my age—early twenties—with long, straight coffee-colored hair, hazel eyes, and full lips. I wondered if she was as aggressive as my late reporter friend, Evie Champagne. Now, there was a dog with a bone. Till someone shot her in the head for asking too many questions. On second thought, this girl didn't strike me as the type.

"Mari Lopez!" a woman said.

Excitement spread quickly. Ignoring the attention, the reporter marched up to the cop in charge. With a serious expression, she asked him something while her cameraman waited behind her. Leering at her chest, he shook his head and pointed at the barricade tape. They'd done this Kabuki dance before. Rolling her eyes, she joined us, choosing to stand next to me for some reason. Even in the rain, I could smell her lavender perfume.

A young boy tugged her sleeve. "Can I have your autograph?"

Side-eyeing him, she kept her attention on the cops.

"No te olvides de tus raíces," an elderly woman said, shaking a crooked finger.

That did the trick. Grabbing a Sharpie from her purse, the reporter signed the boy's Dodgers cap, sending him over the moon. Everyone applauded.

Suddenly, a stunned silence fell like a cloak of liquid darkness. Two stone-faced paramedics emerged from the alley and hurried to the ambulance. One pushed a gurney, and the other held an IV bag. As they got closer, the cops warned people away.

The reporter nudged her partner, who pointed his camera and began recording. Others around him brought out their phones and did the same. I pulled my ball cap low over my eyes and turned up my collar. Despite what Cheech had claimed, the event had to be a random shooting, like the hundreds that happened every year in cities across the country.

That's what I thought anyway. Till I saw the victim.

FIVE

She lay strapped to the gurney, moaning and writhing —a large woman with poofy hair, bad teeth, and way too much blue eye shadow. A gray patient blanket covered everything but her head. Cheech had been right after all. Careful not to draw attention, I pressed in for a better look.

The woman managed to free an arm. Raising it to her face, she shrieked. Someone in the crowd passed out. The wise woman made the Sign of the Cross and covered the boy's eyes. Turning white, Cheech vomited on his shoes as the rest of us dodged the backsplash. And the entire time, the cameraman recorded what was in front of him.

The victim's arm had been stripped clean of skin and flesh, the naked bone and blood vessels intact. A bright orange tourniquet stopped the blood from squirting every-where. It was then I realized what the angel had been trying to tell me. All this time, I thought she was talking about gray-suits. She meant the cutters.

Looking past the ambulance, I noticed a black Escalade cruising past. As it slowed, a gray-suit in the backseat shot rapid-fire photos using a camera equipped with a telephoto lens. Another man sat beside him—gaunt, with close-cropped silver hair and wearing a black suit. A long, shiny purplish scar ran from his temple, past his eye to his jawline. That eye reminded me of the old man's *eye of a vulture* in Poe's "The Tell-Tale Heart." As he studied the crowd, I nearly lost my gorge.

With a gloved hand, a paramedic took the woman's arm and hid it under the blanket. Then, he and his partner loaded the gurney into the ambulance. In another beat, they were off with the siren blaring. The cop in charge signaled the reporter to approach the way a maître d' summons a busboy. It was a gesture that would have royally pissed me off.

She and her cameraman scooted under the tape. After chatting with the officer, she smoothed her hair while her partner lined up the shot. The cop moved out of the way, and Los Angeles Police Chief Lawrence Hughes stepped forward. I recognized him from the news—early fifties, with salt-and-pepper hair, Beverly Hills tan, and a two-thousand-dollar suit. He and the reporter put on their game faces.

A bright light mounted on the camera came on, and Mari Lopez did her standup. The interview went quickly, with the cop dodging questions like a running back in overtime. He dismissed her suggestion that the attack might have been the work of a serial killer. Instead, he followed the standard playbook. Looking soberly into the camera, he assured the public this was a random act—the neighborhood was safe.

What a crock. The bloodbath was just beginning. I listened as the reporter peppered the chief with questions, trying to tease out whether this type of crime had ever happened in LA. But it was denial all the way—the same two words repeated over and over. *Random act.* The cop might as well have blamed the incident on flying monkeys. There was nothing more to be learned till the evening news and tomorrow's newspapers.

After wrapping up, the reporter returned to the van with her cameraman. Several of us drifted into the coffeehouse. Some returned to the drinks and food they'd already purchased but were too upset to consume. Amparo was behind the counter, taking new orders. I paid for my drink and found a seat in the rear, away from the windows.

Scattered images flew through my brain like bats in the belfry. The victim's face and arm. The black Escalade. The gray-suit taking pictures. And that hideous man with the janky eye. He worried me the most. I'd seen him in Mt. Shasta when we raided the secret government lab. He was in the parking lot with Walt Freeman as I escaped in a stolen vehicle. Who was he? And how did he know about the attack?

Never mind. What mattered now was the cutters were loose. I recalled the first ones I'd encountered in Tres Marias. Ordinary Black Dragon guards. Only these had eyes that glowed purple as they calmly chewed the flesh of a man they had flayed with bayonets.

Baseborn Identity Research—*Hellborn*—was behind the massacre in my town. How did I know? Walt Freeman. And now, he'd moved the operation to LA. I couldn't help wondering how far the plague would spread this time. And why the police chief showed up if the attack was nothing more than a random act by some crazy with surgical skills.

I came to Los Angeles to expose the plot that killed Holly and destroyed my home. Maybe I was too late. Walt Freeman was the current face of that evil. Killing him would go a long way towards sating my need for revenge. But the act alone would do little to stop what was already underway. It was like pissing in the wind. Usually, you were the one who got soaked. Still, I was here to end the bastard's life.

Shit, I had lost track of the time. Looking down, I realized I hadn't touched my Ojo Rojo. I took a long swallow and listened to the music track playing in the background—"When You Were Young" by The Killers. I didn't feel young.

The reporter walked in and approached the counter. I thought she'd gone. While waiting for Amparo to make her drink, she asked a lot of questions. The barista didn't know anything—or pretended not to. A minute later, she said *Café de Olla* and handed the customer her drink in a to-go cup. Leaving a large tip, the polished young woman scanned the room. Probably looking for a new rube to interview.

I didn't turn away fast enough. Her hazel eyes settling on me, she headed for my table. I would've walked out, but that kind of move draws attention. As she got closer, I caught a break. The chatty guy with the gold teeth got in her way. His shirt covered in dried sick, he babbled about how he knew the victim and could tell her *all kinds o' shit.*

"Not now, Shorty," she said and tried getting past him.

"Pues, come on, Mari. Don't you want no good tips?"

These two went way back. Covering her nose from the smell, she rolled her eyes as he continued to regale her with bragging and lame half-truths. As a bonus, he threw in a plug for the auto repair shop where he worked in case the camera was still rolling.

"Thanks, Shorty," I said and slipped out the front door.

SIX

It was pouring rain, and my insides ached. Though I'd prepared myself for this day, I was scared—not of dying but of failing. My legs were stiff, and I wanted to vomit. I hated that fear could weaken my determination to avenge Holly's death. Swallowing my bile, I kept walking. The news van was gone. What the...

The familiar clickety-clacking of heels made me stop. It was that pesky reporter. She'd extricated herself from the Shorty Show and followed me. Why? Warily, I watched her skitter towards me, her hair flat and dripping, her nice clothes drenched because she'd forgotten her umbrella. I was determined to make it to my truck, but it was hopeless. Better to play this out.

The sidewalk was slick, and she fell. She looked like a show dog trapped in a car wash. It was hard not to smile. Her knee was bleeding. It was clear she was about to lose her shit —I would have. Though sympathetic, I had no intention of becoming part of her story. She looked up, her eyes begging me for help. *Shit.*

Walking up, I offered my hand. Her mascara trickled

down her face in black, wavy streaks—like Carrie. I noticed the gold crucifix beaded with raindrops dangling from her neck. It resembled the one I buried Holly in. Was God doing this on purpose? I almost laughed at the irony but stopped before she decided I was a lunatic. Gratefully, she took my hand and got to her feet. Her knee was starting to swell.

"You should probably clean that up," I said.

She was sweet—vulnerable even. Then, "¡Puta de madre!" She pulled a few soggy tissues from her purse and pressed them to the wound. "Thanks for the advice."

"So, you're Mari Lopez?"

Despite the pain, she managed a smile. "That's my professional name. My friends call me Maritza."

She was pretty, even without makeup. I warned myself to be careful. The last thing I needed was to get involved. She looked like she was waiting for me to tell her my name. Instead, I stood there with the rain coming down, my expression a cipher.

"Anyway," she said, giving up on the knee. "Do you live around here?"

"I come for the coffee."

"Me too. I grew up in East Los, not far from here."

"I kind of gathered that. The old woman with the boy? And Shorty?"

She laughed. "They watched me grow up." Then, looking at the sky, "Hey, it stopped."

"Can I ask you something? What did she say to you?"

"Oh, that." Clearing her throat, she imitated the wise woman. "*No te olvides de tus raíces.* It means don't forget where you come from. Guess I deserved it."

Though we were drenched, the conversation moved naturally. I wanted to like her, but she was only there for the story.

Even in heels, she was shorter than me and had to look up a lot. The way she gazed into my eyes made me uncomfortable.

"What?" I said.

"Sorry, it's a game I used to play with my sisters when we were little. My dad would always say, *If you look hard enough into a person's eyes, you can see their soul, mija.*"

"Has that ever worked?"

"We knew it was pendejadas—you know, bullshit. But I do it sometimes anyway. Guess it reminds me of Apá. You have nice eyes, by the way."

"Is your father…"

"He passed a few years ago—stomach cancer. He was a real hardass when we were growing up. Very protective of his girls. But he could be sweet too. Gave each of us a quinceañera. I miss him, especially at Christmas. We used to make tamales together."

"Seriously, you should clean that scrape, or it'll get infected." *What am I doing?* "I'll walk you to the coffeehouse. Maybe they have a first-aid kit. Don't worry, I'll deal with Shorty."

She laughed again. Halfway there, she said, "You never told me your name."

"Dave."

She extended a slender hand. "Nice to meet you, David. For a gabacho, you're pretty good-looking." Snorting, she covered her mouth.

"Nice," I said and opened the door for her.

SEVEN

We sat at a wobbly card table in the back room. The area was stacked with boxes of dark-roasted beans, cups, and other supplies. The pleasant coffee aroma made me crave another Ojo Rojo, but I was anxious to leave. After applying Neosporin, Amparo placed a square bandage on Mari's knee and put away the first-aid kit. The rain had started up again. Lighting a cigarette, she stood in the open doorway.

The reporter examined the barista's handiwork. "Thanks, Amparo."

"What happened to the van?" I said.

"I sent Rick to the station with the video."

"There's no way they can show the gory stuff, right?"

"It'll be heavily edited." She laid her hand on mine. "Think you could give me a ride?"

I rubbed the back of my neck. "I need to be somewhere. What's wrong with Uber?"

"It's like this—you owe me."

"How do you figure that?"

"I spilled blood for you." She pointed at her knee. "Look. We're in a sacred pact now."

"Wait. Am I getting shanked here?" I turned to the barista for help.

Giving up nothing, she blew a perfect smoke ring. "Ni modo."

"Fine," I said to Mari. "So what happened to your umbrella?"

"I think Rick might've taken it."

As I pulled into traffic, the reporter gave me the studio's address in Hollywood. She was smart. Instead of interrogating me, she concentrated on gaining my trust. Not that it would do her any good. I knew what she was up to. Other than my name, she had nothing on me. And after today, there was a good chance I would cease to exist. Maybe I'd leave her with a few pleasant memories she could share with her sisters.

"Why do you think the police chief showed up?" I said, driving west through Echo Park and passing the lake.

"Right? That surprised me too. What didn't, though, was what happened to that poor woman. It wasn't the first time, you know. Two weeks ago, someone found a body in the LA River. All that was left was a skeleton with the head intact. The cops attributed it to a revenge killing."

"Or a random act."

"Oh, yeah. Random as it gets. No, I think these events are connected." She was testing me.

"How?"

"Whoever did this took their time. A lot of precision went into it."

"Serial killer?"

"Kill-*ers*."

"You think there's more than one?" Now I was testing her.

"They never leave any traces. I read the coroner's report on the first victim. The angle and variety of the cuts suggest more than one weapon. Take a left at the light."

"Maybe it's one guy, and he's ambidextrous."

"I'm being serious. My gut tells me there are multiple killers."

"Why did you approach me?"

We were in the hills of Silver Lake, cruising the residential streets overlooking Hollywood. She took her time answering. I waited.

"Okay, here it is," she said. "I could tell you didn't belong."

"Because I'm a gabacho, you mean."

She narrowed her eyes at me. "When I work a story, I try to eliminate the obvious and concentrate on the anomaly— the one piece that doesn't fit. It pays off more than you'd think."

"Sounds like you might've been born for this."

"I had an incredible mentor—Karen Rothberg. She never got the opportunity to work on camera, but she was a helluva researcher. Taught me everything I know."

"What, did she suffer from stage fright?"

"She has a withered hand, so the camera didn't exactly love her."

"What about Bob Dole? He was on camera all the time."

"The senator? That's different. His arm was paralyzed, and he always had a pen in his hand. Karen was fine with her situation, though. She knows her strengths."

"You seem kind of young to be doing this."

"My mentor wasn't only smart, she was influential. She convinced the execs to give me a shot. And before you bring up DEI, it was based on merit. I owe everything to her."

"For the record, I wasn't thinking that. So, is she still around?"

"She's retired now. Lives in Santa Barbara. Sorry I got mad."

"Forget it. You said I don't fit."

"Correct. And that's not all. I think you know something about these attacks. Seeing the victim had no effect on you. Yet you got all weird when that black Escalade showed up."

I gripped the wheel even tighter. "You're very observant, Mari."

"You can call me Maritza."

"So we're friends now?"

"You bet." She gave me a toothpaste commercial smile. "And my job is to notice things."

"Does it also require you to be clumsy?"

She laughed. "I fall down constantly. Part of my Chicana charm. Pull into that driveway."

It had finally stopped raining, and the sky was clearing. As I approached the guard shack, a portable radio played Cake's "Short Skirt/Long Jacket"—not what I needed right now. The reporter pulled her ID from her purse and dangled it past my face. Her lavender perfume blended wonderfully with her body's natural scent. For a moment, the effect made me long for a future.

The guard waved us through. I headed past a sea of satellite dishes to the opposite end of the parking lot. Maritza directed me to the nearest building complex. After getting out, she smoothed her skirt and jacket. Then she took a business card from her purse and, using her Sharpie, wrote something on the back.

"In case you decide to come clean," she said, handing me the card. "That's my private mobile number. Call me anytime."

"I really don't know anything."

"Yeah, you do. Thanks for the ride, David."

"It's Dave, remember?"

"I hope those men in the gray suits don't catch you."

"They won't," I said.

Lingering, she smiled in a way that got to me—a little girl trapped in a smokin', grown-up body. If I could've wished for anything, it would be to have those hazel eyes gazing down as I lay dying.

She disappeared into the building, and I realized I was smitten. I knew because minutes had passed, and I hadn't thought about Holly. None of it mattered, though. Everything was already in motion.

"Nice knowing you, Maritza," I said.

EIGHT

My plan was simple—find Walt Freeman and kill him. I didn't care that I was walking into a death trap. The hate I carried had eaten away everything soft, everything warm. And what it left behind was a dry, cauterized shell drenched in bitter-tasting purpose. The smart move would've been to work with the cops—maybe even Maritza. Uncover the secret behind Baseborn Identity Research and expose it to the world before it was too late. As I've said often, no one ever accused me of being bright.

I'd instructed Cuco to wire a large sum to Guthrie in Mt. Shasta. I told the Mexican he could keep the weapons and the rest of the cash for himself. He was a stand-up guy and would do it, no questions asked. The guns and the money would serve as my last will and testament.

Swollen gray clouds rolled in as I parked across the street, half a mile from the industrial park. After locking the truck, I found a park bench that afforded a good view. The property I was interested in consisted of a low, drab building whose color mirrored the leaden sky. Hellborn sat in the middle of the complex—a monolithic rectangular fortress. Wiping the fog from my binoculars, I scanned the area. I'd been through this routine before. Their operation was twenty-four seven, which meant three shifts. The first started at midnight and went till eight, the second from eight to four, and the last from four to midnight.

Trucks came and went at all hours, mainly during the first shift. Every morning, a Sysco truck pulled in, bringing food products and restaurant supplies to the neighboring pizza and sandwich shops. Few deliveries came to Hellborn's main entrance. A private courier service brought mail to the front door, but the driver wasn't permitted to enter the facility. Instead, a security guard would walk outside to sign for the letters and packages. As for the black Escalades, they were everywhere.

My bench was wet from the rain. It was around noon, and I was hungry. People poured out of the building on their way to lunch. I didn't know what they did, but there were a lot of employees—men and women in business attire. One or two wore military uniforms. I waited for everyone to leave. Dodging traffic, I made my way across the street and headed for a side lot where a well-dressed woman walked briskly to her silver Mercedes.

It was Becky, Walt Freeman's assistant. I remembered her from Tres Marias—the reddish-brown hair, red lips, and full figure. I couldn't see her eyes—she had on designer sunglasses—but I knew it was her. No one else was around. It was now or never. As she pulled the car keys from her purse, I walked up behind her and jammed my Glock into the small of her back. Letting out a strangled squeak, she froze.

"Don't scream," I said. Grabbing her arm, I made her face me.

"Dave?" Her voice was warbly. "What are you—"

"Where's Walt Freeman?"

"He…"

I pictured Holly falling onto that cold cave floor, dead from a bullet to the head. The memory made hurting Becky easy. Though Walt hadn't pulled the trigger, he was ultimately responsible. And so was she.

"Where?"

"He's in a meeting." Behind her sunglasses, her startled eyes darted from side to side.

"No one can save you. Take me to him. *Now.*"

I could see she wasn't cut out for this shit. She was nothing more than a voluptuous tool who enjoyed wearing expensive clothes and jewelry. And she wasn't above seducing the occasional city official when called upon. Judging from her manicured nails, she didn't like getting her hands dirty.

"You know I can't do that," she said.

Something told me she wasn't as weak as she pretended to be. So I hit her in the face with my gun, sending her glasses flying.

"I won't ask you again."

Tears sprang from her eyes, spoiling her perfect makeup. She was shaking, which almost made me regret what I'd done. Almost. Touching her lip, she stared in horror at the fresh blood on her fingertips. She backed away from her car and led me to a secure side door.

"I need my ID." She could barely get the words out.

Her hand jittering, she grabbed the badge from her purse and pressed it against the card reader. When the buzzer sounded, I opened the door and used my weapon to urge her through. The long hallway was beige. It smelled like the walls had been freshly painted. We made our way to a set of locked double doors.

"He-he's in a conference room," she said. "But I don't think you'll make it."

"Let me worry about that."

Before she could unlock the doors, a deafening alarm sounded. Emergency lights created a disorienting strobe effect. My pulse quickening, I glanced all around me while pointing my weapon at her head.

"What did you do?"

"Nothing—I swear!"

Shoving her aside, I peered through the wire glass. Men and women moved in an orderly fashion to the walls, like police lineup suspects. Armed security guards descended on the area, searching offices, cubicles, and utility closets.

"What's going on?" I said.

She blanched. "Someone's escaped."

Walt Freeman emerged from a conference room accompanied by the scarred, black-suited undertaker. They joined the others. He looked exactly as I remembered him. Fifties, with thinning gray hair, a ruddy face, and a bulbous nose dotted with burst blood vessels. His gut was as big as ever under his suit jacket.

As the alarm shrilled, the blood pounded in my head. There was no way I was getting to him now—not with all that security. I grabbed Becky by the shoulders. When she tried screaming, I shoved her against the wall and jammed the gun under her chin. With my free hand, I dug through her purse and found her driver's license. *Rebekkah Loring*, with a home address somewhere near West Hollywood. I pointed the weapon at her forehead. Like a robot on the fritz, her eyes went glassy.

"Tell Walt I'm back and that I'm coming for him," I said.

She collapsed onto her heels, twirling her hair like a frightened child. I bolted down the hallway and exited the building. Outside, the rain came down hard, rushing over the asphalt in iridescent, oily sheets. A guard was clearing the parking lot. I ducked behind a row of cars and tried slipping past. But he'd already spotted me.

"Freeze, asshole!" he said.

NINE

Standing, I opened fire as the guard radioed for backup. He wasn't wearing body armor and went down easily, his shirt bright with blood. I spotted movement in the side mirror of a nearby vehicle. A sudden burst of pain buckled my knees. My gun ended up under an Escalade. When I turned, another guard was coming at me with a riot stick. I rolled away and scrambled to my feet.

"You're not going anywhere, son."

He had a toothbrush mustache and looked like an idiot. Grinning at me with small, feral eyes, he threatened me with the stick. I waited for him to advance, then ducked on his swing. Behind me, a car's passenger window shattered, setting off the alarm. When his radio crackled, he took his eyes off me for a sec. I punched him in the throat. Choking, he fell to his knees and grabbed his neck. As he struggled for air, I kicked him in the groin and retrieved my weapon.

I was halfway across the lot when the building's side door burst open. At least half a dozen more guards poured out with their guns up. Someone gave the order to spread out and circle the lot. Scrambling, I bolted towards the street.

"Halt!" a guard said and fired.

The bullet missed me by inches. It struck a passing vehicle, making the driver swerve. As soon as I reached the sidewalk, they stopped shooting. Cars whizzed past dangerously in both directions. Glancing at the approaching hostiles, I ran into traffic. I was nearly halfway across when a semi bore down on me, almost knocking me flat. The driver blared his horn as I worked my way to the other side.

By the time I reached the park, the guards were in the road. Not wanting me to escape, the one in charge proceeded recklessly. A pickup truck struck him and kept going as if nothing had happened. The poor bastard landed hard on the pavement, where a stream of fast-moving vehicles crushed him to death. Incredibly, no one stopped.

My lungs burned, and my knee ached where the guard had hit me. I needed to regroup. There was no way I could ever return to this place. I would have to devise a new plan. My truck was parked in front of a line of cars. I noticed someone's head in the rain, bobbing erratically on the side nearest the park. Whoever it was, they hesitated at each vehicle till they got to mine. I moved closer to get a better look.

It was a girl wearing a white patient gown. I tried to think—there weren't any hospitals in the area. Muttering in a foreign language, she yanked on my passenger door handle. I put away my weapon and approached her.

"Can I help you?"

When she saw me, she tried running. I grabbed her arm.

"I'm not going to hurt you," I said as she struggled. "What do you want with my truck?"

Her cold, naked body was visible through the flimsy gown. Goosebumps had sprouted like bug bites up and down her arms. She had long, light-brown hair. Her frightened blue-gray eyes were ringed with dark circles. Her full lips were pink, her skin fair and blemish free. She couldn't have been more than nineteen or twenty. There was a red sore on her hand. I guessed it was from a hospital IV. There was something familiar about the field of lilacs on the patient gown. Yes! It was the same pattern I'd seen at the isolation facility in Tres Marias.

"Are you in danger?" I said.

Releasing her arm, I stepped away, my hands at my sides. I was positive she'd take off. But she was unsure and stared at her dirty bare feet. I remembered what Becky had said when the alarm went off. *Someone's escaped.* She must've broken out of Hellborn, and now they were looking for her. I couldn't leave her here—not like this. Though I didn't want to get involved, she needed my help. Griffin, the girl Holly and I rescued in Tres Marias, had turned out well—I thanked God for her. I tried convincing myself this situation was totally different. Was it?

"I'm Dave. What's your name?"

She looked at me warily. I had no idea what new hell I was signing up for. Obviously, it would involve more than slipping her twenty bucks and wishing her good luck. When she finally opened her mouth, my blood turned cold.

"Don't let them take me," she said.

Her accent sounded Slavic—possibly Russian. She waited for me to respond. *Someone's escaped.* Was she part of the experiment? Infected with the virus? I needed to think, but there wasn't time. The guards were halfway across the street by now, with cars swerving and horns blaring. When the girl saw them, her eyes got huge. Moving fast, I unlocked the passenger door and waited for her to get in. She hesitated.

"We don't have much time," I said. "You need to trust me."

I pulled out my gun. In another few seconds, it would be

too late, and I'd be forced to shoot. She watched the guards getting closer. One had slipped on the wet asphalt and cursed as the others did their best to hold back the relentless traffic. Chewing her lip, she gave me a quick *Da* and climbed in.

We tore out of there before the guards could make it across. In the rearview mirror, I saw them enter the park. I was pretty sure they hadn't spotted her—or my truck. At this point, I didn't know where to go. What are you supposed to do with an escaped test subject? Better to take it one step at a time.

"We need to get you some clothes," I said.

She didn't acknowledge me. Instead, she kept looking out the rear window.

"It's okay. No one's following us."

Exhaling, she scrunched down in the seat and stared at the beating windshield wipers. "That vas close."

Shivering and holding herself, she closed her eyes and drifted off. Maybe it was the first sleep she'd had in who knew how long. Cranking up the heat, I thought about asking her what had happened but decided to leave her be.

"What did those devils do to you?" I said.

TEN

The rain had stopped. The girl opened her eyes as I pulled into a parking lot in Montebello. Disoriented, she didn't seem to remember how she'd ended up in my truck and stared at me. I wanted to touch her hand to reassure her, but I was afraid she might take it the wrong way.

"It's okay," I said. "Just getting you some clothes."

I could see she still didn't trust me. Then again, why would she? I made it a point to remain calm and reassuring—not really my thing. Maybe she had a family. I could buy her a couple outfits and something to eat, then drop her at a relative's house. That would be best.

There was an Old Navy in the mall. On weekdays, women shoppers and small children filled the place. Though being here was a risk, I was confident I could get in and out fast. So I parked at the end of the lot, far from the other cars. No one paid any attention to us.

"What size are you?"

"Nohl." She gave me a shy smile. Her teeth were straight, which meant she'd been looked after growing up. "Zee-roh."

"And your feet?"

"Five."

"Okay, listen. I need you to lock yourself in. Understand? Keep your head down. I'll be back soon."

"Vhy?" she said.

"Because I don't want anyone to—"

"Vhy are you doing this?"

She'd caught me by surprise, and I had no good answer. As a Black Dragon guard, I'd been trained to protect civilians. Maybe that was why I had gone out of my way to help her.

"I don't know," I said.

Knowing nothing about me, she searched my face. For all she knew, I was setting her up. But I didn't know her either, which meant I was at risk. And so, without words, we established a tenuous trust—enough to get us through the next few hours. I stood outside the truck and waited for her to lock the doors.

Old Navy wasn't crowded. Jet's "Are You Gonna Be My Girl" played over the sound system. *Come on.* I headed to the women's jeans section and began flipping through the stacks on the wall. What in holy hell were boyfriend jeans? Thankfully, a young woman with purple hair and piercings came to my rescue.

"Help you find somethin'?" she said.

"I'm looking for size zero women's jeans."

Waving me back, she pulled out multiple pairs in various colors. I felt embarrassed and checked to see if anyone was watching.

She looked me over. "Girlfriend?"

"Niece. My sister works, and I told her I'd help out."

"So, no girlfriend, then."

She pulled my arms straight out and dropped a stack of jeans on them. Despite being uncomfortable, I didn't mind the treatment. The salesgirl seemed to know I was in a hurry. She made the process as efficient as possible.

"What about tops?" she said.

Twenty minutes later, I returned to the truck carrying two enormous bags. Leaning over, my mysterious passenger unlocked the driver's side door. I shoved the bags through, and she arranged them in the footwell. Stopping, she rubbed her temples.

"What's wrong?" I said.

"Headache. I get them now." She pretended nothing was the matter and peeked at the clothes. "Like Christmas." She examined the receipt. Giving me a knowing smile, she held it up. "New girlfriend?"

The salesgirl had written her phone number on the back. Grabbing it, I balled it up. "Let's find a place so you can change."

I scanned the streets, searching for black Escalades. By now, Walt Freeman would have any number of people out looking for the girl. Whatever their plan, they'd stop at nothing to reacquire her. She dug through a bag and pulled out a pair of black lace-up boots and a gray sweater-knit pom-pom hat. Holding up the beanie, she looked at me with wide eyes.

"Things got a little tense back there," I said. "I blame the salesgirl."

I cruised the neighborhood for fifteen frustrating minutes. It wasn't easy finding a gas station that didn't have a mini-mart attached and security cameras. Then, I got lucky. This one was old school. I pulled around to the rear by the restrooms and parked.

We were alone. I jogged around to the front to get the

restroom key. When I returned, I stood next to the truck, keeping an eye out for anything suspicious. The girl got out, and struggling with both bags, let herself in. I sensed we were safe and placed my gun in the glove compartment.

"What am I doing?" I said to the crow eyeing me from a nearby wall.

My brilliant plan was going great. So far, I'd hit a woman in the face and killed a security guard. Now, I was picking out prom dresses. Seriously... What. The. Hell. I reminded myself why I came to LA in the first place. But I was in a dark tunnel with no sense of direction. Cutters were on the loose, and this girl was somehow part of it.

I needed the angel to provide answers. But she wasn't a dog who came when you called. I remembered a prayer my mother taught me when I was little. We used to say it together every night before I went to sleep. I gave it a shot.

> *Angel of God,*
> *My guardian dear,*
> *To whom God's love commits me here,*
> *Ever this day be at my side,*
> *To light and guard, to rule and guide.*
> *Amen.*

Nothing. The girl came out of the restroom fully dressed. I almost didn't recognize her. She was cute in her pink sweater, gray jeans, and fuzzy hat. A chic waif fresh off a catwalk. She climbed into the truck with the bags and waited for me to return the restroom key.

"Thank you for remembering panties," she said without irony. "But no bras?"

I stared straight ahead, my neck burning. "I, um, I didn't know your size."

"Are you going to have sex vith me now?"

I almost went through a red light and hit the brakes. From her expression, she was serious.

"I have no interest in that."

"Oh. I didn't know you vere—"

"I'm not," I said. "Let's get you something to eat."

Though I was angry, I reminded myself that this girl didn't know me from Ted Bundy. Most men would've taken advantage of the opportunity and demanded a violent quickie under a bridge. My goal was to deposit her safely with her family.

Up ahead, an Asian man in a green suit and carrying a bright yellow umbrella hurried to catch a bus. A dog behind a chain-link fence yapped at him as he walked past. Someone at the back door cursed in Spanish and threw a shoe at the animal. This was how it was supposed to be—ordinary people living ordinary lives. No gray-suits, no cutters. No Walt Freeman.

"I'll find us a food truck. No surveillance cameras that way."

"You avoid the cameras?"

"Always." I caught her expression. "I'm not a bad person if that's what you're thinking. What about you?"

"I am not bad also. They..." She made herself small against the seat.

"It's okay," I said and turned at the corner.

Watching the girl inhale the tacos al pastor made me smile. "When's the last time you ate?"

"They fed us, but it was never enough."

"*Us?*"

"Me."

"Who fed you?"

"The bad men. I don't vant to talk about it."

The rain had started again. We ate in the truck next to a park. When she'd finished, she leaned back and sighed with satisfaction. Then she let out a belch that sounded like a miniature foghorn.

"Izvinite," she said, laughing.

"That was quite a performance. Want me to get you some more?"

"No, thank you."

I didn't want to ask too many questions—not yet. Thanks to the cops, I was well acquainted with being on the receiving end of an interrogation.

"It's Sasha," she said as if reading my mind. "Sasha Drakonova."

"Dra-ko…"

"Sasha is fine."

I dumped our trash into a nearby receptacle. When I climbed into the truck, I found the glove compartment door open and the Russian girl holding my Glock. She looked at me without embarrassment. Carefully, I took the gun from her and put it away.

"I vasn't going to steal it," she said. "Are you a cop?"

"Maybe we should go somewhere and talk."

Her face darkened. "Thank you for the clothes and the food." She grabbed the door handle. "I must go. I vill tell no one about the gun."

"I won't stop you. But you need help, right?"

Her voice became tiny, more foreign. "No one can help me."

"Okay. Like the cops on TV say, you're free to go."

Grabbing her bags, she started to get out. As I buckled my

seatbelt, she changed her mind, and slamming the door, locked it.

"What is it?"

"Drive, please."

Pulling into traffic, I checked the rearview mirror. Impossible. How did they find me? I didn't believe in fate. There were only actions and consequences, with God watching from a safe distance. I made sure not to go too fast so we wouldn't stick out. Maybe they hadn't seen us. But they had.

"Better buckle up," I said.

ELEVEN

A black Escalade barreled towards us, swerving dangerously around vehicles to catch up. In minutes, we'd gone from calmness to staring down death. I didn't think they were after Sasha—she wasn't recognizable in her clothes and hat. Signaling her to scrunch down, I considered my options.

Hard rain pelted my windshield. Checking the rearview mirror, I floored it, barely making it through the congested intersection on a yellow light. Behind me, the sound of a collision. When I looked again, the Escalade had ignored the signal and, picking up speed, tore past the wreckage. I wasn't sure, but I thought I spotted the undertaker.

"Do you know those guys?" I said.

"The bad men."

As we neared the next intersection, another Escalade turned into traffic ahead of me. I'd already guessed how this would play out. First, the lead driver would slow to a crawl as the vehicle behind us caught up. Then they would box us in. Finally, a third Escalade would attempt a takeout, which would send us spinning helplessly out of control. Before the cops could get there, they'd put a bullet in my brain and take the Russian girl. End of story.

I spotted a police officer coming out of a convenience store. Getting pulled over was not my first choice. But anything was better than being executed by government goons. Slowing, I turned to Sasha.

"You need to listen—no questions," I said. "Get my gun."

Obediently, she retrieved the weapon from the glove compartment. Keeping my eyes on the road, I walked her through the steps to disassemble a Glock 19.

"Press the button behind the trigger guard and remove the magazine."

She did as instructed. The mag dropped into her lap.

"Perfect. The mag holds—"

"Fifteen rounds, I know."

I was all set to give her the next instruction when she removed the bullets and, giving me a sly smile, held them in her hand.

"Vhat should I do vith them?"

"Toss them out the window."

She looked at me like I was crazy but did as I asked.

"Now, the magazine. Okay, next you want to…"

But she'd already retracted the slide and inspected the gun for ammunition. She squeezed the trigger, pressed the slide locks, and removed the slide from the frame. When she was done, she stared at the pieces in her lap.

The lead Escalade decelerated as expected. Checking the rearview mirror, I saw the other one—and a cop cruiser.

"Throw the pieces out the window one by one," I said. "Wait a few seconds in between."

Soon, the weapon disappeared. Even if someone found one or more parts, with the rain and the traffic, it would be difficult to recover everything.

I glanced at her. "How do you know about guns?"

"My brother."

"You have a brother? Why didn't you—"

"Ve are not talking." She craned her neck to watch our pursuers. "Vhat now?"

"We bring in the cops."

"Nyet, I don't vant this."

"We have no choice," I said. "Those men will kill me."

To the right of us, an old man putted along in an ancient Nissan sedan with faded paint. Waiting for the right moment, I hit the brakes and swerved in behind him, surprising the hostiles. Checking my side mirrors, I shot past the geezer and blasted my horn like a joyriding teenager.

It took only a second for the cop to react. When he hit his lights and siren, all three Escalades disappeared down a side street. Slowing, I pulled into a loading zone. The cruiser screeched to a stop behind us.

Fuming, Sasha side-eyed me. "I told you, I don't like cops."

"Neither do I, but at least we're alive."

I rolled down my window, letting in the rain. Voices on the police radio chattered over the traffic noise. When the officer approached my car, I noticed his hand on his weapon and signaled the Russian girl to sit up straight.

"Can I help you, Officer?" I said.

Based on my experience with the Tres Marias police, I assumed the encounter would be tense. And it was at first. He looked me over through yellow-tinted aviator sunglasses. Then his demeanor changed when he saw Sasha. She seemed to have that effect on men.

"License and registration."

Reaching over, I removed the paper from the glove

compartment. I retrieved my driver's license from my wallet and handed over both documents.

"Did I do something wrong?" I said.

"Wait here." He returned to the cruiser.

She tugged at my sleeve. "He vill use his computer."

"You need to not look so suspicious. Try smiling for a change."

She gave me a hideous, mental-patient grin. As the cop approached our truck, I grabbed her side and tickled her. Yelping, she burst into helpless laughter.

"Mr. Callahan?" the cop said.

"I know how this looks. But I was getting back at my sister for tickling me while I was driving."

He made a frowny face. "I'm going to let you off with a warning this time. But you should be more careful." Then to her, "And no more distracting your brother, young lady."

Ashamed, she nodded. He handed me my license and registration. Sneaking a glance at the rearview mirror, I spotted an Escalade parked down the street with its head-lights on. The undertaker was in the backseat.

"Have a nice day," the cop said, walking away.

"Officer? Actually, we were looking for City Hall. We adopted a rescue, and I need to get a dog license. Can you point me in the right direction? I don't really know this area."

"You guys don't have smartphones?"

"Money's a little tight."

"It's near LAPD Headquarters. I'm going there now if you want to follow me."

"That would be awesome—thank you."

"What kind of dog is it?"

"Mixed breed. Best I can tell, she's German shepherd and dachshund."

"That must've been some wild date," he said, laughing. "Wait for me to pull out."

The hostiles kept their eyes on the cop as he got into his vehicle and nosed the cruiser into traffic. The undertaker leaned forward and said something. They pulled out too. I swung out behind the cop and followed closely. Turning off at an intersection, the Escalade vanished.

"Udachlivyy," the Russian girl said. "Means *lucky*, Mr. Callahan."

"Hey, about the tickling..."

"It's okay. You're a pretty good liar."

"That was nothing," I said.

TWELVE

After arriving in LA, I'd purchased several fake IDs from a guy on Alvarado Street who Guthrie recommended. Now that Mr. Callahan was on record with the police, I needed a new identity. The same went for my truck. Most likely, Walt Freeman had access to law enforcement databases and would have no problem tracking me down.

"Vhere are ve going now?" the Russian girl said.

To avoid suspicion, I followed through on my story and parked in a public lot off City Hall. Then we went inside. After ten minutes of waiting, we got on the road again. I checked my mirrors to make sure we weren't being followed.

"We have to lose the truck," I said. "Then I want to find your brother."

"No."

"Why not? He must be worried."

"I can't go back, that's all."

"Fine, we'll discuss it later. In the meantime, I need to take you somewhere safe."

"I am safe vith you."

And there it was. I knew it the second I first laid eyes on her. It's true God puts things in your path. And you can choose to step around them, or you can face them. He'd done that with Holly. I was on a bad road, getting drunk every day with my friend Jim. God had given me a wife to save me. Then, He took her away.

Sasha pretended to be tough. In reality, she was scared. I didn't know how she'd gotten mixed up with Hellborn. But I was sure that if Walt Freeman was involved, she was as good as dead. Would I choose to walk away? I'd made plans—a mission that was certain to get *me* dead. And that was my choice. The angel had warned me not to go through with it, but I wasn't having it. Like they say in Texas, Walt Freeman needed killing.

"I'm not the best guy to be around right now," I said.

She worried her sweater sleeve. "Do you vant to kill me?"

"No, of course not."

"Then I stay vith you."

It was no longer raining, but the sky looked threatening as we made our way to an industrial section of LA near the Los Angeles River. Though I'd never been here before, I recognized the iconic Sixth Street Bridge from movies like *To Live and Die in LA*. Oddly appropriate.

I'd memorized the address Guthrie gave me in Mt. Shasta. When I found the location, I pulled up to a junkyard surrounded by a high chain-link fence topped with razor wire. Security lights on rusty metal poles surrounded the property. Patches of motor oil choked the sparse weeds growing in the dirt. Somewhere, a passing train's horn blared.

The gate was locked. As we approached it, scarred-up pit bulls with yellow teeth and myopic eyes attacked the fence. They barked and snapped at us. Terrified, the Russian girl remained behind me. I gave her frozen hand a squeeze. Soon, a heavyset Korean wearing blue overalls and tan work boots came out of the office and walked towards us across the muddy lot. He was packing a sidearm—and chewing.

"Jeori ga!" he said to the dogs. Chastened, they swung around and trotted away. Then to me, "What do you want?"

"Are you Jeong?"

Suspicious, he rested his hand on the holster. Even after everything I'd been through, this guy intimidated the shit out of me.

I looked at him steadily. "Guthrie Manson sent me."

"Guthrie Manson sent me."

The name worked its magic, and he gave me a crooked smile. "I am Jeong."

"I need a vehicle."

Grunting, he gave Sasha the once-over and unlocked the padlock securing a heavy chain. After we drove through, he locked the gate. He gave his testicles a scratch and held out his hand. *Right, my keys.*

It took him all of ten minutes to examine everything—engine, suspension, bed, and interior. Crawling out from underneath the truck, he pulled the papers from the glove compartment. He squinted at something inside and shook his head. Taking my hand, he flipped it over and, with grease-stained fingers, dropped a shiny object into it—a 9mm bullet.

"You should be more careful, Mr. Callahan," he said.

Side-eyeing the Russian girl, I ignored the heat coming off my cheeks. I thought I'd taken every precaution since leaving Northern California. If that cop had searched my vehicle...

"Do you have any trucks?"

"Not today. Come back tomorrow."

"No time. What else have you got?"

"I can put you in a Lexus. Black with entertainment package. Very nice."

Sasha's eyes lit up. When she pulled at my sleeve, I ignored her and focused on the transaction.

"Too fancy. What else?"

"Wait in the office," he said. "I made coffee."

After changing into clean overalls, he jumped into my truck and drove it around back. The office was surprisingly neat—furnished in IKEA. A fifty-gallon saltwater tank stood in a corner. There was a generic laptop on the desk, next to cartons of Korean takeout and an open Coke can. Along one wall were a row of file cabinets and an expensive-looking color printer. A gift basket sat beside it, filled with cans of Spam individually wrapped in colored cellophane.

The Russian girl studied the fish. "Sure you trust this guy?"

"About as much as you trust me."

I picked up a can of Spam, trying to guess the joke. Some minutes later, I heard a vehicle approaching. It was a late-model black Chevy Tahoe. The Korean climbed out and waved us over.

"Best I can do today," he said, handing me the keys.

I walked around the vehicle. It was clean—not even a scratch. Though there wasn't a lot of room in the back, it wasn't a bad choice.

"What do you think?" I said to Sasha.

"Sweet ride."

"Where did you hear that?"

"*Napoleon Dynamite.* I like that movie."

"I'll take it," I said to Jeong. "How do we do this?"

"You're a good friend of Guthrie?"

"I am."

He looked up as if doing math in his head. "Even trade."

"Wow, you sure?"

"Guthrie is like a brother."

"Okay, then. What about the registration?"

"You give me the name and address, and I make it out. Also, I left an extra set of license plates in the tire well."

I'd memorized all the names, Social Security numbers, and addresses of the identities I owned. After giving him a new fake driver's license, he sat at the computer and went to work. In minutes, the printer came on. He handed me fresh documents, including a valid low-cost auto insurance policy, and the garage remote I had forgotten.

"Here you go, Mr. Wales," he said.

I turned over my old driver's license. "What happens to Mr. Callahan now?"

"You didn't hear? He died." He placed the plastic card in the crosscut shredder, where it disintegrated.

Outside, I shook the Korean's hand, and we were off. The late afternoon sun had broken through, revealing a thin watercolor strip of blue sky. The Russian girl looked at where I was pointing.

"Maybe that's a good sign," I said.

THIRTEEN

I stared at the street through the parking garage gate. The engine was off, and it was cold inside the Tahoe. I'd already texted Cuco to let him know I was driving a new vehicle. The last thing I wanted was to bring the Russian girl to my apartment. But I couldn't just dump her somewhere. Still, it was a risk. Whatever connection she had to Hellborn, she kept to herself. And she sure as hell didn't want her brother getting involved.

"You can stay with me—for now," I said. "But we are having that talk."

"Yes, Mr. Vales."

The Mexican spotted us and walked over, holding a brush and a gallon can of outdoor paint. We climbed out and met him.

"You're not dead," he said.

"I got sidetracked. Cuco, this is Sasha. Sasha, my bodyguard."

"Pleasure to meet you," she said, enunciating each word.

He squinted at her, starting with the combat boots and working his way up to the skinny jeans and a sweater that betrayed the coldness of the garage. Looking at me again, he grinned with approval.

"It's not like that," I said. "She's my sister."

"Por supuesto."

"There's nothing going on."

"Ni modo."

The Russian girl seemed to enjoy the misunderstanding and looped her arm through mine like someone in love. We headed to the elevator, each carrying an Old Navy bag.

"They're getting close," the Mexican said.

"I know."

"I overheard two gray-suits asking questions at the tienda on the corner."

"Appreciate the warning." We arrived at the elevator. "Listen, I might need someplace to lay low."

"Pues... You can stay with me in Highland Park."

"Don't you have a family?"

"In Mexico."

"Okay, I'll let you know."

I tried slipping him some cash. Declining, he gave us a wave and walked off as the elevator doors closed. We rode up four floors. As we made our way down the hallway, the cooking smells made me hungry. Spanish TV shows blared over squalling babies and arguing parents.

It felt good to be among the living, but I worried my presence was dangerous for these innocent people. When we arrived at my apartment, I dug out my key and made sure the door hadn't been compromised.

"You are vorse than my brother," she said.

Ignoring her, I unlocked the door. When I flicked on the lights, everything seemed in order. I crossed to the living room window and peeked out. There was a mild drizzle. Fog bathed the streetlights in a receding line of gentle yellow halos. Satisfied, I closed the curtains.

"I'll grab us some food," I said. "There's a chicken place around the corner. Make yourself comfortable. Take a shower if you want."

"You know vhat's good vith chicken?" She removed her beanie and flung it on the sofa. "Wodka."

"Forget it—you're too young. And I don't drink."

"Vhat kind of man doesn't drink?"

"The kind who doesn't know when to stop."

"In Russia, there are no stop signs."

I walked her to the worn sofa with the shot springs. "Take a seat." Settling in beside her, I held her ice-cold hands in mine. "I want you to tell me what happened to you."

I'd caught her off guard, which was my intention. She was a strange girl with a big secret. And I needed to know what I was up against. Turning away, she pretended to be interested in the cheesy yard sale décor. She ran her hand along the arm of the sofa, smoothing the rough fabric.

She spoke in a quiet voice. "They took me off the street. You call them gray-suits."

"When?"

"Two months, maybe."

Two months ago, I was in Tres Marias, up to my neck in draggers with Holly and my friends. Though we saw evidence that the virus had mutated, there were no such things as cutters. Yet. What had these gray-suit devils been prepping Sasha for all this time?

Reluctantly, she described her life on the streets. She was living with her older brother, Vladimir, and another Russian family in a crowded apartment on the west side. The siblings were from Moscow originally. They'd lost their parents in an automobile accident when she was five. Though she didn't say, I had the impression her father was drunk behind the wheel. When she spoke of him, it was with anger.

Vlad was ex-military and knew people in government. He got his sister and him visas to the US. On their arrival in LA, Russian friends took them in. They helped him get a job as a limo driver, working for a countryman who had a side hustle selling illegal weapons. It wasn't long before her brother had saved enough to start his own limo business.

From the way she described their life in LA, it was clear the Russian girl was a handful and difficult to control. Bored and lonely, she fell in with the wrong people—Vlad's words. The last time she saw her brother, they'd fought over her coming home at all hours. Fed up, he kicked her out to teach her a lesson.

She wandered the streets for days, begging for money to buy food. One time, she was nearly raped but managed to get away. Starving, she walked into a 7-Eleven, intending to steal food. When the store manager confronted her, a well-dressed woman appeared and offered to pay. Then, she introduced herself.

"She told me her name vas Rebekkah," Sasha said.

FOURTEEN

My stomach did a somersault when I heard that name. I thought of the trashy admin I'd seen in Tres Marias and again at Hellborn. I should've killed her when I had the chance. Becky told the Russian girl she worked for a charitable organization that got young people off the streets. And she convinced Sasha to accompany her to a coffee shop, where the woman bought her a meal.

"Did she give you anything?" I said.

"Money. She told me, if I vant, I can have a safe place to stay."

"So, she didn't force you?"

"She asked lots of questions. Vhere am I from? Do I have family? I said my parents are dead—there is no one else."

"Did she believe you?"

"She vas happy. After I finished my food, she asked if I vant to go to the safe place. I didn't know vhat to do—I didn't vant to be on the street no more. She took me to her car."

"And that's when the gray-suits took you."

She looked away. "Behind the restaurant. They threw me into a black car like the ones that chased us."

"And Rebekkah?"

"She vatched. I tried to scream, but they covered my mouth. They... How do you say it?" She made a fist and pushed down her thumb.

"They injected you?"

"Vhen I voke up, I vas in a strange place vith no vindows."

"How did you escape?"

"I hid in the, ah, laundry cart. Vhen the man finished, he smoked by the truck. I ran."

"Udachlivyy." I pretended she didn't cringe at my accent. "After everything that's happened, you don't think Vlad will forgive you?"

"He is too proud."

"But he's your flesh and blood."

"He von't, that's all."

I decided to leave the other questions for later. As I got up, she grabbed my arm.

"Vhat about Highland Park?" she said.

"That's my deal."

With lips parted, she stared at me, her eyes searching for something. Getting to her feet, she peeled off her sweater. Her breasts were firm, her pale skin flawless.

"Let me stay, and I'll give you vhatever you vant."

"Stop it."

"Anything, Dave!"

She came at me, rubbing herself against my body and trying to undo my belt. Filled with an overpowering sexual urge flavored with loneliness, I pulled her hands away. There was no question she was desirable, with a lithe body, milky skin, and killer legs. If I were anyone else, I would've screwed her six ways from Sunday.

I could've lost myself in the Russian girl—her hair, her eyes, her warm breath. But I couldn't. It hurt so much to see her throwing herself at me. I kept my voice quiet but firm, even as I fought the urge to take her there on the sofa. Again and again.

"Put on your sweater," I said and handed it to her.

She stared at me with haunted eyes. Then, with tears cascading, she covered her breasts. "Please don't send me avay."

"You don't need to do anything for me except be truthful."

Burning with shame, she pulled the sweater over her head and sank onto the sofa. I tried imagining her brother having to deal with this kid. And though we'd never met, I sympathized. He had neither the tools nor the training. The same went for me. I went into the bathroom and splashed cold water on my face and neck. When I came out, she was standing there, looking contrite.

"Izvinite," she said.

That was the second time she'd used that word. Maybe it was an apology. I wished I could do more to help her.

"Let's forget it. Look, I know you've done things you aren't proud of. I have too. But don't ever offer yourself up like that again—to me or anyone. You're better than that. I want you to promise me."

It must've been hard for her to promise anything. So many people had let her down. Her father, her brother. Becky. And though I hadn't harmed her, I was a stranger with potential.

"I promise," she said.

She began straightening up the room. Amused, I watched as she fluffed the sofa cushions and gathered the empty plastic water bottles.

"Tell me. Vhy aren't you like other men?"

"It's the pain. Keeps me focused."

"I know pain too."

A tear rolled down her cheek. Not knowing what else to

do, I held her and stroked her hair. She was thin, like a wisp of smoke made flesh. Gazing into my eyes, she tried pressing her lips to mine. Holding her tear-streaked face, I kissed her forehead.

"You can stay with me—on one condition," I said. "I must speak to your brother."

"No, he—"

"You don't have to see him. Just tell me how to get in touch. I won't let him know where you are—I promise."

Wiping her eyes, she thought it over. "I vill tell you."

"Who knows? He might surprise you. I'd better get the food. We can talk more later. Don't go near the window."

Smiling naturally had always been hard for me since the drinking. But on the way out, I gave it a shot, hoping it wasn't too *American Psycho*. She followed me as I slipped into the hallway. I heard a snick as she locked the door, followed by her muffled voice.

"Bud' ostorozhen," she said.

FIFTEEN

The departing rain left behind an eerie mist. The sky was thick with clouds, and the streetlights strained to light the way. I didn't want to leave Sasha alone for too long and hurried on foot to the takeout place. Midway past the park, I heard a rhythmic clicking, followed by a yelp. The cry sounded human.

"No, please!" It was a child's voice.

I should've left things to the police. Instead, I ventured closer. Past the playground equipment, in the shelter of the trees, something moved. Peering into the darkness, I could just make out a circle of human figures. Their bodies weaved lazily like candle flames. Where had I seen that image before?

A noise startled me. When I turned around, a swing came to rest. The only weapon I had was my stun gun. I watched the circle awhile longer. Maybe I could take out one or two, but... On second thought, better not to get involved. I could always call 911.

Before I could get out of there, a stranger stopped me cold. He was a lean, muscular man covered in scars and wearing only jeans. His spiky, white-blond hair reminded me of

Rutger Hauer's Roy Batty character in *Blade Runner*. He grinned like Satan, his eyes glowing iridescent purple. Licking fresh blood from his lips, he showed me his butterfly knife. Panicking, I ran the wrong way.

The circle opened, revealing what was inside. Revulsion swept over me—I wished I had a gun. One cutter was on his knees, slicing. Their victim was a Latino boy, maybe eight or nine. Already dead, he lay on the wet grass. One arm was skinless and bloody, and his chest was cored out like a Halloween pumpkin. His vacant eyes stared at me accusingly. *Why didn't you save me?*

I grabbed my stun gun and zapped the nearest hostile in the neck. He fell, shivering in a St. Vitus's dance of retching and clawing. I lunged at the next one, but a hand took hold of my wrist and spun me around, sending my weapon flying. Once again, I was face-to-face with the blond cutter.

With little effort, he held me in a death grip while studying my face. His head was cocked to one side like a curious dog. It was the first time I'd been this close to one of them. He appeared normal in every way except for the glowing eyes. Despite the cold, his touch was warm. He smelled of sweat. As he raised the knife, a huge German shepherd bounded towards us and sank its teeth into the cutter's leg. The owner, a middle-aged man with glasses, came running, a leather leash dangling from one hand.

"Cindy, aus!"

The dog didn't let go. Hissing, Roy Batty tried getting loose. I blocked his arm before he could cut the animal. Then I sent a haymaker to his jaw, knocking him off balance. As he hit the ground, the dog released him. He stared at his bleeding leg. Sneering, he ran barefoot into the night to join his friends.

"Sitz," I said, and the dog obeyed.

The owner clipped the leash to Cindy's collar. "She listened to you."

"I used to have a German shepherd."

He gave the animal a pat. "She's a retired police dog—very protective."

"She saved my life." I glanced behind me. "You'd better get out of here. They might be back."

Horrified, he stared at the young victim. "Oh, Lord."

"I'll handle this."

Taking my advice, the man hurried his dog to the safety of the sidewalk. I retrieved my stun gun and ran. A car almost struck me in the street when I slipped. On the other side, I entered a neighborhood market. The suspicious clerk reached under the counter the second he saw me.

"Call 911," I said.

Used to the drill, he dialed and handed me the receiver. I ignored the call script and told the emergency dispatch operator what happened. Despite her needling, I declined to identify myself. Before she could ask any more questions, I hung up and thanked the clerk.

I wasn't hungry, but I'd promised to bring food. Grabbing a shopping basket, I hurried up and down the aisles. At the register, I pulled out my wallet and noticed my shaking hands. Maritza's card fell onto the counter. I paid for the groceries and went next door to an electronics shop to purchase a burner—something I should've done sooner.

"Is it charged?" I said to the disinterested clerk.

"I think so?"

Outside on the wet street, I did what I thought I'd never do. The call went to voicemail. I waited for the greeting to finish.

"It's Dave," I said. "It happened again—you need to get down here. The police are on their way."

I gave her the location and disconnected. Police sirens wailed in the distance. I had no intention of waiting for the cops. On the way to my apartment, I thought about the blond cutter. How many more innocents would die before I could put an end to this? The angel's words came back to me, playing in my head like a prayer stuck on repeat.

You'll know them by the bodies they leave behind.

PART TWO

AFTERSHOCK

SIXTEEN

I got off the elevator, carrying the weight of the dead boy on my shoulders. Though there was nothing I could've done to save him, searing guilt ate at me like cancer. It was those staring eyes. Sasha opened the door, and taking the bags, touched my face. Her hair was wet. All she had on was a pink T-shirt and underwear. She must have sensed my discomfort.

"I vas in the shower." Handing me the food, she disappeared into the bathroom.

I laid out milk, bread, packaged meat, cheese, and fruit. As I unwrapped the bread, she reappeared fully dressed. Pushing away my hands, she made us sandwiches while I poured two glasses of milk.

"No soda?" she said.

"Milk's better for you."

"Okay, Dr. Vales. The chicken place vas closed?"

"There was a situation."

Sirens blared as the police and fire department descended on the park. I wondered if Maritza had gotten my message. The Russian girl devoured her sandwich—she could eat.

When she'd finished, I slid over my untouched plate, and she started in again.

While confronting Roy Batty, I'd felt closer to death than ever—worse than the shitshow at Hellborn. There was something in his crazy, purple eyes that petrified me. Maybe it was his calm determination, even as the police dog shredded his leg. Over these past months, I'd found that kind of fear useful. Often, it's what keeps us alive.

The cutters weren't afraid of anything. And it occurred to me that, in some ways, Walt Freeman had succeeded in creating the perfect soldier. They would complete their mission regardless of the odds. The only problem was they got hungry afterwards.

"You are nervous," she said, biting into an apple.

I met her blue-gray eyes and gave her a distracted smile. Though she'd been through bad experiences here and in Moscow, there was an innocence about her. And I wished I had that. But I felt old—much older than my twenty-four years.

"I was almost killed tonight," I said.

She took my hand. "The gray-suits?"

"I call them *cutters*. People who—"

"Eat the flesh of others." Her eyes were distant.

"You've seen them?"

"In that place."

"How many?"

"Twenty or thirty, maybe."

She wasn't afraid, so I told her everything. I described the blond cutter, who I assumed was their leader.

"He is the vorst one," she said.

"When you saw them, were they restrained?" On her puzzlement, I held up my fists and crossed them. "You know, not free."

"They vere in clear boxes. Many doctors vere there. They shot guns at them."

"Guns? What were they trying to do?"

"Learn."

"Where were you?"

"Also in a box."

"Were there other girls?"

She got up and rinsed out our glasses. Her silence told me there were others. Becky had been busy.

"What did they do to you?"

She remained at the sink, her back to me. "Tested me—blood and pee."

"What else?"

"Nothing."

I stood beside her and made her look at me. "Tell me what they did to you."

She shook her head violently. "Only tests."

"Not just tests. They did something."

I grabbed her by the shoulders and realized I was scaring her. So I backed off. She slipped away and cleared the table. A buzzing sound got my attention. I pulled out the burner and looked at the number. It was the reporter. I took a beat to calm down.

"Hello?"

"You give me an exclusive and don't even stick around for a thank-you? I assume this isn't your permanent number."

"Where are you?"

"At the park. We're wrapping up."

I walked over to the window and pulled back the curtain. I couldn't see far, but the street traffic was backed up. Helicopters flew low over our building, beaming powerful searchlights.

"They've already taken away the body," she said. "We've got plenty of footage in the can. David?"

"Still here."

"Why did you call me?"

"I wanted you to have the story first. You know, because we're in a sacred pact."

"Not good enough." Damn it—the woman was relentless.

"What? You think I like you now?"

"You're angry. Look, this is serious—we need to talk. You know what's going on, so don't try denying it. Why don't we work together? Can't we meet for coffee?"

Part of me wanted to take her up on it. There was so much more I could tell her. But it would mean getting involved with someone besides Sasha. And my plate was full.

"I'm leaving the area soon," I said.

She sighed. "When can I see you?"

"Not a good idea."

"No cameras—I promise. I know you think I'm this eager-beaver reporter looking for a story. Fine, so I am. But I'm also worried about you. Anyone can see you're in trouble. And you're scared."

"I can take care of myself."

"And don't go all macho on me. It doesn't suit you."

Despite my best efforts to blow her off, talking to Maritza calmed me. I wanted to believe she wasn't playing me. But it was in my nature to be suspicious. And I didn't want to involve her any further for her sake. Walt Freeman would have no compunction about taking care of a reporter from the local news. He'd done it before in Tres Marias. On the other hand, getting the media involved might be the only way to expose the truth. I needed advice. If only the angel would return.

"Listen to me. What's happening in LA is going to get

worse very soon. More people will die, and I don't think I can stop it. But maybe you can—you and the police."

"Are you saying this is bigger than serial killings?"

"I have to go."

"No, don't—"

"Goodbye, Maritza," I said.

SEVENTEEN

Sasha had retreated to the bedroom. Now she was standing next to me. How much had she heard? It didn't matter. My phone vibrated again—I ignored it.

"Who vas that?" she said.

"A reporter."

"You like her?"

"She's a friend. Look, this isn't—"

"Sure—*friend.*" She squeezed my hand till it hurt.

She was jealous. I had to remind myself that although she was younger than me, she was a woman. And a strong-willed one at that. In my past life, I learned two crucial lessons about women. The first was with Holly, and the second with a she-devil who almost destroyed me. Once they claim you, you have two choices—stay or run. In my wife's case, I did the right thing. Okay, so I was one for two.

"Go to the bedroom and open the closet," I said. "You'll find two duffels on the floor. Take one and use it for your stuff. We leave in the morning."

"Vhat's happening?"

"I'm taking you to Highland Park."

Getting on her tiptoes, she kissed my cheek and ran into the bedroom. I peeked out the window. On the opposite side of the street, a black Escalade cruised slowly towards our building. I closed my eyes, praying it would keep going. But this time, the driver pulled over.

Five men got out—four gray-suits and the undertaker. They faced the building. As the gray-suits waited to cross the street, I hurried to the bedroom. The Russian girl had laid her clothes neatly on the bed. I grabbed a handful and stuffed them into a duffel.

"This is vhy men must never pack," she said, taking back a sweater.

"They found us. Put my stuff in the other one. We need to leave." When she tried embracing me, I backed away. "*Now*, Sasha."

I moved to the other side of the bed and, reaching underneath, pulled out a Kel-Tec shotgun. I checked both tubes to make sure it was loaded. Next, I put on a tactical vest bursting with ammo. As I crossed to the living room window, I tucked a handgun into the waist of my jeans.

Outside on the street, the gray-suits had split up. Two approached the front of the building. I assumed the others would enter from the alley. Checking his phone, the undertaker waited next to the vehicle. Sasha joined me at the window, wearing a sweater and gray bucket hat.

"The man in the black suit," I said. "Do you know him?"

"His name is Trower."

I took her trembling hands in mine to calm her. "Can you drive?" I didn't wait for an answer and gave her the car keys. "Take the bags and use the elevator."

"But those men."

"They'll use the stairs. When you leave the building, don't speed."

"Vhat if Trower sees me?"

I pulled her hat down low and gave her a smile. She kissed my hand.

"There's no way he could know you're with me. Turn left and drive about a mile. There's a McDonald's on the corner. Wait for me."

"How long?"

"Thirty minutes." I texted myself a number and handed the phone to her. "If I don't make it, call Cuco and tell him you're coming. He'll look after you."

She didn't want to leave. I touched her face and held her.

"I know you can do this. Now go."

"Don't get dead," she said and kissed my lips.

I walked her to the door. She headed for the elevator, struggling with the bags. As she stepped in, a Latino couple with a squirmy toddler exited their apartment. The man waved.

"Por favor," he said, and she let them in.

Locking the door, I begged God to keep the Russian girl safe. I hurried to the window to watch for the Tahoe. In a little while, a two-door compact pulled out of the building. After a beat, the SUV followed and turned left. Trower hadn't noticed.

The emergency exit door on my floor had always squeaked. I meant to tell Cuco but was glad I didn't. I tried guessing how they would know which apartment was mine. Most likely, they would have obtained a list of tenants and focused on single men in the building. It's what I would've done.

Outside, door hinges squealed. Gripping the bullpup, I moved to the windows. I thought of trying the fire escape. Trower would spot me and take me out. I decided to wait. This wasn't what I wanted—dying without avenging Holly.

And putting down a few gray-suits would mean nothing in the grand scheme.

I listened to the sound of approaching footsteps. They stopped in front of my door. I positioned myself behind the sofa. Kneeling, I pointed my weapon and waited.

"Please, God. Let them be stupid," I said.

EIGHTEEN

An explosion of glass rained down as a gray-suit lumbered through the window. I shot him point-blank. The blast knocked him back. But it didn't kill him because of his body armor. I fired again. This time, his face exploded. A pastel of pink and red coated the curtains and left the half-headed body falling backwards—arms windmilling—through the window. What was left lay motionless on the fire escape, wrapped grotesquely around the railing.

The apartment door burst open. A second hostile marched in, firing his weapon as he came at me. I blasted his legs out from under him, sending him crashing to his knees. Before he could recover, I picked up his gun and put a bullet in his head. Then I ran down the hallway to the emergency stairs. Frightened voices cried out in Spanish behind locked doors. The cops would arrive in minutes. I still had two gray-suits—and Trower—to take care of. Pausing, I loaded more shells.

I stood in the stairwell and looked down. Then, I started my descent and made it to the garage in no time. When I came out, a gray-suit was waiting for me. He fired, striking me in the side. My vest had slowed the bullet, and with adrenalin surging, I hardly felt the pain. I smacked him with the bullpup's barrel and kicked him backwards.

As he stumbled, I fired mercilessly at his raised hands. His fingers exploded in a blossom of bloody fish sticks. When he hit the ground, I bashed his skull with the butt of my weapon. Then, clutching my bleeding side, I staggered to the garage gate. It was raining. The Escalade was still there, but Trower was nowhere in sight.

Fighting shock, I limped across the garage to a service entrance, where I took an excruciating breath and opened the door. Cautiously, I entered the alley. Racking my brain, I tried thinking of a way to get to Sasha without being conspicuous. Maybe in the downpour, no one would notice the blood. I'd have to ditch the guns and the vest, making me vulnerable. Two more hostiles were out there somewhere. I started towards the street. Halfway there, I heard a noise.

Turning, I spotted a dark figure—the last gray-suit. He pointed his weapon with both hands. I leveled my shotgun at him and almost squeezed the trigger when I heard the approaching sound of Linkin Park's "Bleed It Out."

High beams blinded me as a speeding vehicle bore down on the gray-suit. Ignoring it, he fired, missing me by inches. The SUV knocked him flat with a sickening thud. He screamed only for a second as his arms and legs were crushed.

My Tahoe screeched to a stop in front of me. The Russian girl peered at me through the wet windshield, the wipers distorting her features. Her eyes were wide. Her hands clutched the steering wheel in a white-knuckle grip. Urgently, she waved me over and flung open the passenger door.

I looked past the SUV at the writhing meat suit clawing

the asphalt. Marching past the vehicle, I stared at the fallen gray-suit. He tried to speak, coughing up blood instead. The back of his head had a hole in it. Rain washed away the gore, revealing his brain. He no longer had a nose, and one eye was deflated. As bad off as he was, there was a chance he might talk. I didn't want that. Drawing a bead with my handgun, I sent a bullet through his good eye. Now, the only sound was the music coming from the Tahoe.

Trower stood in the faint light of a glitchy flood lamp. But he wasn't looking at me. His eyes were laser focused on Sasha. I should've gone after him, but I was weak from blood loss. Ignoring the intense pain, I tore off my vest and tossed it and the weapons in the backseat. Once I was safely inside, she continued down the alley. I watched from the side mirror as Trower took a knee to examine his dead foot soldier. I turned off the music.

"I thought I told you to wait for me," I said, applying pressure to my side.

Entering the busy street, she noted the blood on my hands. "*Thank you* vould be nice. Hospital now?"

"No hospitals."

We pulled into a CVS. I handed her some cash and gave her my list. The parking lot was deserted except for a stewbum singing a holiday song. In a few minutes, she returned with the supplies. We drove down a lonely street to an abandoned rail line, where I told her to pull over.

My side throbbed as I eased myself out of the vehicle. We found shelter in an old corrugated metal storage shed. Inside, lay a crusty sleeping bag among the leaves and trash. A wood workbench ran along one wall. She dragged over an empty 55-gallon oil drum for me to sit on. Then, she set up an LED flashlight on the workbench and aimed the beam at me.

I lifted my shirt to examine the wound. It wasn't bleeding

as much now. Thanks to the vest, the bullet hadn't gone in deep. I rinsed my hands with Betadine and used my index finger to probe the area. A blinding bolt of pain shot through me like a red-hot railroad spike. Biting down on a scream, I felt around for the slug.

"I think it missed my liver," I said. "Use the rubbing alcohol to sterilize the forceps."

After doing that, she handed me the instrument. Gingerly, I pulled open the wound with one hand while inserting the forceps with the other. But the pain was so intense, I couldn't keep my hand steady.

"Let me," she said.

Like a pro, she inserted the instrument and removed the bullet while ignoring my pathetic howling. After pouring Betadine into the wound, she did her best to close it using butterfly bandages. Panting, I examined the slug. Thank God it hadn't fragmented. She handed me a bottle of ibuprofen. I swallowed four and chased them down with bottled water.

"Thank you," I said and touched her hand.

"Nichego strashnogo." Closing her eyes, she rubbed her temples.

"Another headache?"

"I am fine."

As the rain pattered on the metal roof, I recalled the night's events. I was sure I would die in the alley. But God had seen fit to let me live one more day. Did that mean I was on the right path? I pictured Trower standing in the rain, staring at the Russian girl. The more I thought about it, the more I was convinced he knew I was the one who'd rescued his precious test subject.

Sasha gathered the supplies and helped me into the Tahoe. "Highland Park now?"

"I need to make a stop first," I said.

NINETEEN

Icy rain fell like boning knives as we pulled up to the gate. Careful not to tear open my wound, I climbed out and approached a gray keypad fastened to a metal post. I punched in the code. A motor squealed into life, and the gate rolled back. The storage facility was deserted. We headed for the last aisle and pulled up to my space.

"Wait here," I said, taking the keys.

Yawning, Sasha snuggled into the seat and closed her eyes. In her hat and sweater, she resembled a tired refugee. Wincing, I knelt in front of the Tahoe to examine the bumper. The rain had washed away the blood, but there was visible damage. I removed the unit's padlock and prepared myself for the pain. Gritting my teeth, I lifted the metal roll-up door. Searing blades of agony tore at my side like a harpy's fingers. I suppressed a scream.

The interior was a void except for the outlines of three black storage containers. I'd packed my weapons carefully and knew which box I wanted. Suddenly, I sensed movement. Slivers of light glimmered in a corner through the darkness like fireflies trapped in a killing jar.

The angel came forward. Though she was far from human, I worried she might be cold in her T-shirt and shorts. The concern she felt for me was evident in her eyes. Nervous, I glanced behind me. The Russian girl was sound asleep.

"Tell me what to do," I said.

"You're free to do whatever."

"Every time I try that, I end up with a new problem. Sasha, for instance."

"She is important."

"Why? Can't you tell me what's going on?"

She gazed at the guns without judgment. I wondered what was going through her mind. What did angels think about all day?

"Why didn't I die?"

"Do you want to?"

"Only after I kill my enemies."

"That won't bring back Holly."

She took my hand. Walking me to a container, she waited for me to sit. She was so small and frail beside me. It was as if she weighed nothing at all. Why would God send me a child when I needed a warrior?

"The gray-suits are dangerous," she said. "But there's someone worse."

"Trower? Is he the one who does me?"

"Stay in the light. Protect the girl."

"Dammit, answer my question! Does Trower kill me?"

"No one knows the day or hour when these things will happen, not even the angels in heaven."

I hated it when she quoted Scripture. Instead of providing comfort, it was just a convenient trick to misdirect. I glowered at her, my back to the entrance. Patiently, she waited for me to settle down.

"Fine. I'll see to it that Sasha is safe, but she can't stay with me. I'm taking her to her brother. Let him deal with her. I'm not kidding, I—"

"Dave?" It was the Russian girl.

She stood shivering at the entrance. Silhouetted by the security lights, her warm breath was visible in the night air. For a moment, she reminded me of the angel. When I turned back, my guardian was gone.

"I, um… I was doing a weapons inventory," I said.

"Do you alvays talk to yourself?"

"It's a habit I'm trying to break."

I grabbed the handle of a container and dragged it over the wet concrete onto the asphalt. Ignoring the rain, I opened the vehicle's rear door and removed the floor panel. The Korean had anticipated me—everything was gone, including the spare. The extra license plates lay at the bottom of the tire well.

While I switched out the plates, Sasha inspected the box's contents. Long guns and handguns lay neatly stacked, along with black nylon bags filled with ammo and cash. I should've been an arms dealer.

"Vhich country are ve invading?" she said.

I slammed the lid down and tried lifting the container by myself. But with my injury, it proved to be too much. She touched my arm.

"That vill not fit. Ve can transfer the guns."

"I knew that."

She helped me fill the back with weapons and cash. I replaced the floor panel and shut the rear door. After locking up the storage unit, I got behind the wheel. We drove off into the chilly night.

"How is your side?" she said.

"I need my phone."

She removed it from her back pocket and handed it over. I

called Cuco to let him know the score. He gave me his address in Highland Park and promised to wait for us.

This was how it would be from now on—the kind of life I was used to. No regular place to sleep. Moving frantically from one safe house to another. I was determined to reunite the Russian girl with her brother and get her out of my life. It was the only way. I had to survive long enough to find Walt Freeman before Trower could take me out.

After that, death would be a blessing.

I'd heard Highland Park was a rough neighborhood. But the streets were tree-lined and pleasant, unlike my earlier impression. The rain had let up. Cuco stood on the porch of a small post-war bungalow. I took in the manicured lawn, wrought-iron fence, and white awnings over the front windows. His car was parked on the street.

The Mexican rolled back the gate, and I pulled into the driveway. He took the keys and backed the Tahoe into the garage. He was about to close the door when he noticed something. Crouching, he felt the front bumper and shook his head. After closing the garage door and gate, he invited us inside.

The house smelled like Mexican cooking. It was modestly furnished with inexpensive furniture and beige walls without pictures. I got the sense that, like me, Cuco was a loner. Though he had a family in Mexico who he visited off and on, he seemed to live in a perpetual twilight of unbelonging.

"I'll get that bumper fixed," he said to me. "¿Algo para comer?"

"That would be great."

We followed our host into the kitchen. A young Latino

boy sat at the table, drinking milk. The remnants of a PB&J lay on a plate in front of him. I side-eyed Sasha.

"That's Ernie, my neighbor," the Mexican said.

I didn't like it. "You're taking care of him?"

"His mother works. I look after him when I can."

He tousled the boy's hair and said something in Spanish. Wiping away his milk mustache, Ernie got up and ran out the back door.

My friend had prepared spicy beef that we now used to make tacos. He was aware I didn't drink and offered me a soda. Taking two beers from the refrigerator, he handed one to the Russian girl.

"Provecho."

"How long have you lived here?" I said.

"Fifteen years."

"Any problems?"

"A few burglaries in the neighborhood. But they know to leave me alone."

Sasha looked like she was in heaven as she helped herself to more beans and rice. "Best food I ever ate."

"In Juarez, my wife does all the cooking. Here, I'm on my own."

I hadn't realized how hungry I was. "You have a real talent for it."

He took a long swallow and belched, making the Russian girl giggle. Now it was her turn, and the competition was on. Finally, my friend put down his empty beer bottle and looked at me with a baleful expression.

"Dígame," he said.

I told him what I could—about Sasha and me. After clearing the table, she brought Cuco another beer and sat between us, content.

"I don't want us to be a burden. We need a few days to—"

"No hay bronca." He winked. "O-kay."

"Awesome—thank you." Then to the Russian girl, "Tomorrow, I'm calling your brother."

She looked at her hands, then at the Mexican, who quirked his eyebrows at me.

"Look, I promised I wouldn't tell him where you are."

"I know."

"I want you to be safe."

"I *am* safe," she said, her eyes darkening. "Vith you."

Cuco's face told me there was trouble ahead. I didn't want Sasha running away, especially now that she'd killed a man. That must have affected her. Who knew what feelings she was holding back? Softening my voice, I squeezed her hand.

"If there's even a hint that Vlad will be a problem, I'll cut off all communication. But he's your only family. And he needs to know you're alive."

Though she didn't say anything, it was clear I wasn't getting through. Our host left the kitchen. When he returned, he was carrying a box of tissues. He set them on the table in front of her. She grabbed a few and blew her nose.

"I am such a girl," she said.

"I promise I won't let anything happen to you. You know that, right?"

Grabbing the tissues, she bolted out of the kitchen. A door slammed, followed by a click.

"She's locked herself in the bathroom," Cuco said. As I stood, he grabbed my arm. "Déjala en paz."

"Fine. I'll leave her alone—for now. But I mean, seriously. How bad can her brother be?"

"Pendejo, this has nothing to do with him."

"What are you talking about?"

"Can't you see she's in love with you?" he said.

TWENTY

Cuco tidied up the kitchen while I sat watching with my mouth open. I wanted to believe he'd pulled that comment out of his ass. I didn't even know Sasha. How could she… Turning around, he gave me a wise look. Shit. Women were exhausting. I covered my eyes, and I might have moaned.

"Perfect," I said. "Are you sure this isn't Stockholm syndrome?"

He laid the tea towel on the counter and sat across from me. "What do you know about her?"

"Other than she's a Russian immigrant, nothing."

"You told me she was kidnapped. Trafficking?"

"Worse—experimentation. They did something to her, but she won't talk about it. And she doesn't want her brother finding out."

"Give her time. What else?"

I told him the whole story. How the plague began in Tres Marias and how we battled the undead for months. I described what it was like watching Holly die. Then, I mentioned Walt Freeman. Surprisingly, he took it well.

"At least you know what happened to your wife. In Mexico, victims of feminicidio disappear forever."

"I heard about women and girls going missing. And the, uh, maqui…"

"Maquiladoras."

"Those factories in Juarez, right? Did you lose someone?"

He looked away. "My younger sister." He placed the remaining pots in the dishwasher and slammed the door shut. "And now you come to LA to die."

"Well, I hope to take a few others with me."

He hurled a glass into the sink, sending the wet shards everywhere. My nerves were already on high alert, and the noise made me jump.

"Estás bien pendejo," he said.

So now I was an idiot? He grabbed another beer from the fridge and pulled up a chair beside me, the feet scraping. I worried he would backhand me.

"You don't think I would give anything to find the monsters who killed my sister? Not a day goes by when I don't imagine tearing out their throats with my bare hands. But that's not living, güey. I have a wife and kids. And my parents and her parents. My job is to live."

He was right. I was a dick, acting like I was the only person in the world who'd ever lost someone.

"I'm not like you," I said. "I don't have anyone."

"Alli está, te va a morder." He pointed towards the bathroom. "Any closer, it'll bite you."

"What—Sasha? No no no—no way. I promised to help her. But once I find her brother, I'm out."

"What if El Señor brought her to you?"

"God? Now you're just trying to make me feel guilty."

"Pues…"

He showed me his missing molar through a sloppy grin.

Finishing his beer, he turned on the dishwasher. My head and side throbbed. I drifted into the living room and, flicking on the TV, saw *SpongeBob SquarePants*. It was "The Camping Episode"—my favorite.

The Russian girl cried out from the bathroom. Thinking someone had broken in, I ran to her and banged on the door. In another beat, Cuco appeared.

"Sasha? Are you okay?"

"Dave…"

I tried the door. Locked. Before I could force my way in, the Mexican pushed me aside. He reached up to the top of the door frame and grabbed an emergency key. We found the Russian girl on the floor next to the toilet, holding her stomach. As I knelt beside her, she gripped my hand.

"It hurts," she said.

"Are you nauseous?" Then to Cuco, "Maybe the food was too spicy."

She shook her head and swallowed. "Not the food. It happens for a vhile. Only now, feels vorse."

Gently, I brushed the damp hair from her face. "Why didn't you tell me?"

Gritting her teeth, she squeezed my hand harder. "I thought it vould get better when I left that place."

"Did they give you drugs?"

She hesitated. Then, "Sometimes."

"You need to rest. Can you walk?" I helped her to her feet and looked at my friend. "Where can she lie down?"

"This way," he said.

Ignoring my wound, I carried her as the Mexican led us to a guest bedroom. Everything was made up and ready. There was a double bed with nightstands, a dresser, and pale yellow curtains on the windows—a girl's room.

I laid her on the bed and removed her boots. Then I

covered her with the duvet. Cuco left the room and returned with a glass of water. Setting it on the nightstand, he pointed urgently at the door. Feverish, she grabbed my hand as I tried to leave.

"Nyet—ne ukhodi!"

"I promise I'll be back," I said, withdrawing my hand.

We sat at the kitchen table in the gloom of eternal night. Somewhere, a clock ticked. Rain fell softly outside. The Mexican's expression was grim.

"Those men did something to her," he said.

"And either she doesn't know because they drugged her, or she's afraid to tell us."

"You mentioned a plague before. She might be contagious."

"If it's the same virus we encountered in Tres Marias, it would have to be passed by blood. The infected we fought bit people. That's how the disease spread. She needs a doctor, but I can't risk it."

"I have a friend—un buen hombre. He won't ask questions."

"I don't know…"

"He's used to dealing with illegals. Very discreet."

"We'll need blood tests—the works. Can you arrange it?"

"I'll call him in the morning." He grabbed his car keys. "What about el hermano?"

"Vlad will have to wait."

"I need to pick up some food," he said and slipped out through the back door.

I lingered at the kitchen table. Rubbing my eyes, I tried dealing with the curveballs God was firing at me. Even with the constant pain in my side, it was hard to keep my eyes open. I returned to the bedroom. Sasha stirred as I walked in.

"It's only me," I said.

Lying there, she looked like a helpless child. My brain told me to get her off my hands as soon as possible. But my heart said I needed to protect her, even if it meant risking my life. *Stay in the light. Protect the girl.* This overwhelming feeling of responsibility was the angel's doing.

I pulled off my shoes and lay on the bed next to her. Sleepily, she groaned and turned onto her side. Throwing her arm across my chest, she snuggled her head against my shoulder and snored softly. As much as I wanted the feeling to be unpleasant, it wasn't.

"Why did you come back for me?" I said.

"Bad men... They kill you... Don't vant that."

"Why?"

"Don't vant..."

"You took a man's life."

"Bad man."

"Right. He was a very bad man."

Stroking her hair, I waited as she fell into a deep sleep. I'd intended to keep watch all night. But somewhere along the way, I began drifting off with her fragrant body warming me. Her gentle breathing soothed me, and the soft cascade of secret Russian whispers brought me peace.

"Bad men," I said and closed my eyes to the world.

TWENTY-ONE

When I awoke, Ernie was standing near the bed, gnawing on a corn tortilla.

"Don't you have school?" I said.

"¡Está despierto!" Grinning, he ran to the door and stopped. "You stink."

The yellow curtains glowed in the morning light. Voices drifted in from another room, and I thought I heard laughter. There was a sharp pain in my side—worse than before. I felt feverish. Sitting up, I looked down to find my wound had leaked through the dressing and emitted a foul odor. When I walked into the kitchen, Sasha, Cuco, and Ernie were eating a breakfast of chorizo with eggs, beans, and rice. The Russian girl gave me a warm smile.

"Want some coffee?" our host said.

Playfully, she pushed him back into his chair and poured me a cup.

"Thanks," I said. Then to Cuco, "Okay if I turn on the TV?"

I switched on the tiny set on the counter and turned to Channel 7. The morning show had broken away to local

"

news. Maritza was on-screen, reporting from the murder scene in the park the night before. Curious locals pressed up against the barricade tape, watching the activities of the police and Emergency Medical Services.

As the reporter described the grisly discovery, the scene jumped to an overhead shot from a news helicopter. The police had cordoned off the streets surrounding the park. I wondered if the dead boy's parents were among the hundred or so bystanders. I spotted a black Escalade just before the scene returned to Maritza.

"So far, the police have no leads in the gruesome slaying," she said. "Mari Lopez reporting."

The news anchor reminded us of the previous attack at Holy Grounds. Footage of the female victim being loaded into the ambulance came on, followed by the reporter's interview with the police captain. I turned off the TV and looked at Sasha.

"Te ves mal," the Mexican said to me.

"I'm worse than bad. I think I might have an infection."

"Lucky we have a doctor's appointment."

As I sank into a chair, the Russian girl set a plate in front of me. I pushed it away and swallowed more coffee.

"Let me see," she said, unbuttoning my shirt.

Too weak to protest, I scooted away from the table as she knelt beside me. With the efficiency of a nurse, she peeled away the bandage, exposing the livid gash oozing yellow pus. That was enough for the kid, and he bolted out the back door.

She peered at the wound. "Disgusting. And it smells. I vill clean it now." Then to Cuco, "Do you have, ah, plastic wrap?"

Annoyed, I pulled down my shirt. "Why?"

"So you can shower, Mr. Vales."

She touched my face and hurried to the bathroom to get

what she needed. My friend swallowed the last of his coffee, his eyes sparkling like jewels.

"What?"

"Gonna bite you."

"Shut up," I said.

The waiting room was packed with Spanish-speaking patients —primarily children and the elderly. No one asked us to fill out any paperwork. Whatever Cuco had arranged, this visit was off the books. Sasha fidgeted. On the ride over, she'd been preoccupied with my infection, worried something would happen to me. But now that she was about to be examined, reality set in.

A young woman with long, curly dark hair appeared. "Señorita Castillo?"

The Mexican patted Sasha's hand. "That's you."

"You'll be fine," I said to her.

In a couple minutes, the same woman called for Señor Wales. I followed her into a typical examination room—a table covered in butcher paper, a plastic chair, and a stainless-steel sink with white cabinets above it. There were notices and medical diagrams on the pale blue walls. Everything was in Spanish and, from what I could make out, warned of the dangers of herpes, drug abuse, and head lice.

There was a brief knock. A middle-aged physician assistant entered, wearing a stethoscope around her neck. The name RIOS was printed on her nameplate. All business, she gave my hand a quick pump.

"Señor Wales? Let's have a look."

I sat on the table and removed my shirt. She washed her hands and put on surgical gloves. Then, peeling away the fresh bandage, she probed the wound with her index finger. I tried not to wince.

"When did this happen?" she said.

"Last night. I've been shot before."

"Yes, I can see."

"This is the first time the wound has gotten infected, though."

"It's called gunshot sepsis. Pretty rare, but... Who removed the bullet?"

"A friend."

After taking my temperature and blood pressure, she asked me to lie down. She used a medical penlight to make a closer examination. The area was tender. Although she did her best not to cause me any pain, I had to grit my teeth against the warm, intense throbbing.

"No organ damage, and I don't see any bullet fragments. I'm going to irrigate the wound, then suture it. I'll prescribe an antibiotic. Oh, and something for the pain."

"I'll stick with ibuprofen."

"As you wish. This won't take long."

She left the room and returned seconds later with a surgical tray containing a hypodermic needle and syringe, a suture needle and thread, and bandages. I braced myself as she injected the area with lidocaine. Using what looked like a turkey baster, she flushed the wound with Betadine and sewed me up. The procedure took less than ten minutes. As I buttoned my shirt, the PA gathered everything and waited by the door.

She gave my hand another pump. "I'm glad you came in when you did, Señor Wales."

"Oh? Why?"

"Another twelve hours, and you'd be dead," she said and walked out.

TWENTY-TWO

Rios handed me a prescription in the waiting room. Thanking her, I sat next to Cuco to wait for Sasha. There were even more patients than before. With so many sick children, it was getting noisy.

"Thanks for bringing me here," I said.

He glanced up from a Spanish-language newspaper and responded in a flawless American accent. "No problemo."

"It's really *no hay bronca*, right?"

"You're learning."

Another fifteen minutes had gone by when they called us in to see Dr. Fernandes. The office was sparsely decorated with diplomas from the US and Colombia on the wall. He was a pleasant-looking man in his early fifties. Short, with a shiny bald head and gold rimless glasses. There was a framed photo of his family on his desk—a wife and three teenage daughters. The Russian girl sat with her hands folded as the Latinos exchanged greetings in Spanish.

"Mr. Wales, I've taken blood and urine and ordered tests," the doctor said. "At Cuco's request, I put a rush on them. We should have the results within two hours."

"That fast?"

"The lab is in the same building."

"Did you notice anything unusual?"

"Unusual?"

"Wounds of any kind." I side-eyed Sasha. "Or bite marks."

"Only on her hand where they inserted an IV."

He must've sensed my skepticism and flipped through the patient's chart. "So far, everything appears normal."

"What about her abdominal pain?"

"We'll know more when I see the test results."

"Okay, I guess we'll wait outside."

The doctor stood. "There's an excellent Salvadoran restaurant not far from here. I know the owner very well. I suggest you go there. Have coffee. And mention my name. I'll let Cuco know when we have the results."

I was relieved he hadn't found anything. Maybe I was wrong, and Hellborn had done nothing invasive. As the others left, I thanked Dr. Fernandes.

"What are you looking for, Señor Wales?"

"The truth," I said.

There was a pharmacy off the lobby. Unlike the big chains, they filled my prescription right away. We walked farther down the street to the restaurant the doctor had recommended. It was early, and the place wasn't crowded. The interior was beige and brown, with a brightly lit bar that extended the length of the room. Plants hung from the ceiling, and photos of Latin American soccer teams covered the walls. Large TVs with the sound off were mounted everywhere, tuned to various games. Behind the bar hung the blue-and-white flag of El Salvador.

We found a table away from the windows. The owner

came over and chatted with Cuco in Spanish. He was short and stocky, with wavy black hair, a formidable mustache, and perfect teeth. Though they spoke rapidly, I thought I heard my friend mention the doctor. Immediately, the owner went away, returning with coffee and a tray of delicious-looking pastries.

Two hours was a long time to wait, but the time passed quickly. The owner brought us plate after plate of food. At first, I ate only to be polite. But soon, I found myself sampling everything. When we were done, I took my medication and wished I could loosen my belt like an old man after the early-bird special.

"You didn't like the food?" the Mexican said.

I belched, making Sasha laugh. "So good. I need to walk around."

"There are shops up and down this street."

When the owner presented the bill, I wanted to laugh. He'd charged us twenty-five bucks for what must have cost a hundred. I paid him, leaving a generous tip.

Next to the restaurant, there was a Guatemalan shop that smelled of leather. Intrigued, the Russian girl went in. Cuco and I waited outside. Reappearing, she shoved a colorful worry doll in my face. Bits of fabric had been used to fashion its clothing and head covering. In her other hand, she held a dark pouch that contained the rest of the dolls.

"I don't have money," she said, pouting.

Rolling my eyes, I took the stuff to the counter and paid. Outside, she made the doll kiss my cheek.

"Thank you for saving me," it said.

We returned to the doctor's office and spent the remainder of the time in the waiting room. While I flipped through a magazine, Sasha played with her dolls. Though she was a grown woman, there was something childlike about her, which I found endearing.

In a few minutes, the woman with the curly dark hair called us into the doctor's office. We found him poring over the lab report. Looking concerned, he signaled us to sit.

"What's the verdict?" I said.

He addressed the patient. "I can say you are a very healthy young woman. CBC, basic metabolic panel, enzymes—all good. Everything, in fact. However…"

I leaned in. "What?"

"The lab suspected something and called me. I told them to run an additional test."

"What kind of test?"

The doctor looked at me gravely. "Rabies."

The others stared at me. Unlike them, I took the news calmly. Everyone waited for me to say something.

"Is she contagious?"

"No. But the lab found traces of the antibodies." Then to the Russian girl, "I didn't notice any bite marks when I examined you. Is it possible you got bit by an animal? A bat, perhaps?"

She shook her head and looked at me.

"You don't seem surprised, Mr. Wales."

"I was expecting it." I placed ten crisp hundred-dollar bills on the desk and got up to leave.

"Wait." Ignoring the cash, the doctor came around the desk. "There's something else."

Of course, there was. Once again, I was being pulled down a well, and I didn't want to hear any more. Hellborn had done something to Sasha, after all. I prepared myself for the bad news. But when Dr. Fernandes turned to her, he was beaming.

"Congratulations, Señorita Castillo," he said. "You're pregnant."

TWENTY-THREE

"It's a lie!" Sasha said and left to use the restroom.

By the time Cuco and I realized where she'd gone, the Russian girl was huddled on the curb outside, surrounded by locals chattering in Spanish. A kid on a bike told us she ran into the street, where a car almost hit her. I helped her up, and taking her by the shoulders, made her face me. She looked desolate.

"It's going to be okay," I said.

She pressed her head against me. Unsure what to do or say, I turned to the Mexican. He squinted at the prescription the doctor had given him. Then he went back to the pharmacy to get her prenatal vitamins. I didn't want to care this much, but I couldn't help it. She was alone—I knew what that was like.

I took her hand. "Come on."

A constant rain fell as I helped her into the backseat of Cuco's car and climbed in after her. Though I was never good at giving comfort, I imitated what my mother had done for me after my father's funeral. Pressing Sasha's head against my shoulder, I stroked her hair, which seemed to calm her.

"How can it be true?" she said.

"Getting a soda," I said as we came in through the front door. "Anyone want anything?" A minute later, Cuco joined me in the kitchen. "Where is she?"

"In her room."

I slammed the refrigerator door shut. "Hellborn did this."

"Hellborn?"

"Baseborn Identity Research. I need to talk to her."

He grabbed my arm. "She doesn't need your anger."

Nodding, I stopped and took a calming breath. The bedroom door was closed. I knocked once and walked in. Sasha lay on the bed, facing the window. Her hair covered her face. Humming softly, she twirled a worry doll in the light, making it dance. I sat beside her.

"Vhy did they give me rabies?" she said.

"It's *not* rabies. It's a drug they manufactured using the virus."

"And you knew?"

"I suspected."

"Vhat else did they do?"

"Well, I have a theory."

Desperate, she took my hand. "Tell me."

"I think they used IVF—in vitro fertilization. Understand?"

"No man ever—"

"I know."

Grabbing her abdomen, she moaned. "It hurts!"

There was nothing I could do for her except wait. After the last wave passed, she sat up and slid next to me. I put my arm around her. She felt warm.

"And you had no idea?" I said.

She looked at me, her eyes pleading. "I svear. They took me and the other girls to the special room."

"That's what they called it?"

"Because ve are so special. They put the needle in our hands, and I know I vill go to sleep again. Vhen I open my eyes, I am in my bed. The other girls, they…"

"What happened to them?"

"They got sick. Those men took them avay, and I vas alone. But I didn't get sick. This made them happy, and they gave me treats like a dog. They said they vill move me to a new place in the desert. I knew I must get out. Am I going to become like those things—cutters?"

"You won't." I prayed I was right.

If she suspected I was lying, she let it pass. I stood near the window and looked out at the street. The glare from the wet asphalt was blinding. The rain had let up. White rays of sunlight shone through the cloud cover. We were safe for now, but it was only a matter of time before Trower found us. When she reached for my hand, I returned to the bed.

Holding her, I tried guessing what Hellborn was up to. I went over everything I knew about Robbin-Sear, Bob Creasy, and the protocol. It all began as an experiment to create the perfect soldier—immune to fear and capable of fighting even after getting shot. But what they got were cutters. And Roy Batty was their poster child.

The protocol. I could almost picture it—a thick black binder with the words TOP SECRET printed across the cover. The book would describe the program's phases. They'd already shipped draggers from the Mt. Shasta lab to LA. But Hellborn couldn't continue unleashing them into the wild like they did in Tres Marias. They would have to find a new way to evolve the virus in a more controlled manner. Genetics?

It made sense now. The scientists could've impregnated young women with semen from sick patients, hoping to create what? A superhuman? This was the stuff of science fiction—*The Boys from Brazil.* And yet what other explanation could there be?

If the Russian girl was carrying the progeny of some mutant, wouldn't it be best to get rid of it? How could God expect an innocent girl to give birth to a monster? I thought of the baby Holly carried in her womb when she was viciously gunned down. That little life—my child's life—was gone in an instant. But that was different. We weren't talking about a baby conceived from love. This was something evil. Something hellborn.

I was a fallen Catholic who'd racked up enough sins to last an eternity. Yet, with all the misdeeds in my past, I didn't think I could end an innocent life, even one created in a lab. Despite how it had been conceived, wasn't this child innocent too? Okay, so maybe if this were up to me, I would try to save it. But it wasn't my decision. That responsibility belonged to Sasha.

"What will you do about the…"

I couldn't bring myself to say the word. But she knew what I meant and looked at me with the kind of human expression that manifests whenever death is on the table.

"I vant to see my brother," she said.

be nice. He asked me to follow him. I was a stupid girl, so I vent. He tried to…"

"It's okay, we get it."

"I didn't let him do nothing. Vhen I got home, Vlad saw my arms and face. He made me tell him who hurt me. I said the name, and he vent out. Later, he told me the boy vill not bother me again. I asked him vhat he did. He said only that he teach him a lesson."

A tear fell on her hand. "The next day in school, they said this boy fell and broke both arms. I never saw him again."

"If he's so protective, why did he kick you out?"

"He had enough of my lies. I vas not good to him. Alvays complaining, alvays disobeying."

I turned to the Mexican. "What do you think?"

"Pues, no sé. When he finds out she's embarazada…"

"What will he do? Shit, you don't mean—like an honor killing?"

"Ve are from Moscow," she said. "Not Chechnya."

Getting to my feet, I handed Cuco my keys. "Can you drop me? I want to scope out the place."

She gawped at me like I was nuts. "My brother vill think of that. I'm sure he is going there now."

"What else can I do? We have less than two hours."

She rolled her eyes at us. "You Americans."

Our host pretended to be offended. "Hey, I'm Mexican."

"Cuco takes you, right?" she said. "You vait in the car vhile he checks everything. And he calls you when it's safe."

The Mexican nodded. "I like that idea."

I had to admit, it was a good plan. Besides, we didn't have many options. I changed clothes and, grabbing my Glock, did a weapons check. Sasha touched my hand.

"Don't kill my brother."

"You'd better pray he doesn't kill me," I said. Then to

Cuco, "I want to move my car away from the house. Is there a private garage around here somewhere?"

"On the way. You can follow me."

I held the Russian girl's hands. "Watch the street, and make sure no one sees you."

"I vait for you," she said and kissed me.

TWENTY-FIVE

I t was late afternoon when we arrived. Cuco parked on Wilshire and headed to the lake while I waited in the front passenger seat. Traffic was heavy. The sidewalks bustled with the working class. Though it was a weekday, a surprising number of people were enjoying the break from the rain.

A toothless panhandler shuffled up to my window, his grimy hand extended. I ignored him. With a blackened finger, he drew a greasy bunny on my window and smiled through diseased gums. I dug into my wallet and, cracking the window, handed him some cash. He muttered his thanks in Spanish.

There was nothing for me to do but wait for the Mexican's call. He'd disappeared past the palm trees and through a crowd of Latinas and their laughing children. Now that we were here, I felt better about the plan. Sasha was safe at home. Once I was confident her brother would act reasonably, I would let him see her. Not wanting to be recognized by the gray-suits, I already had on the jacket and baseball cap. Bad idea.

Someone approached the vehicle's passenger side. I assumed it was another panhandler. When I turned around, a beefy, redheaded man glared at me. He was dressed in a black suit and white silk shirt open halfway down his furry chest. He tried the door handle, but it was locked.

I heard tapping. Another man, equally large and wearing a similar black suit and gold chains, stood ominously on the driver's side. He showed me his gun. Cuco was nowhere in sight. Surrounded by humorless Russians, I unlocked my door.

The fire crotch grabbed me by the shoulders and made me face west. I started walking. There was a black town car parked on the street half a block away. From the reflection on the windshield, it was hard to see who was behind the wheel. I guessed it was Sasha's brother.

Opening the rear door, the fire crotch waited for me to get in. Gold Chains had already climbed in on the other side. The first Russian shoved me over, which put me between two gorillas wearing heavy cologne that gave me a headache. In another beat, the car lurched into traffic.

"Empty your pockets," the driver said.

All I could see were his eyes in the rearview mirror. "Vlad?"

The fire crotch smacked me on the ear with his wrist. His oversize gold watch sent a sharp pain up the side of my head. Tears sprang from my eyes. I saw where this was going and handed over my wallet, phone, and Glock.

"This is nice," Gold Chains said, admiring the gun.

After slipping it into his jacket pocket, he lowered the window and tossed my phone into the street, where a passing car obliterated it.

"Thanks," I said. "I was due for an upgrade anyway."

The fire crotch went through my wallet. Ignoring the

cash, he said something to the others in Russian and returned it.

"You are holding Sasha?" the driver said.

"Not holding. Protecting."

"You better not be lying, asshole." These jokers had seen way too many Quentin Tarantino movies. "How do you know her?"

"She escaped from some very bad people. I decided to help her."

"Vhy vould you do this?"

Strange question, and one I couldn't easily answer. "Because she didn't have anyone."

The driver said something to the other two in Russian. They responded in kind. I tried reading their expressions, but these bastards were inscrutable.

"She has her brother," the driver said.

Sure, the one responsible for her being kidnapped in the first place—that brother. Better not to say it out loud. As we got onto the freeway going west, I noticed we were headed towards Santa Monica. As expected, the afternoon traffic was heavy.

Getting off at Fairfax, we headed south to an industrial section of town. We weaved our way past an electrical substation using side streets till we arrived at a nondescript, red brick building with a faded blue-and-white sign that read MOCKBA IMPORT EXPORT.

The driver pulled around to the rear and parked. The two gorillas got out. Not requiring an invitation, I followed them. Faded blue dumpsters covered in graffiti lined the alley. Broken glass littered the ground, sparkling in the late afternoon light. They led me to a heavy steel door. The driver unlocked it, and we went inside.

The interior looked dirty and unused, an open space

dotted with metal load-bearing poles. A faint light leaked in through grimy wire glass. A gray, chipped metal chair stood in the center. And standing next to that, a bulky-looking man with the same light-brown hair as Sasha—except his was curly. He wore a black suit, white shirt, and skinny black tie. This had to be Vlad.

During the early days of the outbreak In Tres Marias, I was repeatedly tortured by the Red Militia, a paramilitary whack job of a group seeking to take control of the town. They whipped my leg repeatedly with a length of rebar. I could still feel the pain as I recalled how they'd hit me for days on end, hoping I would cave. I wondered if Russian-style torture was any worse.

"Vladimir Drakonova?" I said. The others broke into hysterics. "What did I say?"

"I give you a lesson in patronymics for free. *Drakonova* is for girls. I am Vladimir Drakonov."

"My apologies."

The fire crotch nudged me towards the chair. Instead of resisting, I marched to it like I owned the place. The brother's face was neutral—unfinished—like the image of a president stamped on a coin. His hands were folded behind his back. His violet eyes studied me. Wordlessly, he glanced at the chair.

"Thanks, but I prefer to stand."

A blinding pain erupted from the back of my head, and I found myself on my knees. Hands grabbed me from under my arms and dragged me to the chair. My vision grew cloudy. I struggled to recover as they tied my ankles with nylon rope. A searing pain shot through my side when they secured my arms behind me.

Vlad stood before me and, bending down, got up in my grill. He smelled like sour cream and aftershave. I thought about spitting in his face, but I didn't want to encourage any more lousy acting.

"And now, you vill tell me vhere is my sister," he said.

I had no intention of playing games—these guys were hardcore. The Russian girl told me her brother had served in the military. I'd instructed Cuco that, should anything happen to me, he was to wait twenty-four hours, then contact Maritza. He grabbed my face with a paw-like hand and squeezed. The callouses on his fingers scratched me.

"Vhere is Sasha?"

"Safe. I'll tell you if you promise not to hurt her."

"Tell me vhere she is, Mister..." He turned to the fire crotch. Then to me, "Vales? Like *The Outlaw Josey Vales*? This is a very good movie. Not so good in Russian. Clint Eastwood sounds like a drunk Putin."

The other gorillas shared a laugh. Vlad moved in close. Whispering savagely, he spoke the last words I would hear before losing consciousness.

"At the end of the movie, Josey Vales lives," he said. "I don't think you vill be so lucky."

TWENTY-SIX

The sting of icy tap water brought me around. Like a diver bobbing to the surface, I came to as footsteps faded. I expected to find myself bleeding out from a missing hand, but I got lucky. Aside from the pain in my head and the throbbing of my gunshot wound, I wasn't in bad shape.

It was cold. Banks of fluorescent ceiling lights shone harshly, giving the place an eerie, horror-movie pastiche. Across the room, the Russians stood in a circle, speaking softly. Every so often, one of them glanced my way. Something was different, though. There were more now—I counted six. Vlad walked over and studied my face.

"What?" I said.

"In the army, I learned you can see vhat a man fears most by his eyes."

"How's that working out for ya?"

"Vhen I look at you, Mr. Vales, I don't see fear. This creates a problem for me." He bent down. "Vhy aren't you afraid to die? Vhat did you see?"

"You wouldn't believe me."

Side-eyeing his partners, he straightened up and smoothed his jacket. "Then, you are ready?"

I looked away. "I died a long time ago."

He turned to the others and said something in Russian. One of them answered—it was hard to tell which one. Grinning, Sasha's brother faced me again.

"Kha! This line is from *Innocent Blood,*" he said.

"Must've missed that one."

"Directed by John Landis. Best vampire movie ever."

"What are we doing here?"

"I vanted to kill you." He bit off a hangnail. "But I must find my sister."

"So you can kill *her*?"

He took a step back as if I'd slapped him. The fire crotch made a move to strike me, but his boss raised a warning hand. Seeing my chance, I kept going.

"Sasha is afraid of you," I said. "You know that, right? Why do you think I didn't bring her with me?"

"She can't be afraid of her brother."

"She is. Ever since you broke that young boy's arms in Moscow. She never forgot what you did to him. And she's afraid you'll do the same to her."

I was winding him up, and soon he'd blow—but it was worth it. Now I braced myself for the beating of a lifetime, Russian style.

"I have alvays protected her."

"You threw her out on the street."

"Because she…"

"What? She's nineteen. Because of you, some evil men imprisoned her. And they did things to her. Luckily, she escaped and found me."

I'd had enough of these clowns. "I never wanted any part of this. But I helped your sister anyway. And guess what—

those men are coming for her. You know everything now. Kill me if you want. But you'll never see her again."

His shoulders slumping, he joined the others. They argued. The fire crotch—Grigoriy—insisted, probably saying I was a liar and needed to be dead. Whatever. I was done talking. It was up to Vlad now.

Grigoriy pulled a knife from a sheath strapped to his leg and cut the ropes. I was stiff and needed to stretch. Instead, I sucker-punched him in the gut, knocking the wind out of him and sending him on his ass.

"I need my gun," I said.

The fire crotch babbled something, but I could see Sasha's brother had already decided. Gold Chains reached into his pocket and handed me my Glock. I slipped it into my jacket pocket. Vlad said something to the others. They left us alone.

"Is she...all right?" he said.

"She's fine. Staying with a friend."

"I vant to see her."

"You won't harm her?"

"No, I— I promise. She is my sister. She's all I have in the vorld." He seemed sincere.

"So why did you kick her out?"

"I thought she was making a fool of me in front of my friends."

"Okay," I said. "I can take you to her. But I need a phone."

Gunfire erupted outside, the bullets shattering a window. As we spread out, a CS gas canister landed inside, filling the room with a dense fog. Sasha's brother ordered the others to return fire. I had no idea who was shooting at us—or why. Maybe the gray-suits had found me again. He pulled out a Glock similar to mine and waved it at the rear wall.

"Qvickly," he said.

Choking from the gas, I followed him to the exit. We burst

through and came upon stairs leading to the roof. Though he was a large man, he moved nimbly up the rusty metal steps to the top, where there was another steel door. He peered through a small window.

"What do you see?" I said.

"Three men."

"Are they wearing gray suits?"

"How did you know?"

"Those are the men who took your sister."

He pushed open the door and began firing. As they spun around, he shot the closest one in the head. The other two took cover and returned fire. Crouching, I maneuvered sideways while firing a stream of bullets. One hit a hostile in the leg. Screaming, he went down.

"They're up here!" the third one said and reloaded.

The gray-suit crouched near the ledge. I crept behind a massive air conditioning unit and got off several more rounds, striking him in the throat. Gagging, he tottered and fell backwards to his death.

I signaled Vlad. "I'm out!"

He tossed me another mag and ran to the ledge. After reloading, I killed the wounded gray-suit. Standing next to Sasha's brother, I looked down. I wished I hadn't.

The police had surrounded the building, with their lights flashing and radios blaring. Two cops wearing body armor were already halfway up a fire escape ladder. More came from another direction. Soon, they'd surround us.

"Thanks for sparing my life," I said. "But we're dead now."

TWENTY-SEVEN

Vlad grabbed my arm and pointed the way.

"What about your friends?" I said.

"They von't talk."

We ran past the emergency exit. Hidden among the roof ventilators was a trapdoor. The Russian tried opening it, but it was stuck. I moved in to help him, and together, we pulled it open with a screech. He climbed in first. When I was inside, I shut the door firmly, praying no one would discover it.

A dark, narrow passage reeking of rot led us to another building. As we crawled through, distant voices screamed. It was hard to hear what they were saying because of the helicopter hovering above us. Continuing through the darkness, one question played in my head. Were the gray-suits working with the cops now?

We'd gone maybe a hundred feet when Vlad looked up— another trapdoor. Faintly, I could hear the cops swarming over the other building as we climbed onto the roof. A bright beam shone down from the police helicopter's spotlight, illuminating the dead gray-suits.

Keeping to the shadows, we headed for the emergency

exit. Thankfully, the door was unlocked. We made our way down the stairs and found ourselves in a large room filled with wood crates covered in Cyrillic writing.

"This building belongs to us also," he said.

All we had to do was make it to the service entrance and slip away. But as we got closer, I heard a noise. Vlad heard it too and looked at me. It was the sound of feet shuffling. We kept going and eventually reached a metal door. Weapon in hand, the Russian opened it and peeked out. All clear.

Exiting quietly, we found ourselves in a dimly lit, labyrinthine alley. Walls surrounded us, making it impossible to get a sense of direction. Vlad was ahead of me by several feet. I heard another noise and pivoted. Aiming at the darkness, I thought I saw something move. He must've seen it too because he raised his gun. We waited for the figure to become visible. Soon, a shape materialized, turning solid in the weak glow of a rusty light fixture. It was a stewbum.

"Help me," he said.

He staggered out of the shadows, blood seeping from his neck to his navel. Shivering, he gripped his worn overcoat to keep it from falling open. Then, he stopped. There was a slippery noise as his intestines spilled onto the ground. His face ghostly white, he tried screaming, but nothing came out. And he fell dead.

A familiar rhythmic clicking came from somewhere in the blackness. The sound turned my blood to ice. Grabbing the Russian by his jacket, I pulled him away, and we ran. After hitting a dead end, we veered into another short alley as the clicking followed us. Then we turned again through the maze and stopped short, holding our weapons in front of us. The noise seemed to be everywhere.

"Try the door," I said.

He pulled the handle—locked. We went on to the next,

and the next. Finally, we discovered a partially open door. Orange light streamed through the crack. With no other option, we ventured inside.

The interior was large, with broken plaster and debris scattered over the floor. The ceiling was torn away, revealing crisscrossed iron beams the length and breadth of the room. And from those hung human bodies on hooks—dozens of them—stripped clean of flesh, with only the heads untouched. Each face told us of unspeakable pain.

"Kakogo khrena!" he said.

"We need to get out of here."

The clicking pursued us like a curse as we marched backwards to the exit. Shirtless figures emerged from the shadows, their eyes iridescent purple. Cutters. We'd wandered into their nest. Vlad pointed his gun at them. Before he could fire, I grabbed his arm.

"The cops don't know we're here," I said. "If you shoot, they'll come."

"They vill find *this*."

"And they'll arrest us. You'll never see your sister."

A cutter with scars across his chest and abdomen stepped into a pool of light and grinned at the Russian. "Listen to your friend."

I shoved Vlad through and, backing out, closed the door. When I turned around, he was on his knees, clutching his bleeding gun hand. Roy Batty stood over him, holding a deadly sharp butterfly knife dripping red. He licked the blade, then flicked the weapon repeatedly. Unafraid, the hostile acknowledged the gun in my hand and came closer, his eyes boring into me. I felt my strength waning. The cutter studied me, his breath smelling of copper.

"You have questions," he said. "There's only one."

His voice sounded like a bad connection. The hostile

grabbed my wrist, but the sound of an approaching motor-cycle stopped him. In a flash, he disappeared into the building and bolted the door. I helped the Russian to his feet. Soon, we were on a side street, far from the action.

You don't hail taxis in LA, you call. Fortunately, this one responded quickly. In minutes, we were heading southeast towards Highland Park. I borrowed Vlad's phone to let Cuco know I was okay and that Sasha's brother was with me. Then, I called Maritza.

With luck, her story would make the eleven o'clock news.

TWENTY-EIGHT

Sasha bolted out of the house and threw her arms around me. She buried her face in my chest, murmuring things I didn't understand.

"I'm all right," I said.

Glowering at her brother, she let loose a string of invectives. But when she saw the blood dripping from his hand, she stopped. They continued in Russian all the way to the house. Cuco met us in the kitchen and invited everyone to make themselves comfortable.

Ernie brought a first-aid kit and handed it to the Russian girl. After treating her brother, we sat around the table, drinking coffee. I told the others about our narrow escape, leaving out the cutters. Vlad didn't know about his sister's pregnancy. I didn't want to be the one to tell him. As he spoke to her in Russian, she shook her head disapprovingly.

"These are my friends," she said as if addressing a rude child. "Speak English."

Smiling with embarrassment, he looked at me. "About before..."

"Forget it. I would've done the same."

He gave my shoulder a squeeze. "Vhy did these men take my sister? Vhat do they vant?"

Wisely, our host took the boy outside. Me, I thought it was better for Sasha to explain things and started for the living room.

"No, stay," she said. "Please."

It was just the three of us now. I wasn't sure what to do. The Russian had a gun, and I knew what he was capable of. Reluctantly, I sat. His sister moved her chair closer and took his hand.

"Vladimir," she said. "Those men, they made me pregnant."

Tensing, I expected him to start shooting. He didn't budge. Sensing his rising anger, I stood next to his sister to protect her. He went over to the sink. If it had been me, I'd want to break something. Instead, he just stood there, gripping and releasing the edge of the counter. When he turned around, his voice was quiet.

"Vhy did they do this?"

"She wasn't the only one. There were other girls."

I told him about Tres Marias and those horrid experiments, but I wasn't sure he got the connection. The Russian girl kept her eyes on her brother the whole time.

"They've moved the operation to LA," I said.

"The men vith the devil's eyes?"

"Cutters. What I can't understand, though, is why they're being allowed to hunt. Unless…"

"They escaped," his sister said.

That hadn't occurred to me. Maybe cutters running loose was an accident. Which meant that, in addition to coming after us, Walt was trying to recapture the other test subjects. Good luck with that. They were cunning as hell and knew how to hide.

Vlad joined us again at the table. "They made her pregnant. That thing—"

"It wasn't rape," I said. "They used artificial insemination."

"You said there vere other girls."

"Dozens like your sister—runaways."

He looked at her. "Vhat happened to them?"

When she didn't answer, I said, "We think they died."

"And she vill die too?" He pounded the table.

Taking his hand, she kissed it. "I have been to the doctor —I am fine."

She'd neglected to mention rabies, and I wasn't about to wind him up again. I glanced at my watch—almost eleven. They held each other, lost siblings in a death maze with no way out. I left to take my medication.

Cuco and the Russians were in the living room, watching the late news. The lead story was about the mutilated bodies discovered in the industrial building. The news anchor reported that ABC7 Eyewitness News had gotten the exclusive thanks to an anonymous tip.

"And here's Mari Lopez with the story."

As Maritza narrated, the camera panned across the human meat locker where Vlad and I had been only hours earlier. The bodies were gone, but the hooks were in place. Now, shots of blood on the floor and forensic investigators collecting evidence and taking photos. These people had no clue what they were up against.

Sasha took her brother's hand. "You could have died."

"What's it like over there, Mari?" the news anchor said.

"Chaotic. I spoke to Police Chief Lawrence Hughes earlier tonight. He told me the police now believe this is the work of not one but multiple serial killers working together. The internet is calling these the Skeleton Murders."

"We've seen these kinds of killings for weeks. Is the police chief now saying they're connected?"

"Not specifically."

When the reporter had finished, they returned to the studio. I hit the mute button on the remote as they segued to weather.

"They didn't mention anything about the gun battle," I said. "That means Walt Freeman got to the police and the media."

The Russian looked puzzled. "Vhy didn't they hide the bodies?"

"Because I called my friend at the station, remember? She got there before they could kill the story."

The Mexican switched off the TV. I tried guessing Walt's next move. He had two priorities—reacquire the Russian girl and stop the cutters. What would I do? And more importantly, what would Trower do? Me, I'd focus on Sasha—everything depended on her. Vlad's phone vibrated. Recognizing the number, he answered in Russian and looked at me.

"It's Grigoriy. The others are dead."

"Where is he now?"

"Airport. He's returning to Moscow."

"Tell him to watch his back," I said.

Sometime before dawn, Sasha cried out. Vlad and I were asleep on the living room floor. He was the first to get up. She wasn't in her room. Cuco called us over to the bathroom. We found her sitting on the toilet, holding her abdomen. The mewling noises she made were inhuman and frightening. Her brother spoke soothingly, but she didn't seem to hear him. Kneeling, he took her hand and turned her towards him. Her T-shirt was drenched in black.

"Be careful," I said. "That blood is infectious."

Ignoring me, he clasped his sister's head and pressed her close to him. He whispered something in Russian and stroked her hair. I could see how much he cared about her, but I also knew his love wouldn't be enough. She was turning.

In Tres Marias, I saw draggers vomit that same black blood in the early stages. It was only a matter of time. Most likely, this was what had happened to the other girls. The virus was passed on through the semen of those unholy cutters. Eventually, it killed the patients before they could carry a fetus to term. And soon, it would happen to the Russian girl.

My emotions left me—I saw things clearly. The room looked brighter, and every sound dissipated except for the blood pounding in my ears. This could only end one way. The best thing for everyone would be to end Sasha's life before she could turn. I knew what the virus did to people. Eventually, she would infect others. I hoped her brother would understand. And if he couldn't, well.

I reached into my jacket pocket. Feeling the familiar contours of the Glock, I pulled it out. She faced me, her blue-gray eyes a silent question. I pointed my weapon and fired once, the bullet exiting the chamber soundlessly. The round tore through her forehead, leaving a blossom of blood, brain, and bone on the bathroom wall. Her brother wailed. There was no way he would understand now, so I shot him too. All for the best.

Someone grabbed me—Cuco. He stared into my eyes with concern. I realized my hand was still in my pocket, gripping the gun. Vlad was helping his sister to her feet. The episode had passed, and she seemed better. The Mexican signaled me to follow him into the hallway. When I made eye contact, I feigned confusion.

"What happened?" I said.

"No se, pero… I think you went a little loco."

Though I hadn't done anything, I might have. What was happening to me? Even if the Russian girl were infected, killing her and the baby wasn't the solution. There had to be another way.

I gripped his arm. "Thanks for stepping in."

"I only did what you would have done."

"I have to talk to Maritza," I said. "This needs to end."

PART THREE

PRAYER FOR A CREEP

TWENTY-NINE

Maritza and I agreed to meet at Starbucks in Silver Lake. Though it was off the main drag, it afforded a nice view of the surrounding neighborhood. I didn't want Trower surprising me and, as a precaution, drove Cuco's car.

I glanced up from my newspaper as the reporter came in wearing skinny jeans, black booties, and a fuzzy pink cowlneck sweater. Her hair and sunglasses hid most of her face. When she saw me, she gave me a subtle nod and walked faster towards me. There was an espresso macchiato waiting for her.

She swept the room with her eyes. Maybe she'd learned that watching spy thrillers. It was cute. Pressing her fingers to the paper, she slid it around and read the headline—*Skeleton Murders Baffle Police.*

"I don't get why the cops aren't giving us anything," she said, taking a seat across from me.

"Because someone ordered them not to. Good job blending in, by the way."

"Hey, I worked hard on this ensemble—a little respect."

"I'm used to dealing with thieves and scoundrels."

"That explains why you have no life. Which reminds me, weren't you 'leaving the area'?"

"Things are more complicated now."

We kept our voices low. Whenever someone would get too close, we'd pause the conversation and wait it out. Thankfully, no one seemed to recognize her. That or the locals knew to give Mari Lopez her space.

"Thanks for the coffee," she said. "Okay, here's what I know. The cops have definitely bought into the multiple serial killer hypothesis."

I scoffed. "The Skeleton Murders?"

"Catchy, right? The name wasn't my idea."

I pointed at the newspaper. "It looks like the feds have joined the investigation."

She gave me a sly smile that charmed the hell out of me. "I asked the police chief about the rumor. Of course, he denied it." She lowered her sunglasses, her mouth making a perfect *O*. "You believe they're involved."

"Not in the way you think."

Excited, she leaned over the table. I could smell her perfume, and for a sec, lost my train of thought.

"Okay, spill," she said.

"Am I off the record?"

"There is no *off the record*. But I promise not to reveal you as my source. Besides, I don't even know your last name."

"It's Wales."

She scrunched her nose. Again, cute. "Wait, like Josey Wales?"

"Stop."

"I knew a David Wales at UCLA. Tall, skinny... Played the autoharp. Not gay, though. At least, I don't—"

"Do you want the story or not?"

"Cálmate." She dug into her bag and produced a digital voice recorder. "Okay, go."

"No recordings."

"No one else is going to hear this."

"I said no."

"Fine. My fourth-grade teacher, Mrs. McGuinness, said my penmanship was like a cry from Purgatory. Guess I'll have to manage."

Pouting, she pulled out a composition book and pen. It took us two hours and several rounds of coffee. When I was done, she knew as much as I did about Robbin-Sear, Hell-born, Walt Freeman, and the cutters. And she was up to speed on Sasha and the other girls who were abducted.

"I can't believe it," she said. "This is, like, a major conspiracy. Why didn't you go to the media before?"

"It wasn't the right time."

"There's no way I can break the story yet—I need proof. And I have to talk to Karen."

"Why?"

"I told you, she's my mentor. I might be out of my depth. If what you're saying is true—"

"It is—all of it."

She pressed the pen to her mouth, getting lipstick on it. "Even with proof, I can't reveal everything all at once. It'll sound preposterous."

Reaching down, I grabbed the manila envelope lying on my lap and handed it to her. When she started to open it, I shook my head. Nodding, she shoved it into her bag.

"You said you wanted proof. That envelope contains Sasha's lab tests and a vial of her blood. When they test it, they'll find it carries a virus they won't be able to identify. You can start with that."

"I appreciate this, but I'm worried about Walt Freeman. If

he's the kind of man you say he is, he'll do whatever it takes to suppress it."

"He already tried. Last night, I was involved in a shootout with the gray-suits in the same area the police discovered those bodies. Several Russians died."

"Russians now? You're kidding, right?"

"There's a reason it never made the news."

"And Walt couldn't suppress my story because—"

"You were already there with your camera, thanks to me."

It took her a beat to put everything together. Then, "I need to lie down."

"Let me ask you something. Have you noticed anything strange going on at the station? Management taking private meetings with people you've never seen before?"

"Funny you should ask. My news director has been on a lot of conference calls. Sometimes, they go late into the evening. He won't tell me what they're about. It's weird because Nate and I are friends, and he never keeps anything from me."

"He could be protecting you."

I happened to look up and noticed a guy sitting by the window, aiming his phone at us. The tool was taking pictures. Pretending to laugh at something, I laid my hand on hers.

"We need to get out of here," I said. "Don't turn around."

She put away her notebook and pen. "My place isn't far."

Casually, I walked her past the celebrity stalker and out of the store to her car, a black BMW 5 Series.

"Nice wheels." I opened the door for her.

"You can follow me."

"Give me the address," I said. "There's something I need to do first."

THIRTY

The celebrity stalker was still inside, staring at his phone like a kid with a Pokémon card. After a couple minutes, he exited the store. I got out of my car as he approached the parking lot. Making sure we were alone, I waited for him to walk past. When he spotted me, he tried going a different way. I went after him. He was younger but out of shape—too many Caramel Frappuccinos. I caught up to him and grabbed his arm.

"I don't have any money!" he said.

"Give me your phone."

"What? I'm not—"

I smacked him, making his nose bleed. Terrified, he dug into his jeans pocket and handed over the device, nearly dropping it.

"Why were you photographing us? Don't lie."

"I-I took pictures of Mari Lopez, that's all. It's for a class project, I swear."

An elderly couple had just left Starbucks, heading our way. I released the kid and showed him my gun.

"Act like we're having a good time. And wipe your nose."

He managed a weak chuckle as I scanned the photos of the other celebrities he'd documented all around LA. By now, the other couple had driven off. I found the ones I wanted. There were six in all, and I deleted them one by one. I went through his social media apps to make sure he hadn't posted anything.

"This your girlfriend?" I said. "I wonder if she knows you're a stalker."

"I told you, it's for a class I'm taking. We're trying to show how the media influences us, even when—"

"Don't care."

I resisted the urge to beat him senseless. He was just a kid after all—nineteen or twenty. Maybe he'd told me the truth. What was it about LA and celebrities? I demanded his wallet and pulled out his student ID card.

"Loyola-Marymount—nice. What year?"

"Sophomore." He was shaking, and I could smell urine. "Are you gonna kill me now?"

"Relax." I returned everything. "Here's what you're going to do. Forget we ever met. And if those photos appear anywhere online, I'll come looking for you."

I waited for him to drive off. Then, I jumped into my car and headed towards the Hollywood Hills. In truth, I'd have no idea whether he posted the pics. But he didn't know that.

Maritza lived a long way from East LA in a condo complex that looked new. I parked on the street several blocks away and made my way to her unit. Agave plants in big pots stood on either side of the front door, which was decorated with a holiday wreath made from pine branches. I'd forgotten it was almost Christmas.

Greeting me with a surprising peck on the cheek, she invited me in. She'd changed into a white French-cut T-shirt that looked amazing. The one-bedroom condo was neat and sparse—not girly. It was furnished in IKEA because she had used most of her savings to buy the property.

"Want a beer?" she said.

"I don't drink."

"I also have bottled water."

After escorting me to the living room, she stepped into the kitchen. Framed black-and-white photos decorated the pale walls. I recognized Ansel Adams's "Moonrise, Hernandez, New Mexico."

"Are you a photographer?" I said.

She handed me my water. "I wish. I've always loved black-and-white photography." She pointed. "That's Irving Penn. Next to that, Henri Cartier-Bresson. And over there, Diane Arbus."

I caught her looking me over. "What?"

"Why have you never asked me if I was in a relationship?"

"Because we're not in high school."

"¡Hijole! You are one strange gringo."

I crossed to the sofa and sat. "I suppose guys are hitting on you all the time. Makes sense."

"It's ridiculous." She parked next to me—closer than I expected. "And it's always the creeps. You know the type. They drive Porsches and eat lunch at The Ivy and…"

"Sounds like you're not comfortable around money."

"My parents weren't poor. But when I was little, my mother sewed our clothes. She worked in the garment district. Sometimes, she'd bring home these great patterns and turn out cute little dresses, vests, and jackets. My sisters and I were the coolest kids at 4th Street Elementary."

"So, no Catholic school?"

"Trust me, my family is very religious. But my parents are firm believers in not paying tuition. *That's what taxes are for, mija.* Are you Catholic?"

"Was. Am, I guess. My wife…"

She slid away from me like I'd announced I was radioactive.

"She died," I said.

"During the outbreak?"

"Sort of. She was murdered—are you sure you want to hear this?"

"Oh, David. You didn't mention her when…"

"I didn't think it was relevant." Sipping my water, I studied the photographs.

"Can I ask what her name was?"

"Holly."

I always hated it when people trotted out the family pictures. But here I was, flipping open my wallet. She reached for the photo.

"Wow, she's beautiful."

She touched my arm. I didn't know what she wanted, so I concentrated on the wall like I knew who in hell Irving Penn was. Moving closer, she took my face in her hands.

"This is why you're going after Walt Freeman," she said.

"Okay, you got me."

"But you know what he'll do, right?"

"Do you remember when I drove you to the station the other day? After I dropped you, I went to confront him. That's how I ended up rescuing Sasha."

"Whoa, stop the presses. Are you saying you left me to go get *killed*?"

"Why are you mad?"

"Because…"

She raised her fist to punch me. Fuming, she snatched my

hand. I was bewildered. Why would any of this matter to her? I was some random dude she didn't even know. A source. Yet here she was, holding back tears like a little girl determined to be brave.

"Maritza, I—"

"Shut up."

She kissed me. My instinct was to walk out. I didn't want to feel anything. Didn't want to dampen the hatred burning bright like a coal fire in a locomotive. But she wouldn't stop. I felt myself falling—hard. Closing my eyes, I let her caress my beard.

"Please don't do this," I said. "I'm broken."

Still holding my hand, she led me to her bedroom. Her lavender scent clouded my brain—I couldn't think straight. Yet the pain inside screamed at me to get out. *Focus on the mission!* But I wasn't sure what that was anymore. I didn't want to get involved with this woman because she'd end up dead like all the others. Dammit, why couldn't I leave?

Now, we were under the covers, with afternoon light streaming through the wood blinds. I felt her warm body close as she stroked my face and kissed my eyes. Her slender fingers probed the scars from all the violence I'd endured since July. When she found the bandage on my side, she withdrew her hand, afraid to expose what lay beneath.

This wasn't what I wanted—it was what she wanted. And though I didn't know why, I let it happen. I needed to feel something, enough to satisfy her hunger. Me, I was beyond desire—past living. I was a ghost, unaware that I'd already died. Going through the motions of what I used to do in life. But I would try again for Maritza. Just this once, I would pretend to be alive.

"David," she said, her voice breathy. She opened a nightstand drawer and took out a condom. "For emergencies."

She straddled me, and the wall I'd built between us turned to dust. I felt hot, losing myself in her warm breasts and fragrant hair. Letting her passion fill me up, I didn't care about anything.

I was utterly, hopelessly lost.

THIRTY-ONE

Maritza lay in my arms, twirling the hairs on my chest with her finger. I wondered if it was possible to remain there forever. No Hellborn, no cutters. No memories—a new life. The trouble with daydreams is they scatter like dandelion seeds on an angel's breath. Soon, the darkness would close in on me again, my fate in its hands.

"What will you do about Sasha?" she said.

"What do you mean?"

"You told me she's sick. Aren't you trying to save her?"

Save the Russian girl. Right. That's what I was supposed to be doing right now.

"Is she... Is she planning to keep the baby?"

"I don't know."

"I hope she does."

I looked into her eyes. "Why?"

"Because it's a baby—an innocent life. It might be all right. Aren't there drugs they could try to..."

Moved beyond words, I kissed her forehead.

"What?" she said, smiling.

"Nothing, it's... It's something Holly would've said. When they killed her, she was carrying our child." I hadn't meant to tell her that.

She covered my face in kisses. "Lo siento."

Filled with compassion, she repeated the phrase several more times. I pressed her head to my chest, and we lay there awhile longer. It surprised me how easily it had happened, going from dead to alive.

"Sasha told me Hellborn injected all the girls," I said. "At the time, she didn't know she was pregnant. What if they were suppressing the virus with a drug to protect the fetuses?"

"That might explain why she didn't get sick until now. She isn't getting the treatments."

"Maybe. But the other patients had the treatments, and they still died."

I couldn't take my eyes off her as she climbed out of bed. Though it was hard to admit, I wanted her—again and again. She caught me checking out her butt and performed an impressive arabesque, followed by a curtsy.

"Three years of ballet lessons," she said. "The only thing my parents ever splurged on."

"Why'd you quit?"

"I discovered ice skating. Way more fun."

"You should try hockey."

She threw on a robe and picked out clean underwear from her dresser. "I need to go to the station. You can hang out if you want."

"Will there be snacks?"

"Sure, the healthy kind."

"Sounds tempting. But I have to leave."

"David, promise me you're not on your way to an execution."

"I promise."

Leaning over the bed, she kissed me. "Your beard is scratchy."

She slipped into the bathroom and closed the door. In another beat, the shower came on. She began singing in Spanish. Okay, so she was no Selena, but her voice wasn't bad. After getting dressed, I made the bed and went into the living room. Out of habit, I peeked out the front window.

A black Escalade was parked across the street. I backed away and turned around. Maritza looked at me from across the room, wearing a black skirt and jacket, royal-blue top, and black high-heel ankle boots. In any other scenario, I would've dragged her back into the bedroom for another go.

"What's wrong?" she said.

I clasped her hands in mine. "Take a breath. We've got company."

She scooted to the window. I opened the curtain a crack for her to see.

"I don't understand. Why would they come here?"

The vehicle's rear door swung open. Instead of an agent, a short man with pale skin and reddish wavy hair stepped out. He was wearing a white shirt with the sleeves rolled up, a tie, and suit pants. The undertaker was with him.

"That's Nate Fleischman, my boss. Who's he with? Ew!"

"His name's Trower, and he's bad news—like a planet-killer asteroid."

Her friend's eyes darted from side to side—like a police informant—as they crossed the street and approached the front steps.

"Your boss is here to tell you to back off the story," I said.

"He would never do that. ¡Hijo! He looks so scared."

"They don't know I'm here. Is there another way out?"

"There's a glass door leading to a balcony. But it's like a twenty-foot drop."

I decided to hide in the bedroom. Taking her hand, I walked her back and stood in the doorway.

"This is important. Listen to what they have to say. Put up a fight, then agree to everything. If things go sideways, remember. I have a gun."

"Dios mio," she said.

THIRTY-TWO

The doorbell rang, startling Maritza. I wasn't sure how to make this better and kissed her hand. She embraced me.

"It'll be okay," I said. "Try not to act nervous. And don't stare at the scar. Or his janky eye."

"No problemo." She shot me a worried look and went to answer the door.

Opening a dresser drawer, I found a clean bra and tossed it on the duvet. I spotted the top she'd worn earlier and threw it on the floor haphazardly. Then, leaving the door open a bit, I hid behind it, gripping my gun. The doorbell rang a second time.

"Nate? This is a surprise. I was about to head over to the station."

"We need to talk, Maritza. I didn't want to do it there. Um, this is Mr. Trower."

"Pleasure to meet you," Trower said.

"Well, come in, I guess." Footsteps, followed by the sound of a door closing. "Can I make you guys some coffee?"

"We're good," Fleischman said.

"Let's go into the living room."

More footsteps. Though it was hard to hear, I managed to piece together the conversation.

"So, what's up?" Maritza said. "Did I get the anchor job?"

"This is about the Skeleton Murders."

"Great. Did we get a new lead?"

"Legal has advised us to kill the story."

"Wait, what?"

"I know. Look, you're an awesome reporter, and this is no reflection on you. But this is—"

"You see, Ms. Lopez, there are other considerations," Trower said. "As you know, there's a police investigation going on. Also, the FBI is looking into the matter. We don't want to cause undue panic. Does that make sense?"

"This sucks! Nate, have you seen the ratings?"

"The directive came from the top. I was in a meeting this morning with the general counsel. They're serious—we have to play ball."

"You do realize we were on our way to an Emmy nomination."

The hairs on the back of my neck stiffened at the sound of approaching footsteps. It was Trower—he was checking out the place. I prayed he'd notice the mess I'd staged and decide not to enter.

"There'll be other stories," he said just outside the door. His hand appeared in the crack.

Maritza marched over. "Excuse me. I don't believe I was talking to you. And I'd appreciate you not snooping around my bedroom."

She snapped the door shut, and everyone returned to the living room.

"Maritza, come on," Fleischman said, his voice practically rising an octave.

"No, *you* come on, Nate. This is messed up, and you know it."

"Look, I'm ordering you not to pursue this."

There was a long silence. Then, "Fine."

"There's something else. The police want you to give them a statement."

"What? Why?"

"They wouldn't tell me. I'm guessing it's because of those anonymous tips you've been receiving. Kid, you scooped everybody in town. And the police chief wants to know why."

"Well, I'm not revealing my source, if that's what he's hoping for."

"No, of course not. He wants a statement, though. A couple of detectives are waiting for you at the station."

"Do I have to do this? I mean, legally?"

"The general counsel promised our full cooperation, so yes. Don't worry—I'm going over there with you. Hey, I know how important this story was to you."

She gave them a dramatic sigh worthy of Chekhov. "Not your fault. I'll see you over there in a bit."

"Thanks for understanding. Um, later."

After they'd gone, Maritza opened the bedroom door. When she saw the mess, she put her hands on her hips.

"Perfect," she said. "I finally meet a guy with potential, and he likes trying on women's underwear."

"Only on the weekend."

In the foyer, we peeked through the curtained window next to the front door. Trower and Fleischman were standing by the Escalade, talking. The undertaker looked in our direction. Soon, they were off.

"Outstanding performance," I said. "So, what do you think?"

"I hope they bought it. Seriously, though, I've never seen Nate act like that. He's scared shitless."

"You'd better get over to the police station. What will you tell them?"

"Same thing I told Nate. I won't reveal my source."

I rechecked the street and opened the front door. She fell into my arms before I could leave.

"I'm afraid," she said.

"So am I."

"When will I see you?"

"Not sure."

I pulled a brand-new phone from my jacket pocket and handed it to her. "From now on, only use this to communicate with me. I've already memorized the number. I promise to call you as soon as I get another burner."

We kissed. It was impossible to hold off the darkness any longer. I could feel its cold, spiky fingers enclosing my throat like brambles in a graveyard. Soon, they would tear me apart. A little voice inside told me to hang onto this moment for as long as I could. Maybe it was the angel sending me a message.

"Pray for me," I said.

Though we hadn't known each other long, somehow I felt a deep connection. It was as if our souls were communicating on a level I was incapable of comprehending. And I was sure she felt it too. I kissed her soft lips again and trotted down the steps.

"David!"

I stopped and turned around to gaze at her lovely face.

"Don't die, okay?"

Holly had said something similar once. I tried a smile, but it felt wrong. Studying her eyes, I realized Vlad was right. You *can* tell what a person fears, and also what they treasure most.

In a few minutes, I was driving towards my fate and leaving Maritza to hers. I turned on the radio, and Norteño music blasted. I hit the scanner, looking for an alternative rock station. "Creep" by Radiohead poured out from the speakers. God couldn't have scored this moment any better.

In my head, I was home.

THIRTY-THREE

Everything looked wrong the moment I got out of the car. For one thing, instead of kids playing outside, the street was deserted. Dark clouds laden with rain scudded across an oppressive sky. Somewhere, a dog barked a warning. I didn't have my own replacement burner yet and couldn't call ahead.

The front door was open slightly—Cuco always kept it locked. From inside, the angel looked at me with impassive eyes. I hesitated, afraid of what I would find. Gripping my Glock, I went in. She didn't say anything and instead pointed straight ahead. Holding my weapon with both hands, I cleared the foyer and kept going. When I glanced behind me, she was gone.

"Cuco? Sasha?"

The living room looked okay, except for the television tuned to Cartoon Network with the sound off. That seemed odd. Maybe Ernie was somewhere in the house. I listened again. No other noises. I switched off the TV and continued to the kitchen.

Reaching the entrance, I stopped cold. Blood sprays

covered the walls and floor. I took a labored breath and entered, gun first. Someone's leg poked out from under the table. The shoe belonged to the Mexican. Inching closer, I saw what the gray-suits had done.

Shot multiple times, his body lay face-up, outlined in a pool of dark blood. In his right hand was a kitchen knife with blood on the blade. The back door was partially open. Outside, a hostile lay dead, his throat cut.

Kneeling beside Cuco, I checked for a pulse. He was ice cold. I went through his pockets looking for his phone. Nothing. A hissing noise startled me, and I whipped around, my gun pointed. It was only the coffee maker. After unplugging it, I scanned the kitchen. All clear.

I started down the hallway, holding back tears for my friend. When I reached the bathroom, I hesitated. The door was closed. This was where they must've killed Vlad as he fought to protect his sister. I tried the knob—unlocked. Wiping the sweat from my eyes, I went in.

The pale linoleum was slick with blood. Ernie was huddled in the corner like an animal sacrifice. They'd shot him twice in the chest. Stepping around the shiny pool, I crossed the bathroom and felt his carotid artery. The boy's glassy eyes stared up at me. Like his generous neighbor, he'd died alone.

Since the beginning of the plague, I'd witnessed more violence than most people would in a lifetime. And I'd become inured to it. But seeing the bloodied boy brought stinging tears to my eyes that I couldn't control. Collateral damage, they called it. While looking for the Russian girl, the gray-suits didn't hesitate to kill him. Who would tell his mother? This was my fault.

The medicine cabinet door was open. I grabbed my medication and stared at the label. It was made out to Dave

Wales and listed the prescribing doctor's name. As I slipped it into my pocket, I realized how careless I'd been. What if the gray-suits found it? I needed to warn Dr. Fernandes. They'd probably tapped the Mexican's landline. I'd have to call when I was able.

I went through the stuff in Cuco's bedroom, hoping to find an address book. I discovered one in a dresser drawer and flipped through it. There were lots of people in Juarez, many bearing the same last name. I slipped it into my pocket and searched the rest of the house and garage. No more bodies. It was possible the Russians were holed up somewhere safe. If that were true, they'd left in a hurry. Returning to the house, I packed Sasha's clothes, as well as mine. After locking up, I got on the road.

On the way to the private garage, I tried to decide what to do next. I thought about Cuco's extended family in Mexico. If I hadn't returned, they might never learn what happened to him. And there was no practical way for me to bury him.

If somehow I survived this Kafkaesque nightmare, I vowed to write to his family and send them money. And I'd do the same for Ernie's mom. What bothered me, though, was how easily the gray-suits had tracked us. It meant we were vulnerable to more attacks, no matter where we went.

I didn't see my Tahoe when I arrived—a good sign. Maybe Vlad had driven his sister to safety. After stopping at an electronics store, I called him. I expected him not to answer an unknown number, but he picked up on the second ring.

"Hello." His voice was flat.

"It's me. Hang up and call this number from an outside phone."

I disconnected and waited. Twenty minutes later, my phone buzzed. I heard the Russian girl in the background. She was saying something to her brother.

"Vhere are you?" he said.

"Leaving Highland Park. You?"

"At a friend's house."

"Were either of you hurt? How's Sasha?"

"Ve are fine. But ve almost didn't make it out of there."

"How did you manage it?"

"Cuco knew about the Escalades. Vhen he saw one outside, he sent us out vith your keys. Ve climbed the fence and ran through the streets. Is he..."

"Dead. And so is the boy."

"I am sorry. Better get over here."

"Is it safe?"

"No one knows about this place." He gave me an address in Glendale.

"I'll be there in a couple hours. Don't go anywhere. Get takeout if you want, but stay where you are. And lose your phone. Someone might be tracking it."

"Understood," he said and disconnected.

I called Dr. Fernandes to warn him about the gray-suits but got his answering service. They claimed he'd been unreachable for the past few hours and promised to give him a message. I thanked them and disconnected.

I was too late. The doctor was surely dead.

THIRTY-FOUR

L A traffic was a nightmare, and it took me over an hour to get across town. At least it wasn't raining. Jeong was in the yard, inspecting a vintage Coupe de Ville. The stupid dogs went at it as soon as I got out of the car with my bags. The Korean gave them the death stare, and they retreated.

"How's the Tahoe?" he said through the fence.

"Fine. I have to get rid of this vehicle."

"Too old—can't sell it."

"I don't want money, but I need it to disappear."

He unlocked the gate and came out to inspect Cuco's car. "You want me to destroy it, right?"

"Here are the keys. I could use a ride."

"Try Uber."

I showed him my pathetic flip phone. Rolling his eyes, he pulled out his smartphone and fired up the app.

"Be here in three minutes."

I thanked him and waited outside the gate. A cop cruiser passed by, jangling my nerves. Fortunately, it kept going. Twelve minutes later, my car arrived.

"Uber car for Dave," the driver said in an unfamiliar accent.

Though the dude was late, he seemed pleasant enough. He was around thirty, with dark wavy hair and imposing black eyebrows. His silk shirt was half-unbuttoned, revealing a dense forest of curly chest hair. I thought he might be gay and wanted to impress me.

Most people would assume an Uber driver who owned a Prius meant they were in for a safe, uneventful trip. This one had a busted taillight and a dented rear panel with the paint scraped clean. For a sec, I considered asking the Korean to cancel and book another car. Screw it. After a struggle, I got the passenger door open. The pungent odor of man sweat and falafel greeted me.

I got in with the duffels and rolled down the window. Because Jeong had paid, I didn't want to do anything that would reflect poorly on him. So I sucked it up. He'd given the driver an address a couple miles from where Sasha and Vlad were staying.

"Glendale, right?" the driver said.

"How long will it take?"

He fiddled with a laptop computer lying on the passenger seat. I felt my blood beginning to boil.

"Hey, how long?"

Turning around, he gave me a cheesy smile. "Relax."

We hadn't even left yet, and already I wanted to pimp-slap the asshat. Instead, I buckled my seatbelt and closed my eyes, imagining I was riding in Vlad's nice, clean town car. As we made our way to the 110 freeway, the hyperactive moron kept checking his rearview mirror. I turned to see what he was looking at and spotted a tan Dodge Dart following closely. The driver was around fifty—and angry.

"Who's tailing us?" I said.

"Don't worry about him. Taxi inspector. Ahmagh is always after me because I look foreign."

As if his erratic driving weren't bad enough, he opened the glove compartment and rummaged around inside. Among the debris, I noticed a brightly colored hash pipe. He found a box of orange Tic Tacs and tipped back a mouthful. Then, with zero EQ, he reached around and offered me some. In a matter of minutes, I'd gone from annoyed to worried I might not make it to Glendale. I craned my neck. The Dart was still behind us.

"Is that guy going to pull us over?"

"Take it easy, boss."

He glanced at his rearview mirror. Hitting the gas, he flew dangerously through a red light. Behind us, the squeal of brakes, followed by the sound of a collision. When I turned around, the tan car was nowhere in sight. The driver sped onto a freeway on-ramp, zooming past the slower cars.

"You're lucky," he said. "Traffic's not bad."

I planned to shoot this guy in the neck the second we arrived. An iPhone mounted on the windshield went off. He picked up, using the car's microphone and speakers. A woman with a shrill voice began talking fast in a foreign language. He did likewise, screaming at the phone. After disconnecting, he glanced past me and shot across three lanes of traffic, barely avoiding a semi in the slow lane. We got off near the convention center.

"I need to make a quick stop."

"What? No!"

"It will only take a minute."

Street traffic was heavy. The driver was forced to make his way slowly past a line of parked cars. He pulled into a red zone in front of a club where hundreds of people were lined up.

A petite woman with long, dark hair waited near the curb. She wore a skimpy, shimmery red top, black leather pants, and black stilettos. Her arms were folded tight across her chest. The driver flicked on his hazard lights. As soon as he was out of the car, they got into it. I was afraid he would beat her right there on the street.

Someone rapped on my door, startling me. It was the taxi inspector. Giving me a smile, he leaned into the open window.

"If I were you, I'd get out and walk," he said.

"What are you talking about?"

He pointed behind him. "As you can see, Mr. Ghorbani is a menace. It might be safer if you left now. Your call."

I saw his point. Could this day get any worse? Groaning, I exited the vehicle with my stuff. By now, another dark-haired man in a shiny black suit had joined the fun. Speaking the same language, he said something threatening. He took the woman's arm and escorted her hastily up the steps as the doors to the club opened. Ghorbani screamed at them, then faced the street.

Balling my fist, I glared at him. "What did he say to her?"

The inspector shrugged. "I don't speak Farsi."

When Ghorbani realized who I was with, he bolted down the sidewalk, pushing through the thick line of well-dressed people. He knocked down a woman and kept going. Everyone yelled at him as he disappeared around a corner. I heard a beep and stared at the iPhone inside the Prius. Someone needed a ride.

"Come on," the inspector said. "I'll give you a lift."

THIRTY-FIVE

We hiked a couple blocks to where the taxi inspector's vehicle was parked. I was nervous about going anywhere with the stranger. Still, I was already late and didn't want to wait for a taxi. When I opened the rear passenger door to toss in the duffels, I found a Costco-size package of Depends adult diapers. I hopped into the front seat, and we were off.

"The freeway is hell at this hour," he said, sticking to surface streets. "Where ya headed?"

"Meeting a friend at the Americana."

"The mall in Glendale?"

"That's the one. I really appreciate this."

He caught me eyeing the diapers. "Ass cancer. It's a bitch, lemme tell you. What's worse, the wife couldn't cope and bailed."

"Wow, that sucks."

"It's what I get for marrying a girl twenty years my junior. Used to have a hell of an ego back in the day. Good job... plenty of money. Pride, that's what it was. One of the seven deadly sins. Guess God's punishing me now."

I didn't know what to say as we passed Dodger Stadium, so I redirected. "What's going to happen to that Uber driver?"

He sighed with the weariness of Job on a Monday. "Nothing, prob'ly. But I'll file a report. Won't go anywhere. Company's lawyered up pretty good."

"On the plus side, they do seem to conduct thorough background checks."

He coughed up a hoarse laugh like a stubborn fur ball. "I've been tracking Mr. Ghorbani for weeks. Officially, he's a full-time student at UCLA. Unofficially, he's a low-life. Nothing like other Persians I've known. That girl you saw? His sister."

"And the other guy?"

"Boyfriend, maybe. I don't expect to put him out of business, but I have to try."

The inspector was Catholic and used to be in sales. He and his wife never had kids. No relatives to speak of. He lived alone in the city without even a dog to keep him company. When he asked what I did, I told him I'd recently moved from Seattle. Divorced with a baby girl I would probably never see again. We made good time and soon pulled up to the mall entrance on Brand Boulevard.

"Thanks again," I said. "I hope everything works out, you know, with your situation."

"If it doesn't, I plan to shit myself into an early grave."

"What do I owe you?"

"Forget it. You've had enough trouble. See ya."

As he pulled into traffic, I realized I never got his name. Holly would've prayed for a guy like that. There were holiday decorations everywhere, reminding me that Christmas was around the corner. I tried not to let that depress me. Making my way past throngs of shoppers, I set out to find Vlad's address.

I headed north, thinking about my first Christmas with Holly. We hardly had any money in those days. Somehow, we'd scraped together a few bucks for a scrawny tree and generic ornaments from Target. There were only two presents underneath. Instead of waiting till Christmas morning, we opened them around midnight. Her gift to me was a book—*Masterpieces* by Khalil Gibran. I gave her a tiny bottle of Chloé. I recalled how wonderfully it combined with her natural scent. Sometimes at night, I could swear I smelled it on my pillow.

The house was farther than I thought. It took me forty-five minutes to cross over the freeway and make my way to a quiet residential neighborhood. When I arrived, I noticed the Tahoe wasn't in the driveway. *Good thinking, Vlad.* I rang the bell, and immediately the door flew open. Sasha ran into my arms. I stroked her hair and whispered I was okay. She looked worse than when I last saw her. There were dark circles on her pale skin. Something flickered in her eyes, and then it was gone. I wondered how much time she had left before…

"Are you in pain?" I said.

"Not bad."

"Who lives here?"

Her brother came out and set the duffels in the foyer. "Armenian friends. They are in Moscow on a job."

I had enough to worry about and didn't want to know what kind of job. The Russian girl led me into the spacious living room. The décor looked like something out of the sixties with round, colored-glass lamps and a popcorn ceiling. And the place smelled of stale cooking. I sat on the floral-pattern sofa. She scrunched next to me, refusing to let go of my hand. Ignoring the intimacy, her brother sat across from us.

"Vhat did you find out?" he said.

"The news station won't run any more Skeleton Murder stories. I'm pretty sure that goes for the other media outlets."

"America sounds more like Russia every day."

"We have to get out of the city. The gray-suits found you once. I'm convinced they can do it again."

Holding her abdomen, Sasha doubled over and groaned. Vlad and I helped her into a reclining position.

"She's very sick," he said.

"No, I…"

He spoke to her sternly in Russian. Then to me, "I'm vorried. Vhatever they gave her to control this, ve need more. I don't vant her to die like the others."

"Don't forget—the other girls had the treatment and still didn't make it."

Grabbing my arm, she got to her feet. "Hello? I'm still here. Stop talking about death."

"You're right," I said. "But your brother has a point. What's important now is keeping you safe—and healthy."

"I vant to see my doctor."

"I'll call him in the morning." I hated lying to her, but I needed time to think. "When I tried him earlier, he was out. In the meantime, you should rest."

I pulled Vlad aside. "You and I are on guard duty. I'll take the first watch. Then four hours each."

"You have done this before," he said.

THIRTY-SIX

aked, I stood in the middle of the LA River, looking at the moon through slanted rain. As a torrent of water rushed over my feet, I remained anchored. In front of me, an enormous concrete pile held up the Sixth Street Viaduct. The metallic, rhythmical clicking of a butterfly knife echoed all around me.

At the top of the bridge, a lone figure with glowing eyes stared, far away yet close. Nimbly, it leaped over the railing, performing a perfect somersault. Sliding on the concrete like oil down a steel wire, it landed on its feet in the water and marched towards me.

It was Sasha.

She had on the white patient gown she'd worn the day I found her. Only now, a blood spray obscured the lilacs. As she picked up speed, her eyes glowed iridescent purple. She gripped a butterfly knife in her right hand. Flicking it, she came closer. I couldn't move.

The first cut sheared the skin from my arm, exposing red muscle. The blood was warm as it mixed with the rain. Then,

I watched her skin me alive. Shivering, I tried begging her to stop. But she'd already cut out my tongue and gazed into my eyes like a lover.

"I vill eat your heart," she said.

Something moved under the hem of her short gown. A small gray hand with slimy skin and black, razor-like fingernails appeared. Another hand inched its way out. A sudden gush of birth blood exploded onto the rushing water. Then, a crablike monstrosity with no eyes and too many arms wobbled before me, the hideous body pulsing with its first breaths.

Slowly, it crawled over my feet and, hooking its claws deep into my exposed flesh, climbed me like a rock face. Drawn to the thumping in my chest, it stopped and tilted its praying mantis head. A horrific squeal assaulted my ears as its teeth tore me open.

Now, Roy Batty joined the Russian girl. They held hands like schoolchildren. His blond hair was slick in the rain, and his eyes were glowing. They were a happy couple, admiring the hellish thing they'd made together.

"There, there," Sasha said to the demon child. "There, there."

When I opened my eyes, Vlad was looming over me. I shook myself awake as morning light burned away the remnants of the nightmare.

"What time is it?" I said.

"After five."

While he showered, I made coffee. I'd barely slept four hours, and the exhaustion I felt reminded me of my Black Dragon days. The Russian girl slept peacefully through the night. I decided not to wake her. Her brother found fresh clothes that more or less fit. When he walked into the kitchen, he had on a bright orange shirt, tan pants, and a plaid sport coat.

Chortling, I poured him a cup. "Stylish."

Sheepishly, he took a seat at the kitchen table. "There's plenty of hot vater."

"Let me finish my coffee first."

"I am vorried Sasha is getting vorse. Vill she become like those cutters?"

"They may have injected her with a new strain." I was talking out of my ass.

"And the baby?"

"I wish I had answers, but I don't." Despite my head pounding from a lack of sleep, I tried softening my tone. "Your sister survived longer than any of those other girls. That's why they want her so bad. She might have some kind of immunity."

He stared at his hands. "I thought for her to survive, she must get rid of the baby. I am not religious, but this makes me...uncomfortable."

I could see the frustration in my Russian friend's eyes. Like me, he wanted to protect the person he loved most. But the cost was too high.

"My wife was religious," I said. "And I know where she would stand on the issue. She'd want us to protect the child at all costs."

"But it's killing Sasha. Ve could save her—"

"Terminating the pregnancy is no guarantee she'll survive."

He remained quiet for a while. Then, "This is my fault." He looked away ashamedly. "Muzhestvennost."

"What does it mean?"

"Russian masculinity. I am too proud, that's it. If I vasn't, she vould be okay."

"Have some more coffee," I said. "I'm going to shower."

When I returned to the kitchen, Sasha was sitting at the table, wearing a pair of men's pajamas. Her hair fell gently around her face as she held a steaming cup of tea to her lips.

"You change your bandage?" she said.

I gave her a quick nod and poured myself more coffee. The TV was on in the background. Vlad must've gone into the living room. I thought about our earlier conversation and wondered if the Russian girl would recover. Recalling my dream, I couldn't help thinking of her as a murderous cutter. I put aside the thought and sat next to her.

"Feeling any better?"

Instead of answering, she brushed the hair from her face. Her expression was heavy with Russian secrets. "Do you vant to be rid of me now?"

"I want to help you."

"Even vhen you don't know...vhat I am becoming?"

"No one knows."

She looked down. "This creature I am carrying. Should I keep it? Or..."

"I can't tell you what to do. Only you can decide."

She leaped to her feet and rummaged through drawers till she found the knives. Grabbing the largest one, she held it to her abdomen, her fierce eyes challenging me. I didn't flinch. Instead, I gazed at her with kindness.

"I vill save myself!" she said.

Turning my back on her, I refilled my cup. After a long silence, I heard the knife clatter on the counter. When I turned around, she was shaking. I held her.

"I'm so scared," she said, clinging to me. "Maybe if you loved me, I could— Vhy don't you love me? I vant you so much!" Tearing herself away, she glared at me.

"I care about you."

"But you don't love me."

"I'm not sure I can feel love anymore. I've lost too much."

She studied my eyes—the way she had in my dream. Then she raked my cheek with her fingernail. "Liar!"

When I touched my face, I saw fresh blood on my hand. Her brother walked into the room and observed the two of us in a standoff. Though I wasn't positive he knew what was going on, he was suspicious. Avoiding eye contact, I pressed a wet paper towel to my face.

"Something has happened," he said. "Come and see."

The morning news was on in the living room. Maritza was reporting from a spot that looked familiar. Recognizing the location, my blood turned cold. Behind her, a building was in flames as firefighters fought to gain control of the situation.

"All we know so far is that the fire started in the early morning. Firefighters were inside searching for survivors when they made a grisly discovery. There are two dead. The victims have been identified as Dr. Tomás Fernandes and a physician assistant, Michelle Rios."

She pointed at an ambulance as paramedics loaded a body. "Preliminary evidence suggests both were shot at close range. Police theorize that whoever killed them tried to cover up the evidence. Mari Lopez reporting for ABC7 Eyewitness News."

I switched off the TV and faced the others. "We need to leave—now. It's only a matter of time till they find Sasha."

The Russian girl stared at the black TV screen. "Vhy did they kill them?"

"They're thorough. And they didn't burn the building

because of the bodies. The lab was located there, along with your medical records."

I crossed to the windows and peeked out through a curtain. Three dark objects hovered low in the gray, misty sky —drones.

"Things just got way worse," I said.

THIRTY-SEVEN

I worried the gray-suits had made the Tahoe and were on their way. There wasn't enough time to see the Korean about a new vehicle. Cuco had come through and gotten my front bumper repaired. So at least there was no longer any evidence of Sasha's hit-and-run. Our priority now was to get out of LA unnoticed. Once we were safe, we could figure out what to do next.

Thinking about places we might try, I imagined traveling to Mt. Shasta, where we could stay with Guthrie and Caramel. There, we'd have plenty of guns for protection. But being on the road for four or five hours was risky. And anyway, I didn't know if the Russian girl was up for that kind of trip. Hesitating, I made a call.

"Hello?" Maritza said, her voice quiet and intense.

"I need a favor."

"Where are you?"

"Better not to say. Can we talk?" Then, when she didn't respond, "Maritza?"

"I'll call you back."

I looked up from the kitchen table and found Sasha

watching me. The circles under her eyes were darker, and the veins in her arms more pronounced. She looked skinnier—unusual for a pregnancy, I felt. When my phone vibrated, I picked it up on the first ring.

"Hey."

"I had to step outside. Too many strangers hanging around the station."

"Gray-suits?"

"As a matter of fact."

"I'm with Sasha and her brother. We need a place to hole up outside the city. When they killed Dr. Fernandes—"

"Mierda. I remember his name was on that file you gave me."

"He's the one who examined her. Obviously, they got to him—I can explain later."

"The police are saying it was a robbery gone wrong and that we shouldn't call it anything else."

"They're gaslighting you. He was killed because he helped us. The lab that performed the tests is in the same building."

"¡Qué chingados! How is she?"

I looked up. "She could be better. Can you think of a safe place we can go for a few days?"

"I'll make a call. Give me an hour."

She whispered something. It wasn't what she said, but how she said it. "Be careful, David."

"Always. Later."

I was never any good at picking up cues from women. Though they seemed innocent enough, the words had gotten to me. *Be careful, David.* Dismissing the thought, I poured a cup of coffee and watched the Russian girl treat the wound on her brother's hand.

"I'm arranging for a safe house," I said. "But we don't have a way to get there."

Vlad examined the fresh bandage and patted his sister's arm. "Tahoe is no good?"

"They might be looking for it. Any friends you can call for a clean vehicle?"

He pulled something from his pocket. When I recognized his phone, I reached over and snatched it.

"I thought I told you to buy a burner," I said.

"It's fine. No one has this number."

"Someone does. How else could the gray-suits have found you at Cuco's house?"

In another beat, the phone was in pieces. Flicking on the garbage disposal, I dropped the SIM card in. It vanished with a soft crunch.

I returned the device. "Is there an electronics store near here?"

"Target, a few blocks away."

"You'll have to walk."

"Okay, boss," he said, bristling.

Sasha smirked as her brother checked his wallet. She said something to him in Russian and kissed his cheek. Avoiding eye contact, he headed out the front door. Okay, so he was pissed off, taking orders from a Polish guy. There was probably a whole Soviet Union vibe happening, but I didn't give a shit. We had bigger problems.

I went into the living room and turned on the TV, searching for local news. Flipping around the LA stations, I couldn't find anything except soap operas and game shows. I tried CNN. They were in the middle of a story on holiday travel and busy airports. Disgusted, I pressed and held a button on the remote and watched the channels zip by. The Russian girl joined me, resting her head on my shoulder. When she saw the scratch she'd given me, she kissed her fingertip and pressed it to my face. Then she grabbed my arm.

"Go back."

I clicked in reverse, one channel at a time, until I hit C-SPAN. Pointing at the screen, she turned to me with frightened eyes.

"It's him," she said.

THIRTY-EIGHT

Walt Freeman sat at a long table with microphones, surrounded by military men, their chests bursting with medals. There were other stiffs in suits who looked like attorneys. Though the lower third of the screen identified him as the COO of Robbin-Sear, I'd learned recently that he was also Hellborn's CEO.

"Mr. Freeman," the chairman said. "It's my understanding you are here today representing Robbin-Sear Industries. Is that right?"

"That is correct, Congressman."

"And is it your assertion that the money we allocated for your program last time was not, as some on this committee have suggested, used for human trials?"

With a stony expression, the Hellborn chief leaned forward and spoke into the mic. "Like-uh-said, our protocol called for animal trials. Mice, dogs, monkeys, and so forth. It's all in the report we submitted."

"And you further contend that the military applicability of the serum was appropriate..."

My phone vibrated. I answered right away. "Hello?"

"It's me," Maritza said.

"Don't say my name. Are you near a TV?"

"I decided to come home. What's going on?"

"Turn on C-SPAN. And make sure the sound is off. I'll wait."

She spoke quietly into the phone. "Is that who I think it is?"

"Can you record the program?"

"I can do better than that. I'll—"

"Don't say any more. I need you to step outside."

"Wow, you are paranoid."

"And yet alive. Let me know when you're out of the house."

In another beat, she came back on. "Okay, I'm on the street. Or would you like me on a swan boat in Echo Park?"

"You were telling me about the recording."

"Right. I'll ask one of the news editors to download a copy."

"Be careful."

"Don't worry. I'm pretty sure he has the hots for me. He won't tell anyone."

"Be sure to watch all of it. And bring popcorn."

"Okay, so. You remember me mentioning my friend Karen?"

"The researcher who lives in Santa Barbara?"

"I explained the situation, and she's agreed to let you guys stay with her."

"I can't believe it—that's awesome. When can we go?"

"As soon as you're ready."

"Thank you." I side-eyed Sasha. "I mean that."

"I was thinking I could meet you up there to make introductions."

"Not a good idea. I don't want anyone following you. We can figure out a way to meet later."

"Okay." She sounded disappointed. "I miss you."

"Text me the address. I'll be in touch."

After disconnecting, I turned to the Russian girl. She considered me with a critical eye, her feet tucked beneath her on the sofa like a jealous cat.

"What?" I said.

"I knew you liked this girl. I'm going to pack." She got up and walked away. "And don't help me this time."

This is what happens when you get involved with a nineteen-year-old. They're stupid, harboring these insane, romantic ideas. I didn't have time for this shit. All I wanted was to keep her safe. And that was despite the fact that she might turn into a cutter and gut me like a fish. Whatever. I told myself I was doing it for the baby. Seriously, though, why the jealousy? Whatever happened to gratitude? A simple thank-you, for shit's sake.

My only reason for coming to LA was to kill Walt Freeman and expose the evil he and his people had perpetrated, both at Robbin-Sear and now Hellborn. And I had Sasha to look after. The angel said she was important, but I still couldn't see how. Still, something told me to suck it up and keep going. Seems like I'd done a lot of that lately.

Vlad walked in the front door carrying a new phone. "All set. A vehicle vill come in two hours."

"And it's clean, right?"

"You are not the only guy here vith training."

"You'd better pack. And for God's sake, can you find some less conspicuous clothes? You look like a Bible salesman."

I continued watching the congressional hearing. Mr. Like-Uh-Said was in the middle of outlining the history of the military program. He brought up the founders of Robbin-Sear

Industries, Doctors John Robbin and William Sear. Reading from a prepared statement, he painted a picture of selfless scientists dedicated to helping soldiers and defending freedom in foreign lands. Protecting them from disease and hardship. He made them sound like candidates for sainthood.

"That all sounds very patriotic," a sharp-eyed ranking member said. "Tell us about the botched experiment in Guatemala. I believe it was near Jacaltenango?"

"We were administering vaccines to inoculate people against bubonic plague. It was a humanitarian mission, ma'am. Nothing to do with the program we're discussing."

"But everyone died."

"Unfortunately. It wasn't until it was too late that we discovered the vaccine was contaminated. I'm sure you're aware of the cold chain challenge?"

She side-eyed her colleagues. "Enlighten us."

"A temperature of between approximately thirty-five and forty-six degrees Fahrenheit must be maintained to achieve herd immunity. Conditions in Guatemala couldn't guarantee that."

"You burned the village to the ground."

"We took measures to contain the outbreak with the permission of Guatemala's Ministry of Public Health. It's all in the report."

She referred to her notes, then glared at the witness over her reading glasses. "And who was in charge of the operation?"

He leafed through his papers—what a showman. "Robert Creasy."

"Mr. Creasy was ordered to appear before this committee, was he not?" The congresswoman turned to her colleagues on either side of her. "Why isn't he here?"

Covering his mic, the executive leaned over as an attorney

standing behind him whispered in his ear. Soberly, he faced the panel again.

"We believe Mr. Creasy took his own life."

"I see," the congresswoman said. She was obviously pleased with herself at having connected the dots. "Guilt over Guatemala, I guess."

His expression didn't change. "I'm not a psychiatrist, ma'am. Or a priest."

That last jab brought roars of laughter from the people sitting behind him. The chairman banged his gavel. Over the next hour, I listened carefully to Walt's testimony. There was never any mention of what happened in Tres Marias or Mt. Shasta. And no one referred to the fact that cutters were now hunting openly in LA. Even the well-informed congressional committee hadn't connected those dots. So much for government oversight.

The Hellborn CEO handled the hearing like a pro, leaving the committee with few questions while protecting his program's secrecy. As long as he was alive, the killing would continue—not only here in LA but in other cities. My original instinct had been correct all along.

Walt Freeman needed to die.

THIRTY-NINE

I walked into the alley behind the house, carrying my duffel. There was a tan-and-white Forester motorhome parked there. A skinny emo poser in black jeans and a band T-shirt was crouched on one side, polishing a chrome rim with a microfiber cloth. His head was shaved to almost bald. A cigarette dangled insolently from his lips.

Behind the vehicle, a driver in a black suit waited in a town car with the engine running. Vlad and Sasha joined me. Thankfully, he'd found a pair of jeans and a flannel shirt. He spoke to the undernourished kid, who gave him an irritated *Da* to every question. The Russian girl seemed unimpressed.

"A little obvious, don't you think?" I said.

"Americans... Alvays complaining."

The kid flicked away his cigarette butt and entered the motorhome. We followed, carrying our bags. The interior was roomy, with wood paneling, colorful carpeting, and a sofa. We threw our stuff onto a queen bed in the rear. The kid was about to leave when I took Sasha's brother aside.

"What about weapons?"

He said something to the kid, who rolled his eyes. Making

a show of it, the emo opened a modified wardrobe, revealing a cache of long guns, pistols, and plenty of ammo. He waited for his attaboy. We ignored him and walked out.

Outside, Vlad handed over the cash I'd put up. After counting it, the kid joined his friend. They waited for us to pull out. The Russian girl made herself comfortable on the sofa. As I headed for the driver's seat, her brother stopped me with a beefy forearm.

"Vhat are you doing?" he said.

"I thought I was driving."

"This vehicle is my responsibility."

"Yeah, but I paid for it." I could see he wasn't having it. "Fine."

Moments later, we were on the road. Sitting in the other captain's chair, I felt better knowing my Tahoe was safely tucked away in Glendale. The Russian had arranged for his Armenian friends to keep an eye on it when they returned from Moscow. As we pulled into the busy street, the town car followed us for a bit. Then, turning sharply, it vanished.

Vlad checked his side mirror. "Depending on traffic, ve should be there in two hours."

I turned around. Sasha was curled up in a little ball with her eyes closed. She'd been quiet since my chat with Maritza. I convinced myself she would get over it. As we approached the 134 Freeway, I noticed a police checkpoint up ahead. A black drone hovered in the distance between two office buildings.

"We need to find another way," I said, pointing.

He squinted at the drone and turned at the next corner, heading west. "They are vatching the freeway."

"What can we do?"

"Relax, boss."

We continued on surface streets through unfamiliar

neighborhoods. Soon, we were in Burbank. There was police activity up ahead. Two cop cruisers and a black Escalade were parked along the road. Slowing, the Russian maneuvered around the congestion and made a left at an intersection.

"I vill cut through the park," he said.

I'd heard of Griffith Park. A lot of movies had been shot there over the years. "They have an observatory, right?"

"Remember that scene in *Rebel Vithout a Cause*?"

I did not. The foliage was winterized and sparse. It was Saturday, and as we made our way up a narrow, winding road, we passed families walking with their children. There were picnic tables scattered throughout. And birds and squirrels everywhere.

An ABC7 Eyewitness News van was parked in a small lot. I spotted Maritza speaking to a group of Boy Scouts and their leaders. Her cameraman stood behind her, recording the interview. I wished we could stop.

"Where are we going?" I said.

"On the other side of the park is Los Feliz Boulevard. Ve can go vest from there."

I happened to glance at the large side mirror and saw the news crew disappear. A woman screamed, making Vlad slow down. All of a sudden, people ran in every direction, many carrying frightened children. I was so attuned to mayhem, I knew instinctively what had happened.

Someone was dead.

A throng of screaming park visitors passed in front of us. The Russian slammed on his brakes, but he couldn't avoid grazing a middle-aged man. We watched helplessly as he glanced off the side and rolled away. Frantically, he limped off as more people poured out of picnic areas and onto the road.

"Pull over," I said.

Gripping the steering wheel hard, Vlad found a secluded spot under the trees. I headed for the wardrobe.

"Vhat's happening?" his sister said, rubbing her eyes.

I pointed at the windows. "Shut the day/night shades!"

She did as I asked. Her brother closed the windshield curtains. He waited beside me as I flung open the wardrobe door and brought out two Glocks. I handed one to him and grabbed two extra mags. Without words, we checked our weapons. I jammed mine into my belt, using my shirt to conceal it.Then I took Sasha's hand.

"I need you to remain here," I said.

"Give me a gun."

When Vlad nodded, I handed her mine and got another weapon for myself. "Don't use it unless you have to."

"Cutters?" he said.

"I don't know." Pulling out my phone, I called Maritza, praying she would answer.

"David?"

"Why is everyone panicking?"

"A Boy Scout found a mutilated body just like the ones we — Wait, you're *here*?"

My stomach lurched. "Never mind. You need to get out of there."

"But I wanted to interview the police officer in charge."

"Forget it—too dangerous."

A loud banging on the side of the vehicle startled us. Outside, people screamed in Spanish as they tried to force open the door.

"Don't let them in," I said to the others.

"Hello?" Maritza said.

I waited for them to give up. "Okay, go ahead."

"Where are you?"

"I'm close. Look for a big, tan motorhome. Do you think you can make it over here?"

"Not sure—everything's crazy. ¡Mierda!"

"What is it? Hello?" Silence. *"Hello?"*

A crackling noise was followed by static, and then the connection dropped. I redialed the number. This time, the call didn't go through. I realized there were too many people in the area, jamming the cell service. Afraid it was too late to help Maritza, I grabbed the door handle and turned to the Russians.

"If I don't make it back, keep going," I said.

FORTY

Sasha clung to me, her face pressed against my chest. I thought Vlad would be angry. But when I looked up, her brother's expression was only one of concern.

"This is a bad plan," he said.

"The cutters are out there. I have to help Maritza."

"It might be too late."

"And maybe there's a chance. It's okay—I'll go alone. Stay here and protect your sister."

Gently, I pulled away from the Russian girl. The voices outside sounded far away. Gripping my gun, I peeked out the window. All clear. It was now or never.

"No!" she said, trying to block the door. "Let's go to Santa Barbara!"

"Lock the door and don't open it for anyone except me."

I tried pulling loose, but she held on as if afraid of falling. With my free hand, I caressed her cheek and kissed her forehead. The angel was right—she was important. Still, there was no way I was leaving Maritza to die.

"I'll be fine."

Seeing the futility of it, she relaxed her arms, her eyes glistening. She kissed my lips and hugged me one last time. I took a calming breath and unlocked the door. Raising her weapon, she covered me as I stepped outside. I heard the door lock behind me and wondered if I'd ever see the Russians again.

While clearing the area, I saw something move out of the corner of my eye. A lone cop approached me, his gun in front of him in a two-handed hold. He was young and looked scared. Before he could give the order, I laid my weapon on the ground and raised my hands.

"I have a license to carry," I said. "I'm trying to find my friend."

He lowered his gun and waited for me to retrieve mine. "Better put it away. I'll help you."

We'd only gone a short way when we encountered a screaming mob. They reminded me of the hordes I had seen time and again in Tres Marias. But these weren't draggers—they were ordinary people, out of their minds with fear. Some had blood on their clothes.

The cop and I pushed through to a clearing. Over the heads of the terrorized crowd, I could just make out the news van in the distance. Among the trees, bare-chested men with knives circled. They were gathered around something on the ground. Whatever it was emitted a gurgling noise like a brook. Uncomprehending, the officer started towards them.

"Careful," I said. "They're feeding."

"Where's your friend?"

"See that van over there?"

"You can take it from here, right? I have to stop this."

I grabbed his arm. "Don't. They're more dangerous than they look."

Pulling free, he radioed for backup and continued towards

the blood-soaked hostiles. I sprinted all the way to the van and banged on the door.

"Maritza, it's me!" After a beat, she opened it. I took her hand. "We need to get out of here."

"I can't."

"You've got to." Taking my time, I walked her outside. "Where's your cameraman?"

"He-he went to get help."

Far off, gunshots echoed. "We should go."

Holding hands, we hurried along a deserted path. By now, there were cops everywhere. Ignoring us, they moved in pairs through the trees. Soon, we reached the spot where the young officer and I had discovered the cutters. Two mutilated bodies lay motionless in the dirt. One was the cop, and the other was the cameraman.

"Oh, no! Rick!" She tried tearing herself away from me without success.

"It's too late for him. We have to keep moving." My words had no effect, and she fought me. "Stop it! You can't do anything—he's dead."

She gripped my shirt, her breathing erratic. I turned her head away from the carnage and encouraged her to continue down the path. Eventually, we reached the place where the motorhome was supposed to be. All that remained were tire tracks.

"Is this the right spot?" she said.

"If I wasn't back soon, they were to take off. But it's only been— Something must've happened."

We sat at a picnic table. Digging out my burner, I called the Russian. The connection kept dropping. Finally, after three tries, I got through.

"What happened?" I said.

"Sasha vanted to vait, but the cops made us leave. Ve are at the observatory."

"How far?"

"Less than a mile. Stay on the main road. Did you find her?"

"All good. See you soon."

When I turned around, Maritza was shaking. I touched her hand. It was like ice, and she was pale. All she could do was sit there, staring past me. I gave her a smile.

"They're not far, but we have a bit of a walk." I showed her my gun. "I'll protect you."

"I can't do this." She raised a trembling hand. "I mean, look at me!" She was beautiful. With her black pencil skirt, red silk top, and tailored jacket.

"You're fine," I said, helping her to her feet. "More than fine."

She brushed her fingers across my chest. "I got mascara on your shirt."

Most people weren't equipped for this kind of violence, and Maritza was no exception. Her neatly packaged world was fading away. Soon, it would be replaced by a nightmare you couldn't wake up from. As for me, I'd learned how to stay alive. And there was no trick to it—you just had to keep moving.

I kissed her and wiped away the tears. She gazed into my eyes, which seemed to calm her. Then, she smiled and took my hand.

"Okay," she said. "Which way?"

FORTY-ONE

We kept to the road. The air was cool, and the recent rain intensified the smell of lilac and sage scrub. The panicked crowds had moved on. As we climbed higher, I heard the sound of keening sirens through the trees. Somewhere overhead, a police helicopter circled.

"What were you doing here?" I said.

"Human interest story."

"Long way from reporting on murders."

"After what I saw, there's no way they're keeping this quiet."

"Tell me something about your cameraman."

"Rick was awesome. When everything went sideways, he locked me in the van. He was always thinking of others." Her voice cracked. "I attended his daughter's christening."

"I'm glad you're okay."

There was nothing more to say. I'd lost so many people, I had forgotten how to cry for them. Family, friends, comrades-in-arms. This was just another damn day.

She took my hand and held it to her breast. "Thank you for coming to get me."

"Don't mention it."

"You could've left with your friends."

"The old Dave would have."

She looked like she wanted to be kissed. And I was into it, but it felt dangerous. I was on a short line to death and didn't want to encourage this girl any more than I already had. She deserved better. So I kept walking, and that's when I saw them.

Cutters stood at the crest of the road, backlit by morning light. Hoping they hadn't seen us, I pressed my index finger to her lips and took her hand. We moved to the trees, continuing parallel to the road. The foliage was denser here, and shadows made it hard to see clearly. Twice, she skidded on the shiny, dry oak leaves that littered the park floor. In another minute, we arrived at a shrouded enclosure.

Human bodies were lashed to the tree trunks with bright orange rescue rope. The smallest were children. There were maybe a dozen. Like all the others, each had been skinned. Maritza almost screamed. Covering her mouth, she took in short, quick breaths. Carefully, we moved through the clearing past the blood-soaked specters.

"Don't look at them," I said.

She became faint. I grabbed her arm and forced her to keep going. As we approached the last one, a head twitched, sending a thrill of revulsion up my spine. A woman—or what was left of her—stared at me with hollow eyes, mouthing words I couldn't make out. Her naked body was a raw, bloody puree, but her head was intact. Finally, I got what she was saying. *Kill me.*

Maritza stared at my gun. "Can't you do something?"

"If I shoot, it'll bring the cutters."

"Please, David. Don't leave her like this."

Seeing that poor woman struggling against the horror of what had happened made me lose all perspective. I knew in my gut we should get out of there. She would die eventually. Then, I noticed the bloody engagement ring hanging on her bony finger. Motioning Maritza aside, I sent a bullet through the victim's forehead. The report echoed all around us.

I took Maritza's hand. Somewhere a branch snapped, and we stopped. Two cutters watched us, their iridescent eyes glowing in the shadows. Slowly, I put a hand on her shoulder. When she saw them, her eyes widened in terror.

"What do we do!" she said.

The hostiles flicked their butterfly knives in time to some invisible dinner bell. I raised my weapon to fire. But before I could, they came at us like lightning, their outlines a jittery blur among the trees. A hand grabbed me. When I looked down, my arm was bleeding. Screaming with fury, I jumped in front of Maritza and fired in an arc, striking a cutter. As he wobbled from the shot to his gut, I sent two bullets through his head and waited for him to drop.

"David!"

The second cutter had sliced open her shirt, exposing her bra. Viciously, he leered at me and moved in to finish her as she fell to her knees. Seeing my chance, I fired repeatedly at his back, hitting his lungs. Shuddering, he dropped the knife, gasping for air. I took her hand, and we ran.

"Are you bleeding?" I said.

"I don't think so. Your arm!"

"Never mind that."

I glanced over my shoulder. The cutter was gone. I was right about them. They could withstand almost any kind of body trauma as long as it didn't involve the brain. I pointed my gun at the trees. A blur crossed my vision, and I squeezed the trigger, only to hear a disappointing click. Before I could reload, the injured hostile was in front of me. Maritza screamed, distracting him.

Snatching his knife, I stabbed him in the eye. He reeled, shrieking. I withdrew the blade and sliced his throat, sending bright blood squirting everywhere. The wound gaped like a second mouth. As he tried standing, I rammed the knife into his temple. With a violent shudder, he fell sideways, the glow in his eyes fading to normal.

"There are more of them out there," I said. "We need to keep going."

Her eyes were vacant. I thought she might pass out.

"Here we go—I've got you."

Her legs moved like a marionette's as I helped her along. She was silent and cold, her mind most likely rejecting everything she'd witnessed. At the top of a hill, we returned to the road.

A few hundred feet away, Griffith Observatory appeared. Majestic, its white masonry art deco form gleamed in the morning light. Police cruisers lined the wide driveway. I put away my weapon. Spotting the motorhome, we picked up our pace.

The cops had set up a command post and didn't pay attention to us as we descended the hill. I banged on the motorhome door. Inside, a chink as someone raised a corner of the shade—it was Vlad. He opened the door, and I helped Maritza inside.

"We were attacked," I said. "I think she's in shock."

I guided her to the sofa. Clutching her torn red top, she stared at the floor. Sasha hung back with her brother, giving me the stink eye. Ignoring her, I grabbed a bottle of water from the fridge and placed it in Maritza's frozen hands.

"Drink this."

Blindly, she took a swallow and looked up as if seeing me for the first time. "They could've killed us."

"You should rest."

"She is coming vith us now?" the Russian girl said, her tone petulant.

I scowled at her. Then to Maritza, "We're leaving the city. Do you want us to drop you somewhere?"

The fear in her eyes hardened into resolution. "I'm staying."

"What about your job?"

"I'll call Nate to explain."

"If that's what you want. Do you still have your phone?"

She removed it from her little red Coach purse and handed it to me.

"Here ve go," Vlad said. Then to her, "I hope you don't care about that. No phone is safe around this guy."

I side-eyed the Russian. "We can't let anyone know where we're going."

After disassembling the device, I threw the SIM out the door. Vlad got behind the wheel and started the engine. His sister joined him in the passenger seat. He said something to her in Russian, and she nodded. In another beat, we were heading down the hill towards the Los Feliz District. Soon, we'd be in Santa Barbara. And with luck, we would be safe. Sasha surprised me when she brought Maritza a cherry yogurt.

"I like your shoes," she said.

FORTY-TWO

Vlad's driving turned out to be a blessing. Maintaining a steady speed, he didn't make unsafe lane changes or do anything to arouse suspicion. He was the perfect limo driver. A CHP cruiser followed us as we headed north on the 101. I expected to hear the short siren. You know the one—where your stomach shoots out the top of your head like a bottle rocket. But he kept his distance. Then, his lights came on. Luckily, he changed lanes and accelerated past us.

As I sat dozing in the captain's chair, I thought about everything that had happened since arriving in LA. I'd come alone, and now I had friends again. In Tres Marias, I'd only survived because of others—Holly, Griffin, Warnick, and the rest. I was an idiot for trying to do this by myself. It was a miracle I wasn't dead. Still, it was hard to let anyone in. My gut told me the only way was to trust someone.

"Vhat did you do before all this shit?" the Russian said.

"My wife and I worked at Staples." When he laughed, I sneered at him. "How is that funny?"

"I thought you vere some badass ex-military guy. You had

me fooled, Josey Vales." He turned serious. "Vhat makes a man change like that?"

"Seeing the woman you love gunned down in front of you."

"Blyat'."

"Your sister told me you were in the army."

"One year only—2008. They deployed us to Tskhinvali. Ever hear of that place?"

"I was nineteen and too busy getting drunk with my friend."

"They almost killed me over there—I didn't tell Sasha. The enemy fired mortars at the building ve vere hiding in. My best friend…" He cleared his throat. "After this, I tried to take out every Georgian soldier I could find. Too much blood. Too many bodies."

In Tres Marias, I'd battled draggers. And then there were living enemies like the mayor and Walt Freeman. It was only natural to want revenge. And it was easy to become numb to the carnage. Other than those closest to me, I considered most humans—living or undead—as meat bags that needed to be dealt with in a very permanent way.

"Would you have killed me at the warehouse?" I said.

His ears turned red. "It's not personal."

"Look, I get it. You had a job to do—find your sister."

"Da. And if I believed you hurt her, that vould be the end for you." He gave me a crooked smile. "Fortunately…"

"I'm not an asshole. Did you ever get revenge for your friend's death?"

"I killed many, but it vas not enough."

"It never is."

I checked on the others as we entered Camarillo. Maritza was on the sofa, wearing one of Sasha's T-shirts under her jacket. She stared blankly at the stands of eucalyptus trees on either side of the narrow freeway. Towards the rear, the Russian girl lay on her stomach on the bed, paging through _Cosmo_. I sat next to her.

"Thanks for fixing my arm," I said.

She didn't look up. "No charge."

"You look better."

"I look like shit."

"Are you angry with me?"

Rolling her eyes, she flipped a page, tearing it in the process. "Vhy are you talking to me? Your girlfriend is over there."

"You're right." I got to my feet. "Let me know when you turn twenty-one so we can have an adult conversation."

The magazine struck me in the back, but I didn't give her the satisfaction of turning around. Instead, I joined Maritza.

"She thinks I'm your bae," she said.

"That girl needs to grow up."

"Did you two ever..."

"I bought her clothes."

"Well, in some cultures..." She took my hand. "I keep thinking about the creep who was with Nate."

"Trower? I loved how you shut him down."

"He was about to go through my stuff. But if I'm being honest, he scares the shit out of me." She glanced at Sasha pouting on the bed. "This isn't going to end, is it?"

"We tried stopping it in Tres Marias, but the tentacles are everywhere. You heard Walt testifying on Capitol Hill. The whole operation is well protected—and well funded."

She fingered the crucifix around her neck. "When we were little, my mother would say God is always with us. And I believed her. But sometimes when I pray, I don't feel His presence. It's like I'm alone. Have you ever felt that way?"

I was the last person to preach about faith. But I felt compelled to tell her something. "He's there."

"How do you know?"

"Because if He wasn't, I'd already be dead."

I only said it to make her feel better. In reality, I knew I was destined to die a violent death. But I still had a mission. And I believed God had given me just enough rope to finish it.

She squeezed my hand. Hers was warm. Traffic slowed to a crawl. I patted her arm and returned to my seat. Judging by the number of vehicles, I guessed we'd reached Santa Barbara.

"Almost there," Vlad said, checking the GPS.

We exited at State Street and cruised through historic neighborhoods that reminded me a little of Tres Marias. I wondered if the gray-suits would track us here. Though I was hot to kill Walt Freeman, my priority was to protect the Russian girl and her baby. And now Maritza.

Dark visions of an uncertain future occupied me as we approached an expansive southwestern-style house with stucco walls, a red clay tile roof, and an arched doorway. Surrounded by trees, it sat at the end of a charming cul-de-sac. A fat orange cat lazed on the porch. When he saw us, he trotted off. The Russian parked on the street.

"Velcome to the safe house," he said.

PART FOUR

BLOOD FEVER

FORTY-THREE

Maritza's mentor, Karen Rothberg, kicked off our arrival with an intimate cocktail party. Though I didn't drink, I thought the gesture was classy. The woman's generosity was unparalleled. She welcomed us sight unseen into her home and greeted each of us with a warm hug and a New York-accented *How are ya, doll?*

The five-bedroom house was remarkable. It was filled with precious possessions collected over a lifetime—antique furniture, Oriental rugs, expensive plants, and television news memorabilia. Framed autographed photos of Peter Jennings, Diane Sawyer, Sam Donaldson, and other ABC Network luminaries adorned the walls. And there were hundreds of books on shelves in the living room.

The researcher was in her early sixties—attractive with dark-brown hair, blue eyes, and bright red lips. She wore an expensive suit and minimal jewelry. A white cotton glove covered one hand. As she fawned over her mentee, it was easy to see the love they shared. Karen referred to Maritza as *my little girl.*

"Lunch is almost ready," she said. "Why don't we go into the dining room?"

The table was formally set, and I wished I'd dressed better. As we took our places, a Latina wearing a black dress brought salad in a large bowl. Worried about eavesdroppers, I shot her a questioning look, which our host did not miss.

"Is there a problem?" Karen waited for the Latina to return to the kitchen. "I'll bet you're wondering if Olga will blab." She laughed. "She's been with me for many years—she's family. You have nothing to worry about."

Getting over my embarrassment, I tried the salad. "I apologize."

"Don't," she said. "Maritza explained everything, and I can't blame you, David. Your instincts are what kept you alive." Then to Sasha, "But now, I want to know all about you, young lady."

Lowering her eyes, the Russian girl moved the lettuce around on her plate. "I am pregnant."

"Ha! That's an understatement. You, my dear, are carrying something extraordinary. Considering what's happened, it's a wonder you're alive."

The room was dead silent except for the sound of forks on china. Maritza gave us an apologetic smile.

"You'll find, my dears, that I'm blunt," Karen said. "But I know what I'm talking about, and I have your best interests at heart. You'll see."

"The other girls... I am the only one left."

"And I'm so pleased you're here." Then, like a favorite aunt, she brushed the hair away from Sasha's face.

Olga carried in the main course, breaking the tension. I tried to help, but she insisted I remain seated. Each plate was already made up—roasted chicken with vegetables and mashed potatoes. When everyone had been served, she returned with a steaming bowl of macaroni and cheese.

"I thought we could all use some comfort food," our host said.

After lunch, Karen led us to her expansive home office. Three computer monitors stood side-by-side on the large, antique mahogany desk. Piles of newspapers, bound reports, and yellow legal pads filled with notes lay scattered across the desk and on the floor. A whiteboard with scribbles ran the length of one wall. Behind the desk, leaded glass French doors opened onto a beautiful walled garden. Nothing was in bloom. I tried imagining what it would look like in the spring. Holding our coffee cups, we spread out on chairs and a leather sofa.

"That's some desk," I said.

"Like it? The network gave it to me when I retired." She flipped through her notes. "Okay, we have lots of work ahead of us."

"Excuse me?"

She peered at me over her reading glasses. "Oh, honey. Maritza told me how you tried getting yourself killed going after this..." She referred to the notepad. "Walt Freeman person." She clucked her tongue. "Committing suicide at your age—honestly."

This woman wasn't only blunt—she was pushy. Walt wasn't anyone's business but mine.

"It's not suicide if the other guy gets it first."

She winked at Maritza. "So noble."

"Right?"

The researcher continued the lesson. "Gary Cooper was noble. And of course, John Wayne."

"Vhat about Clint Eastvood?" Vlad said, getting in on the fun.

"If you're referring to Dirty Harry, then yes. But the man with no name was a bit of a—"

"And Josey Vales?"

She gave him a tolerant smile. "He turned out all right, I suppose. And stop interrupting me. I never cared for Russian men. You all seem to lack basic manners."

As they locked eyes, I thought he might smack her. Instead, he chuckled. Simpering, his sister patted his arm.

"Where was I?" Karen said. "Oh, yes. David, I don't think you should try killing Walt Freeman, and here's why. It won't change a thing."

"He'll be dead, so that's something."

"No, *you'll* be dead. This man is more powerful than you can imagine. He has the ear of Congress, the Pentagon, and maybe even the president. I wouldn't do anything to antagonize him."

I pulled my earlobe. "Um, I may have hit his assistant in the face with my gun."

"Why in the world would you do that?"

"Because she's an evil bitch. She was the one who arranged Sasha's kidnapping, not to mention all those other girls."

"What's done is done." Side-eyeing Maritza, she went up to the whiteboard. "As you can see, I've been busy."

She walked us through some of the history, most of which I already knew. Robbin-Sear Industries was a privately held bioscience technology company founded in 1990 by two former government scientists. Their headquarters was in Virginia.

Upon incorporation, the Department of Defense awarded them a contract to provide vaccines to soldiers during the

Gulf War. At first, they focused on diseases like Hepatitis A and B, typhoid, and malaria. Later, they began manufacturing other vaccines to protect against chemical and biological agents.

"After a meeting at the Pentagon in July 2008, the firm undertook new research," she said. "They were looking for a way to inoculate soldiers to prevent PTSD. I was curious why the military was suddenly interested, so I dug deeper."

She circled a date on the whiteboard—July 13, 2008. "On this date, Taliban insurgents carried out what was considered to be the bloodiest attack against American troops during the war in Afghanistan. The Battle of Wanat, for those of you taking notes. I have a hunch that Robbin-Sear began work on what was to become RS-6160 as a direct result of this battle."

"My God," I said. "That was five years before Tres Marias."

FORTY-FOUR

It took me a minute to reorient. Mentally, I reviewed the information I'd gathered in Tres Marias—people, places, snippets of conversation. And RS-6160.

Karen smiled with curiosity. "David?"

"In Tres Marias, we interviewed two scientists," I said. "Originally, the project focused on combinations of drugs they could use to suppress the fear response."

She referred to her notepad. "In the amygdala."

"Right. But then, they discovered they could achieve a better result using a virus that targets the brain."

"Rabies"

Sasha leaned forward. "This is vhy they found rabies in my blood?"

"A modified strain," I said. "But they didn't count on the virus turning people into the undead."

Vlad scoffed. "This is impossible."

"Really? So I guess my friends and I were fighting ghosts for the past six months?" Then to the researcher, "The test subjects have since evolved. They look like you and me now."

She squinted at an area in the center of the whiteboard.

"Tell me, isn't it true that another incident occurred outside the country?"

"Guatemala," Maritza said.

"Walt Freeman testified to the committee that Robbin-Sear was on a humanitarian mission, and that they were responding to an outbreak of—"

"Bubonic plague," I said. "They destroyed the town to cover their tracks."

Karen picked up a different notepad and scanned the pages. "The research facility you discovered in Tres Marias—that was owned by Robbin-Sear, yes?"

"Correct. And we discovered a second lab in Mt. Shasta."

"I'm confused. Freeman works for Robbin-Sear. I was given to understand you're targeting a different company?"

"Baseborn Identity Research. He's the CEO."

She tapped the notepad with her fingernail. "It all makes sense. In the hearing, he testified as the COO of Robbin-Sear. And now I know why. He's using them as the scapegoat."

"I don't understand."

"John Robbin and William Sear are deceased—cancer, apparently. They passed within months of each other."

"Okay, so?"

"The company is defunct. Oy gevalt!" Then to Maritza, "You see where this is going, right?"

Her star pupil sat up straight. "Everything that happened in Guatemala and Tres Marias can be blamed on Robbin-Sear. And now they're gone."

Karen removed her reading glasses. "Along with their sins."

Why hadn't I seen it before? "And that's why Hellborn gets to continue this sick experiment as if nothing had happened."

She returned to her desk and dug through a stack of *Wall*

Street Journal newspapers. "Ah, here it is." She handed me the front section. "Take a look at this."

I read the headline—*Baseborn Identity Research Announces Pricing of Initial Public Offering*. "Great. And this is supposed to—"

"They're going public. Goldman Sachs is handling the transaction. They already have a drug in the pipeline, which might be RS-6160."

"But the damn thing doesn't work!"

"Makes no difference. They simply need to convince investors they have a viable program to secure funding."

"So this whole thing—the infections, the murders—it was about money?"

"My dear, sweet boy," the researcher said, peering at me over her reading glasses. "It's never been about anything else."

"How did she find out all this stuff?" I said as Maritza and I lingered in the garden.

It was getting dark. The first shimmering outline of the moon shone through the tall trees. She took my hand as we walked.

"I warned you she was a badass."

"But isn't she worried about her computer getting hacked?"

"Are you kidding? She has more security than the Pentagon. A hacker who goes by *V. Kulla* set everything up for her."

She stopped near a young apple tree and turned to me. "There's something I need to say."

"Okay..."

"I don't want you to die—don't talk. When we first met, you were ready to take on Walt Freeman and Trower and anyone else who got in your way. Can't you see how crazy that is? You heard Karen—the conspiracy is too big. And there's a lot of money behind it. You won't win—they'll kill you."

"I have to—"

"I know. You want to avenge Holly's death, and I get that. But there might be another way. Listen, I've been thinking. What if we were to expose Hellborn for what they are? Make it so they can never do this again?"

Pulling away, I stood beside a bed of barren rose bushes. I didn't want to get emotional. But somehow, I felt I could be myself with Maritza. The words that poured out brought tears, yet I wasn't embarrassed.

"When they murdered Holly, they took everything from me. My wife, my baby... My future. Look, I knew what we were up against. There were so many times over these last weeks and months when we could've died trying to save ourselves from the evil. But I still had hope. I thought God would protect us. I thought..."

Kneeling, I touched a naked branch that held the promise of spring. "I believed that because I had repented for my sins, I deserved to be happy. But I'd underestimated what bad people are capable of, and I paid the price. Holly paid the price, and so did our child—our baby. An innocent soul who never got the chance to live."

As I got to my feet, she fell into my arms and held me as hard as she could, as if trying to keep the pieces of me from flying apart.

"You can still be happy—with me," she said. "I'm asking you to give us a chance."

"You don't even know me."

"I know you enough."

When I looked up, Karen was approaching us from the house. Her expression was grim.

"You'd better come inside," she said. "It's Sasha."

FORTY-FIVE

Sasha lay tied to the bed with thin polyester rope, her head tossing from side to side. Her outstretched hands and arms were slick with blood. A red stain covered her abdomen. I worried something might've happened to the baby. Inching closer, I noticed the glowing purple irises. This was what I had feared most—she was turning. Unafraid, Vlad remained beside her, dabbing her forehead with a cool washcloth.

"What happened?" I said.

He looked pale. "She vas fine—vatching TV. Then she started shaking. She... She made a noise—horrible. Like D'yavol."

Karen shuddered. "The Devil."

Straining to lift her head, his sister looked at me, her eyes begging me to do something. She struggled to free herself and snapped at me. Opening her mouth wide, she let out a mewling noise that sounded like an animal. I felt helpless to do anything.

"Better double up on the ropes—she's getting stronger." I

side-eyed Maritza. Then to the researcher, "This is your house. What do you want to do?"

"Let's talk outside."

The Russian grabbed a first-aid kit and treated his sister's wound. "I vill stay here."

We sat in the living room, all of us shaken. Karen was silent, unlike the gregarious host who'd welcomed us earlier. She crossed to the drinks trolley and, using her good hand, flipped over a crystal whiskey glass. But when she tried picking up a bottle, she nearly dropped it.

"Let me," Maritza said, walking over.

"Lord, I'm a mess. Four Roses—neat."

"I remember." Then to me, "Want anything?"

"I'm good."

The researcher drained her glass before we could sit. The drink seemed to calm her. Watching her gave me a mean craving. I poured a glass of club soda and rejoined the others.

"After her convulsion, she found a knife in the kitchen," she said. "By the time we realized what was happening, she'd already cut herself."

I set aside my glass. "What about the baby?"

"The cut was superficial, thank God. But there was so much blood. Her behavior—it's because of the virus, right?"

"They had her on some drug at Hellborn. I think they used it to control the negative side effects. But now that she's off it—"

"This is going to get worse. Is she contagious?"

Exasperated, I got to my feet. "Look, if you want us to leave…"

"I didn't say that. And sit down—you make me nervous." She tilted her glass at Maritza, who fixed her a fresh drink.

We were running out of time. Based on everything I knew, it was a matter of days—maybe even hours—before Sasha became uncontrollably violent. Closing my eyes, I traveled back to when Holly and I worked for Black Dragon.

At an abandoned grocery store, we found a Latina who carried the virus. But unlike the rest of the draggers, she hadn't turned. She exhibited the same signs as the Russian girl—the glowing irises and the unpredictable, animal-like behavior. God, and that awful mewling.

"There was a woman in Tres Marias," I said. "When we found her, she was in bad shape."

The researcher took a sip of her drink. "Sick?"

"But not violent. We put her under a doctor's care."

"Did they treat her with anything special?"

Desperately, I tried recalling a vague conversation. We were at the isolation facility. My friend, Dr. Isaac Fallow, explained why Ariel—that's what we called her—had improved. *We've got her on antibiotics. Her recovery is nothing short of miraculous.*

"They had her on fluids and antibiotics," I said. "And it seemed to work."

"Well, I'm no doctor, but it sounds like the treatment might've stabilized her."

"So, what do we do?" Maritza said. "Take her to a hospital?"

Karen shook her head. "Not a good idea. They'll want to know what's wrong, and they'll perform tests. Once they enter her information into their online systems, Walt Freeman will know right where she is."

That made me smile. "You sound like me now." I pulled the phone from my pocket. "We need someone who can treat Sasha and keep her off the grid."

Maritza stopped me before I could dial. "Wait. What happened to her? That other woman?"

I'd only mentioned Ariel to bring a glimmer of hope to the

situation. In truth, there was no fairy tale ending I could spin that would leave them warm and fuzzy. Only the cold, hard reality of what the plague had wrought.

"We had to put her down," I said.

FORTY-SIX

Calling Isaac was risky, and I was less sure now that I should do it. He was my friend, and I was about to put his life in danger. Maritza gave me an encouraging smile. He didn't answer, which I expected. So I left him a two-word voicemail—*It's Dave*. The doctor returned my call in minutes.

When I explained the situation, including the risks, he insisted on driving down. He could be in Santa Barbara in a few hours and would bring medical supplies. In the meantime, we were to do our best to keep the patient stable. Before ending the conversation, I cautioned him to leave his phone behind and purchase a burner.

Deeply tired, I lay back on the sofa. As soon as I closed my eyes, I fell asleep. A little while later, Vlad joined us. Filling a glass with Grey Goose vodka, he drained it in one go. I couldn't blame him.

"How's your sister?" Karen said.

"Sleeping." He poured another drink and sat next to me. "Tell me the truth—she's getting vorse."

"I'm bringing in a doctor to treat her."

"And if he asks questions?"

"He's a close friend."

"But maybe it's not safe to…"

"You have to trust me. He's done this before."

"In Tres Marias."

The Russian stared at his drink, pretending he was okay. I thought about the person who was prepared to kill me when we first met, and I understood completely. No decent human being could remain immune to the torment of what was happening, especially when it involved family.

"I'm going to see what's on the dinner menu," our host said.

Maritza joined her. As she left the room, she gave Vlad's shoulder a gentle squeeze. Then she brushed my hand with her fingers. I decided to check on Sasha.

The four of us had agreed to take two-hour shifts watching the patient till Isaac arrived. I went first, sitting in an over-stuffed chair that faced the bed. Sasha slept fitfully, moaning and turning her head from side to side. I hated seeing her like this and was tempted to untie the ropes. But I couldn't risk her attacking us—or herself.

After a while, she settled down. Her steady breathing lulled me to sleep. I didn't open my eyes again till someone touched my shoulder. When I looked up, Maritza was standing next to me, holding a book.

"Are you hungry?" she said. "Karen and Vlad are in the kitchen."

Stretching, I was about to leave when she pushed down my arms and kissed me. "What was that for?"

"Just because." She settled into the chair and opened her book.

"What are you reading?"

She showed me the cover. It was *The Plague* by Albert Camus. Good choice.

I wondered if she really believed we could have a future together. For me, there was only darkness. Still. Instead of pushing her away, maybe it was better to enjoy what little time we had left. I'd convinced myself I wasn't falling for her. It was the safest route. The angel had told me to let in the light. Did that include Maritza?

The others were in the dining room, drinking coffee with Four Roses. Outside, the rain had started up again. When Karen saw me, she stood. "I'll ask Olga to fix you a plate."

I sat next to Vlad and gripped his arm. "Your sister was asleep when I left."

The Latina came out of the kitchen, carrying a plate of fish with pasta. "Y para tomar?"

"Coffee is fine, Olga. Gracias."

Karen poured more bourbon into her cup and handed the bottle to Vlad, who did the same. I wanted to join them—ceremonially drown my sorrows. But my sadness went much deeper than a couple drinks. If I started down that road again, I'd be lost. And so would the Russian girl.

"So, David," she said. "How do you see this playing out?"

I put down my fork. "Right now, the priority is to keep Sasha stable. Unfortunately, there's no cure. But maybe with Isaac's help, we can manage her symptoms."

The Russian pushed aside his cup. "I heard you tried that, and it did not vork."

"We didn't know what we were dealing with. When Ariel turned violent, we got scared. I keep thinking if we'd only waited, she might've..."

"You're saying there was a chance she could've come out of it?" the researcher said.

"No one can answer that. There were lots of patients in the isolation ward. Isaac treated all of them. But when they became dangerous, he ordered them to be terminated."

"Interesting choice of words."

"You weren't there."

"And now?" Vlad said. "Maybe this doctor vill terminate my sister."

"Her condition is different. She's had the virus longer than any of the others in her test group. That means something. Isaac will do everything he can to help her—I promise."

Karen peered at me over her coffee cup. "Which leads me to my original question. Assuming your doctor friend can successfully treat her symptoms, what then?"

I pushed away my plate and poured myself more coffee. If the Russian girl survived, Hellborn wouldn't stop coming after her. We would never be safe.

"You were right about going after Walt," I said. "It was stupid. We need to find a way to stop the killing. And that means shutting down Hellborn."

She touched my hand. "Without getting yourself killed."

"Have you heard about what's happening in LA?"

"Maritza told me. Maniacs running rampant, committing gruesome murders."

"Escaped test subjects. I call them cutters."

"Cops cannot stop them," the Russian said. "How can ve?"

"I'm working on it. There's something I don't understand, though. Have you noticed they're becoming bolder in their attacks? They used to operate at night in secret. Now, they're out in the open during the day. It's almost as if—"

"They want to be caught," Karen said.

FORTY-SEVEN

Vlad and I hovered over Karen's desk as she googled Baseborn Identity Research and navigated to the company's website.

"The cutters are a problem," she said. "But right now, I'm more interested in the man working for Walt Freeman."

A few clicks later, she had the list of officers. The CEO's headshot was first, followed by other senior executives. No one was under fifty. Scrolling down, she found Eamon Trower, Chief Security Officer. I read his bio.

Eamon Trower is the Chief Security Officer, where he oversees information security, R&D security, investigations, and law enforcement relations. Before joining Baseborn Identity Research, Mr. Trower ran operations at Black Dragon Security, both in the US and abroad. He spent nearly twenty years with the Department of Defense, overseeing a biological weapons reduction program. Mr. Trower is an avid golfer and marksman, and...

"That photo is disturbing," the researcher said to me.

"You haven't seen him in person. Does it say how he got the scar?"

She navigated to an obscure news website. For a one-handed typist, she was pretty fast.

"Looks like in the '80s he was captured by Libyan terrorists while on a peace mission in Jordan. I suppose they tortured him. Hmm, this looks interesting."

A link in the sidebar led us to a YouTube clip from an old *60 Minutes* interview with Mike Wallace. Trower was young and handsome. Wearing his Army uniform, he sat opposite the interviewer, his back ramrod straight. He looked like an All-American boy—nothing like the sociopath I'd encountered.

Wallace began by recapping the soldier's illustrious career. A West Point graduate, Trower came from a long line of military men. He was considered a rising star and, at the time of the interview, had been selected to head up a special diplomatic mission to Jordan. It was hard to reconcile this young, idealistic person with the Trower I knew. But one thing was clear. In those days he loved his country and was eager to serve.

The interviewer delivered his next question in a careful, quiet voice. "Knowing the danger of what you and your team are about to face in the Middle East, do you have any reservations about going?"

Trower paused and looked at his hands. Meeting the interviewer's eyes, he said, "I'm a soldier. It's all I ever wanted to be. I do what's asked of me for the good of my country."

Karen leaned back and stared at the screen. "Wow."

"He's the one sending the gray-suits?" the Russian said.

Exhausted, I wandered over to the sofa. "To reacquire your sister and kill me. Whatever happened to him in Libya changed him profoundly."

Vlad plopped down next to me and brooded. Gathering her notes, the researcher came around the desk. Leaning against it, she glanced at her watch. Soon, it would be time to relieve Maritza.

"David, what do you know about Black Dragon Security?" she said.

"I used to work for them."

The Russian sneered. "You lied to me."

"What I told you was true. Okay, so I omitted a few details. The security firm was contracted to restore order after the outbreak. The new supervisor recruited my wife and me. I guess Holly and I proved ourselves fighting the draggers."

"Earlier, you hinted that you'd met Trower," Karen said.

"I never met him. Recently, the gray-suits came to my apartment building to kill me. Trower was there. Before that, I saw him in Mt. Shasta, where my wife was murdered. I didn't know who he was or that he used to work for Black Dragon."

"And you think he killed her?"

"No, but..."

All this time, I'd assumed Walt killed the mayor when he tried to flee after murdering Holly. But that wasn't the CEO's style. He would've delegated the job. And what better candidate than a soldier?

"Mt. Shasta was a shitshow," I said. "The mayor murdered my wife. Then, at Walt Freeman's direction, Trower took out the bastard because he was a liability. When his people showed up the other day, Sasha rescued me."

Side-eyeing Vlad, Karen made a note. "Brave girl. And now he knows you two are together." She sighed. "You should get some rest." Then to the Russian, "It's almost time for your shift."

As he and I walked out, she erased a section of the whiteboard and began scribbling new notes.

Later, Maritza found me in the den, channel-surfing with the sound low. She sat next to me and rested her head on my shoulder, her eyelids growing heavy. I stopped at Fox News.

"In other news, analysts are saying the Baseborn Identity Research IPO is poised to bring in much-needed cash to fund a clinical trial for a new drug. The firm claims it will revolutionize combat. Earlier today, I had a chance to catch up with the Chairman and CEO, Mr. Walter Freeman. We were at the Century Plaza Hotel, where he had just given a speech."

The scene switched to a brightly lit open area with colorful carpeting. In the background, business executives and military brass poured out of a ballroom. The reporter and the CEO stood off to one side.

"Mr. Freeman—"

"Call me Walt."

"Can you tell me anything about this new drug?"

"Our marketing folks are busy working on the name. We've already trademarked *Surrelis*, but don't quote me on that." He chuckled amiably. "Today, we inoculate our soldiers against malaria and other diseases. Our company wants to protect our military personnel serving overseas from the effects of combat itself."

"Are you saying your drug could eliminate PTSD?"

"I don't want to make any extreme claims. Like-uh-said, if successful, our product will lessen the debilitating effects of war and allow these fine men and women to lead happy, productive lives once they return home."

"Sounds almost too good to be true, Walt."

"Isn't science wonderful? New and exciting discoveries are being made every day."

"Any idea when the drug will be ready to market?"

"After the IPO, we'll seek approval from the FDA to begin clinical trials. In fact, our lawyers are working on that now. It's our hope that we can have an approved drug on the market within three years."

"Amazing. Well, I wish you much success."

Awake now, Maritza sat up. "What happens when the soldiers or their partners get pregnant?"

"That's why they need Sasha," I said.

FORTY-EIGHT

When the knock came, I hurried to the front door and flung it open. Real smart, Dave. It might've been a gray-suit—or Trower. But it was my dear friend, Dr. Isaac Fallow. Giving me a wide grin, he embraced me as the taxi drove off.

"Dave Pulaski," he said. "I decided to take the train so I could get some work done."

"Thank God you're here."

He'd changed in the short time I was away. His white hair was long and unruly, and he could've used a shave. He had two suitcases. Grunting, I grabbed both and waited for him to enter. Maritza and Vlad met us in the foyer.

"Isaac, this is Maritza Lopez and Vlad Drakonov." Then to the Russian, "See? I got it right this time."

The doctor extended his hand. "Pleasure to meet you both."

"Vlad is the patient's brother."

"Mnogo let nazad ya posetil Moskvu," Isaac said. "Eto krasivy gorod."

"Osobenno letom."

"Wow," I said to my friend. "I didn't know you spoke Russian."

"Studied it in college. I did it to impress a girl." He winked at Maritza. Then to me, "Dave, I'll get right to the point. I need a bathroom and some hot coffee, preferably in that order."

"There's a guest bathroom to the right. I'll grab the bags."

"And I'll get the coffee," Maritza said.

Isaac sat with us in the kitchen, devouring the chicken sandwich Olga had prepared. I had a million questions about Tres Marias, Warnick, Griffin, and Fabian. But now it was time to focus on Sasha. So I brought him up to speed on her condition while he ate.

"And how are you holding up?" he said.

I knew what he meant. *Are you thinking about blowing out your brains now that Holly is gone?* We'd last seen each other at her funeral. He had watched me go from a young hockey-playing fool to a poor student with a sore attitude and, later, a mean drinking problem. This man knew the worst in me. And he also knew the good I was capable of when it came to my late wife. Unlike her, he and I had survived the evil that befell our town. Yet here we were once again, ass-deep in the bad place.

"One day at a time," I said.

Maritza smiled at the doctor. "How was your trip?"

"Uneventful." He reached into his pocket and pulled out a flip phone. "I did as Dave suggested and purchased this."

I programmed in my number and handed it back. "Not to spoil your lunch, but Walt Freeman is in the picture again."

He swallowed some coffee. "Doesn't surprise me. This evil spreads like the virus itself."

When our host walked in, Isaac wiped his lips with a napkin and stood. Extending her hand, she gave him a warm smile.

"Our savior. You must be Dr. Fallow. I'm Karen Rothberg, the owner of this humble abode."

"Pleasure. You have a beautiful home. And I appreciate you putting up with us. I'm sure it hasn't been easy under the circumstances."

"What it's been is an education. Can I offer you some spirits for that coffee?"

"Thanks, but I'm tired. I don't want to fall asleep during the exam."

"Well, the girl is awake now, so why don't we—"

"Of course." Then to me, "My equipment?"

"I moved it into Sasha's room."

After washing his hands, Isaac put on surgical gloves. Karen led the way into the bedroom. The Russian girl gazed out the window, her hands and feet bound securely. Her brother whispered something to her in Russian. She nodded.

"Sasha?" our host said. "This is Dr. Fallow. He's going to examine you now, dear."

"Hello, young lady. I'm a friend of Dave's." He picked up his medical bag and stepped into the light cast by the lamp on the nightstand. "I'd like to make a thorough examination. Will that be all right? Nyet prichin boyat'sya." Then to us, "I told her there's nothing to be afraid of. Karen, I'll need a urine sample."

"Okay, I'll ask Olga to assist you. Be right back."

He opened the bag and removed a needle and syringe. Taking out a small bottle of clear liquid, he prepared an injection.

"What is that?" I said.

"Valium."

"You know she's pregnant, right?"

Irritated, he side-eyed me. "As I'm sure you are aware, *Doctor*, Valium is safe for short periods."

"She must have this?" Vlad said.

"It's a precaution for when we untie her."

After checking her heart rate and breathing, Isaac explored the patient's forearm, searching for a suitable vein. He swabbed an area with alcohol and gave her the injection, making her wince. Soon, she relaxed. He lifted her eyelid and retook her pulse.

"I'm going to untie you now, and I want you to be a good girl."

She muttered in Russian as he and Olga undid the ropes. Her brother stroked her hair to calm her.

"I'd like everyone else to leave now," my friend said. Then to Olga, "Help me get her into a sitting position."

Outside in the hallway, Vlad closed the door and sat on the floor, looking forlorn. I tried getting him to join Maritza and me, but he refused. Maybe it was for the best, in case something happened.

"Vámonos," she said to me. "I don't want us to be in the way."

FORTY-NINE

Maritza and I watched television in the den. I went around the dial, looking for more news about Hellborn. Since there wasn't any, we settled for a *Seinfeld* rerun.

"So how would you feel about me returning to the station?" she said.

"It's not about me. If you feel that strongly, then you should go back."

"What do *you* want?"

"I want you to be safe."

Pouting, she folded her arms tight across her chest. "You're no help."

"Hey, I was wondering. How did you explain your absence?"

"I told Nate I was having anxiety attacks after what happened in Griffith Park."

"Did he buy it?"

"I really do get those. Usually, right before reporting on a major story, I go through this little ritual. I say a prayer while looking at a photo on my phone."

"Of your family, I'll bet."

She laughed. "Actually, it's a panda. I can't explain why, but it calms me."

"Does Nate know?"

"No. And he's not going to find out, get it?" She threatened me with a balled-up fist, then hugged my arm. "He told me to take a few days. I'm sure he expects me back soon, though."

My mind drifted as she continued talking. Maybe it was the lack of sleep, but I pictured myself perched on an impossibly high cliff. Watching—helpless—as the Russian girl hurtled into the abyss. Falling... Screaming my name until—

"Hello? Hello?" Maritza said. "Anybody home?"

I took her hand. "We can't stay here. Sasha will only get worse."

"Do you think she'll lose the baby?"

"No idea—I hope not."

"What will you do?"

"What I've always done. Improvise."

That was no lie. I was a million miles from what I'd originally set out to do. And I was good with that—at least I was alive. But we were on a train without a ticket and no clear destination.

"The important thing is to protect Sasha," I said.

She turned off the TV and interlaced her fingers with mine. "When I first met you, I thought you were a bad boy."

"Really?"

"It's what attracted me to you." She laughed again, then became serious. "But when I looked into your eyes, I knew. There was something good in you. It's like Karen said, you're noble."

"That's crazy talk."

"Hey, I come from a superstitious family. We believe in signs. Big ones, little ones…"

"Yeah? What sign did you see with me?"

She took the crucifix she wore around her neck in her fingers. "It's hard to explain. It was the way you looked at this—like you recognized it."

"Are you sure I wasn't checking out your rack?"

She punched me in the arm. "Can you be serious for, like, thirty seconds?"

"Holly wore one similar to yours. But I thought I only glanced at it for a moment."

"It was all I needed."

She kissed me, and I felt myself plummeting again—falling for a woman I hardly knew. I tried telling myself this would end badly, but in reality, I no longer believed that. And I didn't know whether it was her lips or her scent or how she breathed when she pressed her face to mine. Something drew me to her. And in resisting, I was fighting a truth I'd known since that first day. Being with her felt right.

Approaching voices caused us to slide away from each other. I got to my feet as Isaac entered the room with the Russian.

"Sasha is strong enough for a bath," he said. "Olga is helping her. Are we interrupting?"

Maritza stood and, blushing, straightened her clothes. "Not at all."

The doctor found an accent chair and sat. "I've tested her urine and reviewed the lab report from her last exam. But I'd like some fresh blood tests."

"How do we swing that?" I said.

"Glad you asked. I have a colleague at St. Lazarus Institute here in Santa Barbara. They have a very sophisticated setup—exactly what we need."

"You vant to take my sister to a hospital?" Vlad said.

"It'll be very discreet."

"How long?"

"Depends on the tests. My guess is we'll be there all day."

"I vill not allow this."

"It's for her own good," I said.

"Nyet." His face flushed, the Russian left the room.

Isaac turned to me with a bewildered expression. "I don't understand. I thought he'd be happy to hear that—"

"I'll talk to him," I said.

I found Vlad alone in the garden, which was dewy from the last rain. A bank of dark clouds obscured the moon, giving him the appearance of a hulking shadow. He didn't acknowledge me as I joined him.

"She is all I have left," he said.

"I know."

"Trapped in that place. Strangers experimenting on her and those other girls. Now, you and that guy vant to do the same."

"This is different—we're trying to save her. You know she can't stay here, right? It's not fair to Karen."

"Vhen she is better, ve vill leave. I have friends in Seattle."

"But what if she doesn't get better? Isaac has a lot of experience with the virus. If he says these people can help…"

He grabbed me by the shoulders. "I don't vant them to hurt her!"

"We won't let them. Look, I'm not family, and I don't love Sasha the way you do. But I care about her. I hope you know that."

"Vill you come vith us?"

"Try to stop me. And I promise we won't leave your sister there. We'll take the motorhome."

"Vith the veapons."

I was beginning to understand him. There wasn't any problem a gun couldn't fix. I knew the feeling. He gazed at the sky as the first drops of a new rain fell on us. Soon, it would be a downpour. We headed to the house.

"Vhy did you help my sister?"

"Because it was the right thing to do," I said.

FIFTY

Vlad and I found Karen in the kitchen, deep in conversation with Isaac. Each had a drink. When she saw us, she poured one for the Russian. I went to the refrigerator and helped myself to a Jarritos Mandarin.

"Where's Maritza?" I said to our host.

"She's helping Olga." Then to Vlad, "Your sister couldn't wait to get in the tub."

"Thank you for everything."

"It's my pleasure. I'll go and check on them."

The Russian tossed back his drink and looked at Isaac. "Sasha must have these tests."

"I'm glad you feel that way."

Preoccupied, Vlad left us. Isaac took a swallow of his drink and, savoring its warmth, invited me to join him at the table.

"We've made some good progress on the virus recently," he said. "I have a lab and a research team now."

"This is in San Francisco, right?"

"Tres Marias."

I wasn't sure I'd heard him correctly. "But I thought it was a ghost town."

"The governor declared a state of emergency, which freed up all kinds of resources. We're rebuilding. And we're using the isolation facility as a research center."

"Amazing—I can't believe it."

"It's my hope that after we get the test results, I can transfer Sasha to Tres Marias. That way, I can care for her until she delivers."

"Wait, what about security? Is there a police force?"

"We have something better." He paused for effect. "Black Dragon Security is in charge again."

"Really? Who's the new supervisor?"

"Your old friend, Nathan Warnick."

My head was spinning. Warnick had been my rock throughout the nightmare that decimated our town. He stood by me when they murdered Holly. And he had saved me from getting killed by a lone dragger, even though I wanted to die. Finally, he helped me bury my wife. When I last saw him, he was scheduled for a new assignment in Atlanta.

"What about Griffin and Fabian?" I said.

"They're in Georgia."

"I need a drink."

He handed me my soda. "Here you go, my friend."

Later, as I lay in bed listening to the rain, I had an overwhelming urge to see Maritza. I wanted to be with her—lie beside her, feeling her warmth. And it wasn't all about the sex. I wanted her close, holding me. She was the silken thread keeping me connected to...what? Sanity? I only knew that without her, I would tumble headlong into darkness again. It was a stupid, idle fantasy. After Isaac arrived, she moved in with Sasha.

Vlad had drunk too much Four Roses and snored like a walrus in the other bed. I gave up on sleep and drifted into the living room. Standing by the window, I looked out at the street as the rain came down. I thought I heard a nighthawk. The sound transported me to my hometown and those other nights when I'd wander drunk through the forest with my friend Jim. But the sound I heard wasn't a bird.

Pivoting, I spotted a figure standing in a corner, pressed against the wall. When I saw the glowing purple eyes, I realized it was the Russian girl. Adhesive tape dangled from one hand where her IV needle had been. She was holding something—I couldn't tell what.

"Sasha," I said.

Her breathing was like the sound of bellows. She raised her head and, with a shriek, came at me. I almost saw the knife too late. As she tried slicing my arm, I grabbed her wrist and twisted. Sensing her strength, I worried she would overpower me. I directed all my energy to my hands and clamped down harder. Like a feral animal, she hissed.

Voices and quick footsteps now. Soon, others were in the room. Someone switched on the lights, revealing Vlad, Isaac, and the women. When Olga saw the knife, she screamed. The Russian came to my defense, attempting to take away the weapon.

"Noooooo!" his sister said, her voice like burning metal. "Let me do this!"

She twisted her hand free and cut her brother's forearm. When she saw what she'd done, a look of shock washed over her. Then, her eyes returned to their normal color.

"Vlad!"

I'd almost let my guard down when her eyes glowed

fiercely again. I didn't want to punch her body because of the baby, but I had to do something. So I clocked her. Groaning, she lost her footing and staggered back. Seeing his chance, Isaac injected her in the arm. In another beat, her eyes glazed over, and she dropped the knife.

"So hungry," she said, shrinking into her brother's arms.

The Russian and I tied Sasha to the bed while Isaac reinserted the IV. The women stood in the doorway, looking fearful. I sympathized. The Russian girl was getting stronger—more unpredictable.

"I didn't even hear her leave the room," Maritza said, as if this were her fault.

The doctor brought the duvet up to the patient's chin. "She'll sleep now."

Vlad examined his bandaged arm. "I vill stay."

No one felt like sleeping, so we reconvened in the kitchen. One step ahead of us, Olga had already made coffee. The thought of not being able to save Sasha ate at me. Sensing my mood, Maritza handed me a steaming cup. Grateful, I kissed her hand.

"There is some good news," Isaac said.

After burning my tongue, I put down the cup. "Nobody died."

"And something else. Whatever the virus is doing to her, she might possess the ability to control it. Did anyone else notice that she stopped as soon as she realized she'd hurt her brother?"

"She tried to kill me. So, there's that."

"But don't you see? It's something. Those cutters you mentioned don't stop."

"If anything, they enjoy an audience."

"Sasha is something very different," my friend said.

Though sleep was out of the question, I still needed rest. We had a long day ahead of us. Lying in bed, I thought of Ariel. If only we'd given her a chance, she might have overcome the raging hunger the virus induced. But we were too afraid. Instead of waiting, we put a bullet in her. Would we make the same mistake with the Russian girl?

If we did, an innocent child would pay the price.

FIFTY-ONE

What kind of sleep was I supposed to get after drinking all that coffee? Resigned, I wandered into the den and turned on the morning news. More bodies had been discovered. This time, the victims were a homeless family living out of their car—a man and woman and their young son. All were flayed and partially eaten. Their remains stood in a dumpster like discarded mannequins.

An ABC7 reporter—some guy I didn't recognize—interviewed the police chief. As usual, the cop tried downplaying the grisly discovery. And unlike Maritza, this tool's questions were softballs.

"Thanks for speaking with us, Chief Hughes," the reporter said. "Any leads yet on who's responsible for the Skeleton Murders?"

"None that I can talk about at this time."

"I'm sure you're doing everything you can. There's been talk of satanic rituals. Care to comment?"

"We now believe these killings are linked to a dangerous

group operating in the area. Certain items were found at the crime scenes that suggest Satanism."

The reporter deadpanned his next question. "Chief, people are frightened. Is there something you can say to reassure them?"

The cop grabbed the microphone and, with a grim expression, faced the camera. "Our job is to keep the citizens of this community safe. We will catch whoever is responsible and bring them to justice. If you have any information, I urge you to call our tip line." He gave out an 800 number.

"Thank you, sir. Back to you, guys."

Disgusted, I turned to find Maritza standing in the doorway, staring at the screen. Though it was early, she was already dressed.

"Morning," I said. "I thought the station wasn't supposed to report on the story anymore."

She joined me on the sofa. "They must've realized that tactic wasn't working. People are demanding to know what's going on."

"You're right. And they went with misdirection. Give them an enemy to hate."

"I know Jerry, and it's not his fault. The interview was scripted." By the look in her eyes, she was far off somewhere. "I spoke to Nate this morning."

"Which phone did you—"

"Relax, Sherlock. Karen has an encrypted VoIP line. Anyway, they decided to place me on an extended leave of absence."

"For how long?"

"He wouldn't say. I guess they figured I wouldn't go along with their phony story—and they're right. They don't want me reporting the news anymore." Tearing up, she looked away.

"This has Walt Freeman written all over it." I switched off the TV and held her.

"What am I supposed to do? I'm a reporter who knows the real story, and I can't tell anyone."

"Maybe it's better this way. I don't want you getting hurt."

I brushed the hair from her face and kissed her eyes. As we embraced, I could feel the anger coursing through her body. Pulling away, she glared at me.

"It's not fair. I didn't do anything except tell the truth."

"They see you as a threat. Maybe your boss is trying to protect you."

"Maybe. I came in here to tell you Sasha's awake. She looks much better. Her brother's with her now."

"Does she remember anything?"

"She said she had a nightmare. Vlad is wearing a long-sleeved shirt to hide his injury."

"I think I hear Olga. Does that woman ever sleep?"

In the kitchen, a fresh pot of coffee sat on the island. When the Latina saw us, she asked us to sit and handed each of us a cup. The researcher was already at the table, buried in the *Los Angeles Times*. A stack of newspapers lay next to her. I recognized *USA Today*, the *New York Times*, *The Times*, *Le Monde*, and *Pravda*.

"Morning," I said. "Guess you heard about the latest murders."

She didn't look up. "I'm reading about them now. Satanic cult. You'd think Walt Freeman could do better than that."

I was about to say something when Isaac and Sasha's brother led the patient into the kitchen, her IV bag trailing on a stand. Though she looked pale, she seemed calm. She had on a T-shirt and jeans. Someone had painted her toenails bright green.

I gave her a hug. "Hey, how are you feeling?"

"Like the horse rode me." Groggy from the medication, she allowed her brother to help her into a chair.

"I'm going to stop the Valium," the doctor said as he poured himself coffee. "And once she's done with this bag, we'll get her started on oral fluids."

Karen patted his arm. "You've worked a miracle, Doctor."

"That's God's department. I practice medicine."

"Well done." Then to the Russian girl, "Are you hungry, dear? Olga prepared you something special. I hope you like it."

The kitchen door swung open, and the Latina carried in a plate with a thick steak on it. She'd barely set it down when Sasha began cutting off rare, bloody hunks. The steak knife made me nervous as she focused all her attention on devouring the flesh.

"May I have milk?" she said, aware everyone was watching her. "Vhat?"

Her brother kissed her head and reached for the Russian newspaper. For a few precious moments, everything seemed normal. Over breakfast, we chatted about nothing in particular. Our host mentioned she was planning to visit family in New York in the spring.

After finishing her meal, the Russian girl washed down her prenatal vitamins with the milk. Sitting back with a look of satisfaction, she belched unashamedly.

"That vas good."

"So, what's the plan?" I said to Isaac.

"We have an appointment at St. Lazarus this morning. I'm assuming Maritza is coming with us?"

She touched my arm. "I think I should stay here with Karen and Olga."

Draining the last of his coffee, the doctor got up. "I don't want to be late. Dave?"

"I'll gas up the motorhome."

"Who are you seeing at St. Lazarus?" the researcher said.

Isaac beamed. "The director himself, Dr. Franklin Zeles. Why?"

"No reason." She gathered the papers and walked out.

Maritza took Sasha's arm and, with Vlad's help, led her away. When I turned around, my friend was smiling like the Cheshire Cat.

"You're starting to creep me out," I said.

"She's a nice girl. Anyone can see she's crazy about you."

"Who? Maritza? Isaac, don't—"

"Keep an open mind is all I'm saying."

"I've tried to. But it's hard when…"

"You've had it pretty rough these past six months. And unfortunately, it's not over yet. But there is good out there. You'll find it if you open your heart."

"You sound like a greeting card."

"Son, I've known you your whole life—you're strong. Don't give up. And remember, none of this was your fault. What happened, happened. You're a good man."

Maybe it was his voice or the way he looked at me, but a tidal wave of sorrow overcame me. Saying nothing, he held me. Feeling helpless, I thought of everything I'd lost—my home, Holly, the baby… And he was right. I blamed myself, even though there was no way I could've prevented any of it.

I wiped my eyes. "I'm such a pussy."

"The best men cry, you know," he said. "Look it up."

FIFTY-TWO

The air was crisp, filled with the scent of pine. When I walked into the house, everyone was ready to leave. Vlad and Isaac helped Sasha into the motorhome, minus the drip bag. Maritza waited outside to see me off. Slipping her hand around my neck, she kissed me.

"You need to be extra careful," she said.

"I will. But I'm worried about you."

"I'll be fine."

"No, listen. Trower could track you down here."

"I don't see how. Even Nate doesn't know where I am." She kissed me again. "I want you to promise me something. Don't be a hero—you're no good to me dead."

"A little harsh, don't you think?"

"I'm serious."

I lifted her chin with my finger and saw how scared she was. "Don't worry. I plan on sticking around to see where this thing goes."

"You mean us?" As she waited for my response, Vlad blasted the horn.

"Hold that thought," I said.

She remained by the door, her arms folded against the cold. Soon, we were off. I told myself this was a milk run and the Russian girl would be safe. But lately, things had a habit of going sideways. I didn't want to think about it, but there was a chance I might never see Maritza again. When I arrived in LA, the angel told me not to be afraid. But I was.

The hospital was close by in Montecito. As we made our way through wealthy neighborhoods, I continued to worry about Maritza. She might not have told anyone where she was staying, but Trower was smart, and her friendship with Karen wasn't a secret. The plain truth was the star reporter knew too much. And if that pale-eyed freak questioned her, I wasn't sure she'd hold up.

Sasha sat next to Vlad in the other captain's chair. She had on some of the clothes I'd bought her, including the sweater-knit pom-pom hat. Being outside had put her in good spirits, and she seemed happy to be with her brother again. Seeing her took me back to the day we met. I didn't believe in fate, but there was a reason I'd found her.

Isaac was on the sofa, rereading the lab reports from Dr. Fernandes. Once or twice, he paused, his index finger stopping on the page, and shook his head. Closing the manila folder, he removed his glasses and rubbed his eyes. I plopped down beside him.

"Any of it making sense?" I said.

"Maybe. Of course, the lab wasn't equipped to look for the virus, though they did find evidence of rabies. According to the blood tests, the patient is a normal nineteen-year-old woman. Most of the changes are due to her pregnancy. For instance, increased blood volume and a higher white blood cell count."

"That's good, isn't it?"

"It is. But we don't know anything about the fetus."

"Whether it's normal, you mean?"

He lowered his voice to a whisper. "Or if it's even human."

I glanced at Sasha. She gazed out the window, enjoying the view. Was it possible she was carrying something that was against nature? I thought about the angel's admonition. *She is important.* But why? Because of the child? The Russian girl had turned on the radio, and she and Vlad were arguing good-naturedly over the stations. My friend gave me a subtle wave and headed to the rear of the motorhome.

"The only way to know for sure is by performing a procedure," he said. "We could try taking a fetal blood sample, but there are risks. Depending on what we found, we might have to—"

"Terminate the pregnancy?"

"Only as a last resort. After that, we'd be able to examine the fetal tissue under a microscope."

Isaac's words chilled me. Listening to him reminded me that, as much as I loved him, he was a medical man and a scientist. Thinking about the other girls who'd died, I wanted to scream at the irony. Hellborn was the epitome of evil, yet their people were laser-focused on protecting Sasha's unborn child.

"Do you think the hospital can tell us anything?"

"I hope so. I brought a kit we used in Tres Marias to test for the presence of the virus. But that was a different strain. I'm not sure what we'll find now."

"Ve are here," the Russian said.

FIFTY-THREE

The streets were slick from the recent rain. Taking his time, Vlad turned into a driveway. Isaac and I made our way to the front and peered out the wide windshield. The grounds were immaculate, with a vast lawn trimmed with flower beds. There were trees everywhere. I recognized manzanitas, dogwood, and sycamore. In the center of the property stood an impressive multistory white building. The architecture was unfussy and modern. I spotted a narrow service road.

"Go that way and pull around back," I said, pointing.

Sasha made a face. "Vhy?"

"Because we don't know these people, and I'm not about to sit out in the open."

My friend scoffed. "That's ridiculous. St. Lazarus is a well-respected institution with—"

"Dave is right," the Russian said and made the turn.

Eventually, the road dead-ended. There was a deserted alcove behind a detached generator building. Across from that, a short set of stairs led to a side entrance. Vlad backed up the motorhome till it was no longer visible.

"I hope you're not planning to walk in with weapons," Isaac said, his voice stern. "These people are doing me a personal favor."

Every instinct told me to go in packing, but I followed my friend's advice out of respect. After closing the windshield curtains and day/night shades, we helped the Russian girl out and locked up the vehicle.

It was just after nine when we entered the vast lobby. The interior was spare, dotted with contemporary furniture and potted plants. Modern paintings hung on the walls, and light streamed through the tall windows. On one side, there was a bank of elevators. We approached two security guards sitting against the wall behind a curved desk. The doctor handed over his driver's license. The first guard, who seemed crusty, typed something into the computer and pushed over the visitor's log. He gave Isaac a numbered badge.

"I need to see everyone else's IDs," the guard said.

How could I have been so stupid? I had no problem giving them mine since it was a fake. But, as far as I knew, Vlad carried an authentic driver's license. And Sasha had no ID at all. Seeing the look on my face, my friend seemed to understand.

"Excuse me a moment," he said, pulling out his phone.

He stepped to one side and spoke in hushed tones. Side-eyeing his partner, the crusty guard gave the Russians the greasy eye. When he got to me, I grinned like a feeb.

Returning, Isaac leaned over the desk. "Someone's coming down."

Moments later, an elevator dinged. A man wearing an expensive suit without a tie and loafers approached us. He had chiseled features, wavy black hair that looked dyed, and professionally whitened teeth.

"Dr. Fallow, so nice to finally meet you," he said, his hand extended.

"Dr. Zeles, these are my friends."

"Welcome. Frank Zeles."

The three of us declined to give our names. After shaking hands, the director went behind the desk and helped himself to three more visitor badges.

"I'll take you upstairs," he said, handing out the temporary IDs.

"Doctor?" Crusty said. "Only one has signed in."

"It's fine. I'll contact your supervisor later and explain the situation." Then to us, "Follow me."

Butt-hurt, the guard snatched the visitor log and glared at his partner. As we made our way to the elevators, I motioned for my friend to hang back.

"I thought you knew him," I said.

"Only by reputation. I never actually met him in person."

We arrived on the top floor and followed Zeles into a large corner office. Two adjoining walls were pure glass—the view was breathtaking. I could see all the way to the ocean, where dark clouds were already gathering for the next storm. The director brought over an extra chair and slipped behind a sleek, glass-top desk.

"Please sit." He pressed a button on his speakerphone and asked someone to bring in refreshments. "I was so pleased you thought of us, Isaac. I'm honored."

"Nonsense. You come highly recommended."

Moments later, an assistant brought a tray with coffee, tea, bottled water, and apple juice. Then she disappeared, closing the door after her. Zeles took a sip of his water and set the bottle on a coaster.

"I'd like to begin the tests right away," he said.

"Agreed. And I cannot stress enough the confidential nature of this case."

Almost imperceptibly, the director glanced at the patient. "Understood. We'll forgo the standard paperwork."

Usually, I can tell when someone is lying. But this guy was a cipher. And that wasn't necessarily good or bad. Still, it made me want to dig deeper.

"Dr. Zeles, what kind of work do you do here?" I said.

"Great question, um…"

"Dave."

"This is an advanced research facility. We are a team of geneticists, chemists, biologists, and immunologists. We're focused on cutting-edge bioscience technology." He must've practiced that speech.

"How does all that help the patient?"

The room went quiet, and the director reached for his water. Then, instead of responding, he turned to my friend.

We're not sure they will be able to help," Isaac said, irritated. "But these are some of the best scientists around. I thought it was worth a shot."

"And on that note," Zeles said, getting to his feet, "why don't we get started?"

Sasha's movements were halting, and her expression intense. I guessed it was because she was once again in a lab setting under someone else's control. As we walked down a pleasant-looking hallway, she refused to let go of her brother's hand. Speaking Russian, Vlad did his best to calm her.

A female nurse waited for us in the private room, a patient gown draped over her arm. The interior reminded me of a moderately priced hotel. The walls were pale blue. There was a hospital bed, with a nightstand and a decorative lamp on each side. A window afforded a view of the vast lawn. In the center lay a rose garden, where doctors sat on park benches, smoking and chatting.

"This must be our patient." Though her voice was pleasant, it lacked warmth. "Doctor Fallow, after she changes, you can accompany us to the lab. And you gentlemen are free to wait in the lounge."

I didn't like leaving the Russian girl here alone and wished I could stay. But my friend had vouched for them, so I had no choice but to let this play out. Before we left, Vlad gave his sister a hug. We waited in a living room-type setting that featured cable TV, a PlayStation, and a ping-pong table. Next door, there was a kitchen stocked with refrigerated food and snacks.

"How long?" he said.

"Isaac promised to join us for lunch. Maybe we'll know something by then."

"I am thinking about the baby."

"And the fact that you're going to be an uncle?"

He grinned self-consciously. "A baby is good—family is good."

I thought about my lost child, not knowing whether it had been a boy or a girl. Holly died early in her pregnancy, but she'd always insisted we would have a daughter. I couldn't help wondering if, in some cryptic way, God was making amends by giving this strange child to Sasha.

A little after noon, Isaac walked in wearing a medical lab coat. Looking preoccupied, he grabbed a water from the fridge.

"How is she?" I said.

"Nervous. Dr. Zeles is overseeing the testing. One of his team members—an immunologist—is running blood and urine tests. After lunch, they'll do a sonogram."

The director walked in, grinning. "Isaac, we used that test

kit you brought and are well on our way to isolating the virus."

"That was fast."

"Let's break for lunch, then we can show you."

"I can't wait," my friend said, giving me an I-told-you-so grin.

FIFTY-FOUR

Vlad opted to eat lunch with his sister in her private room. So Isaac and I joined Zeles and his team in the top-floor dining room. It was a sprawling space, with large windows and a cook staff headed by a chef rumored to have been stolen from a local one-star Michelin restaurant. As expected, the food was excellent.

"We've never seen anything like her," the director said. "Though the patient carries the virus, there are no symptoms, such as a fever."

Another scientist chimed in. He was a tall, slight man in his late twenties with pale skin, curly dark hair, and brown eyes. "Her white blood cell count has not increased above what would be considered normal during pregnancy."

"Dave, this is Dr. Peter Asimov," my friend said. "He leads the immunology team."

"*Asimov.* That's Russian, right?"

"My great-grandparents were from Odesa, which used to be part of Russia."

"You were saying something about the white blood cell count. What does that indicate?"

"It means her body is not fighting the virus," the scientist said.

"What about the baby?"

Zeles knitted his brow. "The patient isn't far enough along for an amniocentesis. Even if she were, it's invasive. And I don't feel comfortable taking a blood sample from the umbilical cord."

"So that means you have to wait for the baby to be born?"

"Not necessarily," the scientist said. "There are other tests we can perform on the mother since the baby's DNA is also in her blood."

"You'll have to excuse my young friend," Isaac said, patting my back. "He always wanted to be a doctor."

As the others chuckled, my phone vibrated. I recognized Maritza's number and excused myself. The windows afforded a view of the lawn and trees. The wind had kicked up, and the sky was beginning to darken. Tensing, I answered.

"What's up?" I said.

"Are you alone?" She sounded scared.

"Sort of."

"You need to get Sasha out of there. Karen did some research on Dr. Franklin Zeles. It's not good, David."

Sudden laughter got my attention. I craned my neck. "Can you be more specific?"

"He's connected to Walt Freeman."

My skin turned clammy, and cold sweat beaded on my forehead. I lowered my voice. "And she's sure?"

Muffled talking, then the researcher came on. "After you left this morning, I decided to look up St. Lazarus—you know me." She let out a nervous sigh over the sound of rustling papers. "It's all cutting-edge stuff. For the hell of it, I began digging into Dr. Zeles. He used to work for Robbin-Sear at their old headquarters in Virginia."

"Shit."

"That's not all. Five years ago, he took a new job. Guess where."

"Baseborn Identity Research."

"The same. Two years ago, he took over as director of St. Lazarus."

"This can't be a coincidence."

"Last year, he and Walt attended a hearing in Washington, DC. Maritza and I are looking at a press photo of them now. They're seated at a table, surrounded by attorneys. And who's sitting next to Zeles? Your good friend Trower."

I'd been hunched over my phone the entire time, speaking in hushed tones. When I straightened up and looked out the windows again, I saw the angel. She was in the middle of the empty rose garden, her hair blowing in a wind that was like a gale. And that's when I knew—someone was coming.

"I have to go," I said. "Find out everything you can about an immunologist, Dr. Peter Asimov. And tell Maritza not to worry."

"Wait. If these people are working with Walt Freeman, they'll do whatever it takes to keep Sasha there. Capiche?"

"Understood." Disconnecting, I looked for the angel, but she was gone. I turned to find Isaac standing next to me.

"Everything all right?" he said.

I stared past him at our table, where everyone was in deep conversation. "How exactly do you know Dr. Zeles?"

"Well, as I said, I didn't know him personally. A colleague in San Francisco gave me his name. Why?"

"We need to leave asap."

"I thought you wanted to help this girl."

"It's not safe."

"Dave, I realize you don't like him, but—"

"It's not about that. He's connected to Walt Freeman."

"That's preposterous."

I noticed the director observing us. "Keep your voice down. I know what I'm talking about."

As we returned to the table, I tried to think how to do this. Somehow, we'd have to get the Russian girl out of the building without attracting attention.

"Nothing serious, I hope," Zeles said to me.

"My girlfriend and I are fighting. Isaac thought he was being helpful."

Everyone seemed to accept my explanation—all except Asimov, who looked at me like he knew something was up. Ignoring me, the director turned his attention to my friend.

"Anyway, we've been brainstorming. I'd like to keep Sasha overnight. A lot of the remaining tests will be exhausting for her. I feel—and the team agrees—that it would be better if we spread them out."

"Sounds good to me, Dr. Zeles," I said. "Isaac, we should do whatever's necessary, right?"

Catching on, he gave the director a convincing smile. "I agree wholeheartedly."

"It's settled, then." Zeles sat back, obviously pleased with the ruse. "I'm afraid we're not exactly a hotel. But we do have a few rooms available for patients' families. Peter, why don't you show these gentlemen where they can stay?"

The scientist got to his feet. "Happy to."

As we exited the dining room, the director walked beside me. "By the way, I meant to ask. Where's your car? I want to make sure it doesn't get towed."

"Oh, we ubered over here. Didn't really know the area, so."

He didn't look to me like he bought it. If his suspicions got any worse, all he'd need to do was check in with the guards. Chances were they saw our motorhome approaching from the street. I hoped he was too busy to care.

Making our way to another wing, my friend shot me a worried glance. Violence came easy to me, and Vlad and his sister were tough. But Isaac wasn't like us. I worried he wouldn't be up to playing his part. Whatever was about to happen, each of us had to be committed. I prayed he would be. And there was something else.

We were going to need our weapons after all.

FIFTY-FIVE

Z eles stopped at an intersection of two hallways. "I'll leave you here. Peter will show you to your rooms."

I reached out to shake his hand. "I was wondering if we could see the patient before we settle in."

"Of course. We're not quite ready to begin the other tests." Then to Asimov, "Go ahead and take them over."

"We're this way," the scientist said as his boss disappeared around a corner.

We found Sasha sitting up in bed, watching television with the sound off. Vlad dozed in a chair by the window. When we entered, he got up and joined us.

"This is Dr. Asimov," I said to the Russian.

As he extended his hand, Vlad hesitated before shaking it. "You're a Jew."

Bravely, the scientist laughed off the inappropriate comment. "Is that a problem?"

"I knew many in Moscow."

"What a relief." Asimov approached the bed and gave the Russian girl a warm smile. "How's our patient holding up?"

She stared straight ahead. "I don't like hospitals."

Taking out a medical penlight, he examined her pupils. "I'll tell you a secret. Neither do I."

Gently, he brushed the hair from her face. I was sure she'd stop him, but she didn't make a move. He addressed her brother.

"There are a number of additional tests we need to perform."

Scowling, she side-eyed Vlad. Then, "Yebanoye dno."

He shook his head disapprovingly. Whatever profanity she'd used, I was pretty sure the scientist understood too because his ears turned crimson.

"We, uh…we'd like to keep you overnight," he said. "Izvinite za bespokoystvo."

Though I was the only person in the room who didn't speak Russian, I recognized the first word. He'd apologized to her.

She folded her arms tight across her chest. "Fine."

My phone vibrated. Glancing at it, I saw a text message from Maritza.

Asimov is clean.

"Well, if you'll excuse me. I need to make preparations. A nurse will be here in half an hour."

"Thank you, Doctor," Isaac said.

"Yeah, thanks." I was starting to like this guy.

When we were alone, I shut the door. The others watched as I did a sweep of the room, looking for hidden microphones. Catching on, the Russian helped me. With her arms still folded, Sasha rolled her eyes as I checked under the bed. Vlad and I took apart the lamps and removed the light switch covers. Nothing. Finally, I climbed onto a chair and pushed open several acoustic ceiling tiles.

Peering into the darkness, I tried to see if there was a camera.

"Are you quite finished?" my friend said.

There was no way to be a hundred percent sure the room was bug free, and we had no choice but to proceed. There wasn't time to come up with a rock-solid plan, so I decided to wing it. I took the Russian girl's hand. She squeezed mine affectionately.

"We're getting out of here tonight," I said.

Alert, her brother came over. "Vhat has happened?"

"Zeles is working with Walt Freeman. This whole thing is a trap. That's why they insisted on keeping your sister overnight."

Isaac shook his head, defiant. "I still can't believe it. That man is a respected scientist. Why would he be a part of a conspiracy?"

"Let me ask you something. Did anyone here mention Sasha's name? I know I didn't." Then to the Russian girl, "Did you tell them?"

"Nyet."

I turned to my friend. "And Vlad didn't either. So why did the director refer to her as *Sasha* at lunch?"

He scoffed. "This is your argument? One of us must have mentioned her name. Maybe I let something slip when I was with the team earlier."

"Okay, how about this? Zeles used to work for Hellborn. There's a photo from last year of him and Walt Freeman sitting together at a congressional hearing. Look, I know you like thinking the best of people, but it's true. He's in it up to his neck."

"And the others?" Vlad said.

"I don't know about the rest of the team, but Asimov is not involved. Karen already vetted him."

The Russian girl gripped my hand tighter. "I vant to leave now."

"I'm pretty sure they won't let us." Then to Isaac. "I think it's best you stay with her and keep an eye on Zeles. Vlad and I will make some excuse to leave. We'll wait in the motorhome till dark. Later, you can let us back in. Only this time, we'll be armed."

My friend was vehement. "I don't like it. Innocent people could die."

"They already have," I said.

FIFTY-SIX

Vlad and I sat at the table in the motorhome, performing a weapons check. His Russian friends had supplied us with plenty of guns, ammo, and body armor. With all the windows covered up, it felt like we were in a cave. Earlier, we'd made a big show of going out the front, telling everyone we had urgent business and would return in the morning.

"What time is it?" I said.

"Past eight."

"We can assume Isaac and Sasha had dinner. She should be in bed soon."

Though my gunshot wound had nearly healed, I winced as I put on my protective gear. Soon, my friend texted me.

All set. I hope ur right.

I wasn't sure how Isaac would find the correct exit. All he knew was that it was on the east side of the building.

"Let's go." Switching off the lights, I headed for the door. I was just about to open it when the Russian grabbed my arm.

"Comms," he said.

Outside, a flashlight beam played across the shaded windows. A voice crackled over a two-way radio. "10-45... 10-45... Over."

Whoever was outside lowered the flashlight and responded. "This is Lewis. I'm on the east side of the building. There's an unauthorized vehicle parked here. Over."

"10-1... 10-9... Over."

Having worked for Black Dragon Security, I knew most of the codes. The guard inside the building was asking Lewis to repeat the message. Once he confirmed, we were screwed. Gripping the handle, I banged open the door, knocking someone on his butt. Vlad rushed out after me.

Heavily armed, we stood over a young security guard. Thin and gangly, he wore a cap that was too big for him. A voice over the radio repeated the previous code. I pointed my Glock at his face.

"Say '10-26,' or I'll blow your head off."

The Russian tapped my arm. "Vhat does this mean?"

"Disregard last information." Then to the guard, "Tell him."

I thought the kid might piss himself. He spoke into the radio, his hand shaking. "10-26... 10-26. Over."

A long pause. Then a second voice cackled in the background. "Letting your imagination run wild again. Huh, Lewis?"

While I continued to stare him down, he said, "Real funny, guys."

"Awright, come on inside. There's a Milky Way with your name on it."

"10-4. Lewis out."

Kneeling, I grabbed the radio and motioned for the nervous guard to stand. Without resisting, he did as I asked.

He looked like a recent high school graduate who'd gotten his training from an online course.

"What're you gonna do?" he said.

Vlad pointed his weapon at the kid's head. "No vitnesses, yeah?"

"Shit!" He nearly fainted.

As he fell back, I caught him. "Relax. My friend isn't from around here." Then to the Russian, "This could work in our favor."

I took away the guard's gun, riot stick, and mace. Tossing them under the motorhome, I pointed at the side entrance. "Is there an alarm on that door?"

When he didn't respond, Vlad gave him a creepy smile to encourage him.

"Doesn't activate until nine."

I checked my phone. Eight-thirty. I texted Isaac, instructing him to meet us in Sasha's room. With my weapon at his back, the guard unlocked the door. We entered a storage area. There were endless racks of medical equipment and supplies piled high in boxes.

"Where's the service elevator?" I said.

He led us to a set of swinging double doors—the kind you'd find in a supermarket. When he raised his hand to push them open, I grabbed it and peered through the scratched plastic window. In the small beige room, there was an extra-wide stainless-steel freight elevator on one side. Opposite it, mounted on the ceiling, there was a video surveillance camera.

The Russian peered inside. "Any cameras in the elevator?"

The guard was terrified, and I believed him when he shook his head. Reaching down, I grabbed the hunting knife strapped to my leg.

"Okay," I said. "Here's how this goes."

. . .

I pressed the muzzle of my AR-15 against one of the small windows on the swinging door. It was pointed at the kid walking towards the camera. Fortunately, there was a little space behind the setup, and he parked himself out of range of the lens. Gripping the knife, he jumped straight up, attempting to cut the coax cable. There was only one problem —he was too short.

Wiping the sweat from my eyes, I checked my watch as the guard considered his dilemma. There was a large plastic paint bucket next to him in the corner. Using his foot, he slid it over and inverted it. Teetering on top of the bucket, he reached up and, after several tries, severed the cable. When the camera's light went out, Vlad and I walked in. I retrieved my knife and patted the kid on the shoulder.

"Nice work," I said.

The Russian pointed at the knife. "Ve get rid of him now?"

"Not so fast."

I found a spool of sisal rope in the storage area. When I returned, Vlad was tearing a cleaning rag into strips. I sat the guard on the bucket away from the elevator and bound his hands and feet. Then the Russian gagged him. When I was sure the kid couldn't move, I patted him on the head.

By now, the other guards would wonder what happened to their timid mascot, and they might start looking for him. Our destination was on the eighth floor. I hoped we wouldn't have to start shooting when we got there. The elevator doors opened. Before getting in, I made certain there wasn't a camera inside.

"There's video surveillance in all the hallways," I said. "Maybe we can get out without killing anyone."

"You take care of the guards. I vill protect my sister."

The doors opened again on eight. Something was wrong—all the lights were off. Signaling Vlad, I slipped out and, weapon up, peered into the darkness. As we neared the private room, I spotted a thin, ghostly figure standing alone at the end of the hallway in front of a tall window, where streaks of moonlight fell. It was Sasha, wearing the clothes she'd arrived in.

"Dave!"

Zeles emerged from the shadows as her brother and I ran towards her. He grabbed her arm and pointed a handgun at her head, stopping us cold.

"Evening, gentlemen."

"Let her go," I said.

"Mm, I'm thinking no. Lay down your weapons." He chuckled self-consciously. "You know, I'm actually horrible with guns. But at this distance, I don't think even I could miss."

Like a volcano about to erupt, I directed all of this seething rage at myself. Because I was supposed to protect the Russian girl—that's what the angel said. But in doing so, I'd delivered her to Walt Freeman.

I had done everything wrong.

FIFTY-SEVEN

Four security guards appeared behind us. One of them had Isaac by the arm. Judging from my friend's appearance, they'd roughed him up pretty good. I glared at the director, whose gun was still on Sasha. As her eyes met ours, her brother inched forward. I held him back.

"You won't kill her," I said.

"You're right."

Lowering his weapon, Zeles nodded to the guard holding Isaac. The tool threw him against the wall and threatened him with his sidearm.

"But there's always the good doctor."

"You make me sick," my friend said.

"Ouch—that hurt."

Vlad and I side-eyed each other. Seeing no other option, we placed our guns on the floor. Two guards scooped them up while the others patted us down. The director gripped the Russian girl firmly by the arm and sneaked furtive glances out the window. Smiling, he waggled his weapon at us.

"Wasn't even loaded." He stood there like a poker player revealing the losing hand that won the game. Then he pointed at our body armor. "Overdoing it a bit, don't you think?"

"It takes a lot of firepower to stop this kind of bullshit," I said.

He laughed appreciatively. "Very good. I find it curious—a 145 IQ and years of medical training. Yet somehow I managed to slip up. Would you have been as suspicious had I not mentioned Sasha's name at lunch?"

"Pretty sure I would've figured it out."

"That's because you're a smart young man."

"What do you want, Zeles?"

"Me? What I *want* is this patient. She's fascinating. I could spend years studying her and, eventually, her child." He became serious. "Unfortunately, there are other forces at work."

He stroked the Russian girl's hair. Revolted, she tried in vain to pull away.

"Did you know she's having a girl?"

"So you made a deal," I said.

He glanced out the window again. "Seems like research is all about deals these days. It costs millions and takes years to make any real progress in this field. I can't tell you how helpful it is when you find a rich benefactor."

"Someone like Walt Freeman."

"Walt and I go way back. He's agreed to fund my research for the next ten years. In exchange, I deliver the girl."

Before I could stop the Russian, he went after the director. "I vill kill you!"

The hostile holding Isaac shot Vlad in the leg. As the Russian fell, his sister screamed. In the confusion, I punched the guard nearest me and took away his gun. Then I squeezed the trigger, sending a blood spray out the back of his head.

"Sasha, get down!" I said.

She dropped to the floor and lay prone as Zeles watched stupidly. Two guards fired—a round struck me in the chest. I grabbed the third one and used his body as a shield. A barrage of bullets peppered his torso like a meat tenderizer. I let him drop and signaled my friend to get out of the way. As the two slow-witted hostiles reeled from what they'd done, I put them down.

Isaac examined Vlad's leg while the Russian girl held his hand. The pasty-looking director kept checking the window. Then, nodding, he smiled with relief. I checked my body armor. The slug hadn't made it all the way through. Grabbing my AR-15, I marched up to the miscreant.

"Stay down," I said over my shoulder.

As I raised my gun, a horrified expression materialized on Zeles's face. Shutting his eyes, he held himself like a frightened child. I aimed at the window. A steady stream of bullets weakened the plate glass till it exploded, letting in icy wind and rain. Lowering my weapon, I turned to my friend.

"See if you can find a first-aid kit," I said.

Sasha remained with her brother while Isaac hurried off. I looked at the director and, using the rifle, butt-stroked him. Crying out, he fell to his knees and spit out a tooth.

"You bastard! Why did you..." He raised his trembling hands to protect his bloody face. "It's too late—they're here."

I looked out the window through the pouring rain. Below, there were black Escalades stationed at the front of the building. Gray-suits poured out of them like scorpions leaving the nest. Among them was a man in a black suit—Trower.

My friend returned. Working efficiently, he snipped open the Russian's pant leg and examined the wound. We didn't have much time. The gray-suits would be here any minute.

"This is going to hurt," he said, grabbing the forceps.

Vlad gritted his teeth as the doctor probed the wound till

he found the slug. After removing the bullet, he poured Betadine into the hole and covered everything with a QuikClot bandage.

"You're lucky. The bullet missed the artery."

"Can he walk?" I said.

Isaac scowled at me. "The man's just been shot!"

I ignored him. Then to the Russian, "Can you walk?"

He nodded, and using the others for support, got to his feet.

"Get to the elevators and head to the storage area."

My friend hesitated. "What about you?"

"I'll catch up. Go!"

When we were alone, I stared at Zeles as he crouched in a corner, cowering and gibbering, a bloody handkerchief pressed against his swollen cheek.

"I think you broke my jaw."

I laid down my gun. Grabbing him by the collar, I dragged him to the open window, drenching both of us. Below on the sidewalk, Trower watched. The director looked at me in confusion. Realizing what I was about to do, he shut his eyes and whimpered like a dog.

"You can't! Don't you get it—we're saving lives!"

"You can explain when you get to hell."

I hauled him as high as I could and flung him backwards. Screaming, he fell out the window and landed on an Escalade. Trower and I glared at each other. I pointed at him.

"You're next," I said and left to join the others.

FIFTY-EIGHT

Isaac and the Russians were waiting at the elevators when I arrived. Avoiding eye contact, I joined them.

"What's the holdup?" I said.

My friend gave me the stink eye. "I had to change Vlad's bandage. What happened to…"

When the doors opened, Asimov was already inside and gaped at us. We must've been quite a sight. The Russian bleeding, and me armed to the teeth. I waved him back with my gun. Once everyone was inside, I pressed the Basement button.

"Will someone tell me what's going on?" the scientist said. "And stop pointing that thing at me."

I did as he asked. "Zeles is dead."

"What?"

"He was working with some very bad people who want to harm Sasha. And now they're in the building. Can you help us?"

"I don't understand." Desperate, he looked at Isaac, then at the Russian girl.

"I am a science experiment," she said darkly.

Outside, an alarm sounded. Shoving me out of the way, Asimov pulled the red button. The elevator shuddered to a stop, throwing us off balance.

"That's the fire alarm," he said. "The elevators are being recalled to the first floor."

"Where the gray-suits will be waiting. Do you have a phone on you?"

"Left it in my office. I was just coming up to get it."

I scanned the interior. There were flat metal rails mounted on three walls. I laid down my weapons. "Give me a boost."

Together, the scientist and my friend lifted me onto a rail. It took a beat for me to find my balance. While Asimov leaned against me, I repeatedly slammed my foot against the rail. Eventually, it loosened. One side gave completely, and I hopped down. He and I pulled on the metal till it came off.

"How did you get mixed up with these people?" I said.

"I was at Johns Hopkins when they recruited me. I'd always wanted to live in California. You see, I grew up in the East and—"

"Fascinating."

Jamming the end of the rail into the groove between the doors, I worked it back and forth while the scientist used his fingers to widen the gap.

"And you had no idea," I said, grunting.

"I've only been on staff a year."

Isaac touched Asimov's shoulder. "I could use you on my team."

"Assuming we make it out of here."

Eventually, the doors loosened. When there was enough space, we each took one and pulled it open, revealing a corridor. The alarm echoed, and emergency lights flashed. We were only a little below the floor. One by one, we helped the others through. When everyone else was safe, I handed over my weapons and climbed up.

"What's the fastest way out?" I said.

The scientist peered down the corridor. "Looks like we're on the fourth floor. There's a lab that way, which I have access to. Inside, there's a separate emergency exit."

"Great." Then to Vlad, "How are you holding up?"

He grimaced from the pain. "Protect my sister."

I nodded. "Listen, Asimov—"

"Call me Peter."

"I need you to arm yourself. Do you know how to use a gun?"

"No, but I'm a quick study."

Keeping the rifle for myself, I handed him my Glock. After showing him the basics, we went as fast as we could, but the Russian was in a lot of pain. When we reached the lab doors, the scientist swiped his card. The reader buzzed and continued glowing red. He kept trying it till I grabbed his hand.

"Everyone cover your ears," I said.

Using the AR-15, I blasted the panel. The door sprang open, and we entered. We found ourselves in a gigantic room. In the center were rows of long white tables with high-powered microscopes and other electronic equipment. Offices and glass-enclosed conference rooms surrounded the area. Peter led us to another corridor, where I noticed a glowing green Exit sign. Grabbing the door handle, he looked at us gravely.

"Let's hope they didn't outguess us," he said.

The stairwell was clear. As quietly as we could, we

descended two flights of stairs. The noise of a door banging open below stopped us. Holding up my hand, I signaled the scientist to aim his weapon. I trained my rifle, and we waited.

After a few light footsteps, a head appeared. As the figure continued to climb up, I recognized the scrawny guard we'd tied up earlier. When he saw me, his eyes widened, and he lowered his gun.

"Eff me."

Reaching down, I grabbed his arm. "Get your ass up here."

Like an obedient dog, he trotted up the stairs and handed me his weapon without being asked. "Oh hey, Dr. Asimov. Working late?"

"Sorry about this, Lewis. It's nothing personal."

"It's fine. I should've listened to my mother and stayed in school." Then to Sasha, "What's your story?"

"Look, I'm not going to kill you," I said. "But we are getting out of here, understand?"

"Sure, but how will you tie me up this time?"

"Turn around." As he did, I raised my gun to strike him in the head.

"Dave, no!" my friend said.

Vlad exhaled heavily. "Make him a hostage."

I side-eyed Isaac. "Even better."

The kid descended first, and the rest of us followed. As we got closer to the basement, no one showed up to block our path.

"Is he always like this?" Peter said to my friend

"You get used to it."

Before going through the double doors, I peered at the storage area through a window. Incredibly, there were no security guards or gray-suits waiting to ambush us. If we could reach our vehicle, we might have a chance of escaping. I could go back for Maritza and figure out how to get us all safely up north. But as I opened the door leading to the outside, my plan evaporated in smoke.

The motorhome was on fire.

FIFTY-NINE

Heartsick, I stared at the orange flames and black smoke rising out of the charred shell of our escape vehicle. Isaac laid a hand on my shoulder.

"Is there a Plan B?" he said.

I pulled out my phone and dialed 911. As it rang, I handed it to Peter. "Identify yourself and tell them you heard shots being fired."

"What?" When the dispatch operator answered, the scientist spoke in a panicky voice. "H-hello? This is Dr. Peter Asimov at St. Lazarus."

I knew from experience the operator would insist on going through the call script. "Tell her."

"No, listen to me! I know about the fire alarm—it was a mistake. There's an active shooter situation, okay? You need to send the—"

I grabbed the phone and disconnected. "Very convincing. Don't worry, they'll be here."

Vlad was pale from blood loss. His sister looked at me imploringly, and I took her hand.

"We will make it out of here," I said.

My friend scoffed. "So we're just supposed to stay here and wait for the cops?"

"We need another vehicle."

"Mine's in the rear," Lewis said. "I could drive you."

We followed the guard around the building. In the distance, there was a private parking lot where the gray-suits had set up a command post. I couldn't see a way for us to reach the vehicle safely—too many hostiles. I pulled the kid aside.

"You'll have to pick us up."

"Vhat if he tells them?" Sasha said.

Peter handed me my gun. "I'll go with him."

"Wait." I removed the bullets from Lewis's weapon and returned it to him. "Try to act normal."

He holstered his sidearm, and the men marched into the open. When they were close, a gray-suit challenged the guard. The kid looked like he was explaining something and gestured at the scientist. For a slacker, he wasn't bad.

Lowering his weapon, the gray-suit stepped aside and allowed the pair to pass. The headlights came on in a ten-year-old Ford Explorer. Then the engine roared as the vehicle accelerated towards us. Soon, we'd be far away from this godforsaken place.

Out of the darkness, Trower appeared in the middle of the road, surrounded by more gray-suits. Waving his arms, he shouted a command. I prayed Lewis would keep going. But he rolled to a stop and exited the Explorer with the engine still running. The hostile peered inside. When he discovered Peter in the passenger seat, he began his interrogation. As the guard answered the questions, his weight kept shifting from one foot to the other.

Contemplating what Lewis had said, Trower turned to his associates. Without warning, he shot the guard twice in the chest. As the kid crumpled to the ground, he put another bullet in his head. The sound of a revving engine got everyone's attention. The vehicle lurched forward and, just missing the hostiles, barreled towards us as a stream of bullets shattered the rear window.

"Get ready," I said.

The scientist took the corner tight on two wheels—nearly flipping the Explorer—and screeched to a stop in front of us. Isaac and the Russians piled into the back. I hopped into the front passenger seat, and we were off.

"I don't know what I'm doing!" our driver said.

"You're fine—watch the road." I pointed at the gray-suits swarming in front of us. "Don't stop for anything."

He picked up speed as the hostiles formed a line, their weapons pointed at us. "What do I do?"

"Keep going straight."

We broke the line, scattering bodies everywhere in a sickening mixtape of crunching bones and helpless screaming. Gunshots echoed as we followed the driveway out to the street.

"Slow down," I said.

As we reached the main road, a line of fire department, police, and sheriff's vehicles raced in the opposite direction towards St. Lazarus. It would be hard for the gray-suits to make it past them, giving us time to escape.

Peter white-knuckled the steering wheel to keep his hands from shaking. "I had no idea people actually lived like this. How do you do it?"

I side-eyed my friend. "You get used to it."

"Okay, so where to?"

"We need to make a stop."

"Is that wise?" Isaac said.

Vlad coughed. "Ve must get my sister avay from here."

"I'm not leaving Maritza behind," I said. Then to the scientist, "Drop me off up here. I'll find a way to get to her."

Sasha punched the back of my seat. "Nyet!" She excoriated her brother in Russian.

Peter narrowed his eyes. "I'm still paying off school loans, you know. Fine. Give me the address."

As we continued to Karen's house, I noticed him glancing at the Russian girl in the rearview mirror. When she caught him, his cheeks flushed. Perfect—more complications.

The rain had started up again as we parked on the street. All the other houses in the cul-de-sac were dark. By now, the Russian was semiconscious. Peter and I helped him as we made our way to the entrance. Before I could ring the bell, Maritza opened the door.

"Thank God," she said.

"They shot Vlad." The scientist and I helped him into the kitchen and eased him onto a chair.

Karen walked in. "Nice to see— Oh my goodness." Kneeling, she examined his leg. "Olga!" Then to Peter, "Hello, Dr. Asimov."

"Have we met?" Confused, he turned to me.

"She did a background check. It's why we knew we could trust you."

"Good thing. Or I'd be dead too, right?"

Olga appeared and, seeing the Russian, said, "¡Hijo!"

"Let's get him into the bathroom," our host said. Then to Isaac, "Time to work your magic again, Doctor."

When Maritza and I were alone, she sat beside me and took my hand. Noticing the drops of blood on my side, she unbuttoned my shirt and examined the bandage.

"We should change this."

"It's only blood."

Ignoring me, she ran off to get the first-aid kit. When she returned, she tore off the old bandage. Fortunately, the stitches had held. As she treated my wound, we continued our conversation.

"I'm surprised you came back," she said.

"I was worried about you."

"Worried?"

"Where did you get those clothes?"

"Karen bought them for me. Never mind, what's the plan?"

"I want to take Sasha to Tres Marias. Isaac can look after her there till the baby comes."

"And Peter? What's his story?"

"Isaac thinks he can be useful. Also, I think he's got a thing for her."

"Does that make you jealous? Sorry, I—"

"It'll be good to have someone who cares about her—in that way."

"And me?"

"It would be best if you went somewhere safe for a while. Take Karen and Olga."

"Right." She smiled bitterly. "Because you're worried. And?"

I didn't want to admit what I felt—it was too soon. Besides, we had more pressing matters—like saving the Russian girl. But Maritza was insistent. Taking my face in her hands, she forced me to make eye contact.

"And?"

"And I love you."

Kissing me, she held me close and whispered in my ear. "That's what I wanted to hear. I love you too. So much."

Other than my mother, the only other person I'd ever said

that to was Holly. And now, here I was, telling a woman I hardly knew. I waited for the body-wracking guilt to wash over me like broken glass. Instead, I felt a gentle calm. But it didn't last long.

Peter burst in, out of breath. "Outside! Black Escalades—a lot of them!"

I gripped Maritza by the shoulders. "Wait here."

In the foyer, I peeled back the curtain. The rain came down in sheets, punctuated by lightning and thunder. A dozen or more vehicles filled the cul-de-sac, boxing us in. Gray-suits formed a line. Most carried long guns. A lone figure holding an umbrella pushed through and stood on the sidewalk, facing the house.

Once again, Trower had found us.

SIXTY

Trower stood at the door like Death's messenger, with armed gray-suits to his left and right. His vulture's eye glistened. Unblinking, he raised his voice over the pounding rain.

"Give us the Russian girl," he said.

Sasha and Peter stared at me, her hand clasping his. I ran to the kitchen to gather our few guns and handed the scientist a Glock. Together, we waited next to the window. Looking impatient under his umbrella, Trower sighed.

"If you do this, I won't kill you. You have my word."

Peter grabbed my arm. "There are too many of them."

I turned to the others. Vlad wavered at the living room entrance, supported by Isaac and Karen. Where was Olga? At the sound of breaking glass, I signaled the Russian girl to come to me. Raising my weapon, I faced the kitchen with her behind me as two figures emerged—Maritza and a hostile pointing his gun at her head.

"David!"

The front door burst open. I fired point-blank at a gray-suit. Spinning, he slid to the floor, blood spurting from his neck. Trower tossed the umbrella aside and walked in, unafraid and unarmed, his hands raised above his head. Callously, he stepped over the man as he bled out.

"Try that again, and your reporter girlfriend dies," he said.

We laid down our weapons. Feverish, the Russian pressed himself against the wall. Karen and my friend stood beside him, alert but frightened. I turned to find the other hostile grinning as he drilled his muzzle into Maritza's ear to see what she would do. She bit down on a scream, her eyes shut tight.

Minutes seemed to pass with the only sound, the patter of rain on the abandoned umbrella. I wanted to do something, but what? Sasha surveyed the room. Then she released her grip and, before I could stop her, walked towards Trower.

"Sasha, no!"

He grabbed her and passed her to another gray-suit, who tucked his gun barrel under her delicate chin. Vlad said something to her in Russian. All my instincts told me to lunge at them. But if I did, they'd kill Maritza for sure.

"Thank you for everything," the Russian girl said to me in a voice devoid of emotion. "There's been enough killing."

I thought I detected a flicker of purple in her eyes. Then it was gone. Trower seemed gratified his plan had worked and relaxed.

"Smart girl," he said.

Now Sasha's eyes glowed, and she began mewling. Anticipating her, Trower reached into his pocket and produced a clear glass syringe filled with iridescent purple liquid. As his associate held her, he jabbed the needle into her neck. Groaning, she went limp, her irises returning to normal.

"You had a good run, Pulaski," Trower said. "But it's over now. As you can see, this is way above your pay grade. Remember Mt. Shasta? I encouraged Walt to let me put you out of your misery like I did the mayor. But he's a softie, to be honest. He was convinced you'd crawl into a hole and drink yourself to death. Unlike me, he underestimated your determination."

"Know what, Trower? You talk too much."

He took it in stride. "The result of too many years in Washington, I guess."

The one holding Maritza ordered the others into the foyer with the scientist and me. Though the Russian could barely stand, his eyes were defiant. Trower gazed at us with satisfaction.

"This is fine." Then to another gray-suit, "Make it quick."

"Trower!" I said. "What about your word?"

He studied me as if I were a bug on the sidewalk. "Never believe anything you hear. Unless it's in writing."

"You were a soldier—you used to care. What happened?"

For a second, he looked sad. Then, his face hardening, he stared at me with that pale blue eye I hated.

"Things change," he said. "People change."

Numb, I watched as he retreated through the rain, his arm looped through the prisoner's. I kept going over it in my head. If I hadn't insisted on coming back, everything would be all right. But then I realized something. No matter where we went, Trower would be there. I glared at the hostile stationed at the front door, his Glock pointed at us. Behind me, Maritza struggled.

"Let go of me!"

Her captor drove her to her knees and aimed his weapon at the back of her head. Hyperventilating, she collapsed in a dead faint.

"Maritza!"

I went to a dark place. It was like witnessing an execution, and the condemned was a stranger. I felt nothing because I'd been here before. Peter and the others shouted something, but I couldn't make out the words. Time slowed. Then, cutting through the mad rush of blood in my ears, the angel spoke to me.

"Do not be afraid."

An explosion tore through the blackness, raining flesh and bone. The gray-suit behind Maritza fell, half his face missing. Olga stood in the doorway, clutching my smoking bullpup. Confusion as I went for the gun on the floor. Rolling, I fired at the last hostile, filling him with death. He stumbled backwards and, collapsing, smeared the wall with red.

The wind blew a sharp, cold downpour into the foyer. Lowering my Glock, I marched past the forgotten umbrella to the curb. Only one Escalade remained. A whirring noise came through the rain. Looking up, I spotted something. It was a drone with two glowing red lights—demon's eyes. I ran inside and grabbed the bullpup from Olga's trembling hands.

Outside, I fired at the drone. It attempted to flee, but another blast hit a propeller, and it spun wildly. A last burst knocked it out of the sky. I lifted the carbon fiber carcass. There was a video surveillance camera mounted securely underneath. I stared into the lens and, using my weapon, destroyed it.

In the living room, I held Maritza and looked around. Karen and Isaac were on the sofa on either side of Olga, who was in shock over what she'd done. The scientist helped Vlad into a chair. As he sat, the Russian glared at me with a look of intense hatred.

Because I had failed him.

PART FIVE

WELCOME TO HELL

SIXTY-ONE

I sat slumped in a chair in the kitchen, contemplating the Four Roses on the table. Maybe Walt was right—better to drink myself to death. Outside, the rain beat against the kitchen door like a chorus of tiny hammers. A pool of water formed on the floor where the glass had broken. Saying nothing, Maritza put away the bottle. Then she kissed my head and hugged me. Her eyes were red from crying.

"I was so afraid of losing you," she said.

"You're better off thinking about yourself."

She grabbed my arms. "No one is blaming you. You know Trower would've found Sasha eventually, right?"

I kissed her warm hand. Taking a water from the fridge, I assessed the damage to the door. "I'm not sure Vlad would agree."

"Okay, so he's angry—they have his sister. But deep down, he must know the truth."

I searched the cabinets, looking for aluminum foil and some tape. The least I could do was stop the rain from coming in. I found what I needed and began covering the broken window.

"What are you doing?" she said.

"Fixing this."

"Leave it." She took my hand. "Come on, we need to talk as a group."

I didn't want to look at her, so I watched the falling rain. "This is all on me."

"Stop saying that. You've done nothing but protect that girl from the beginning. You're a good man."

Taking a deep breath, I let her lead me to the others. When we got to the living room, I glanced at the foyer. The bodies of the two gray-suits lay where we'd left them. Only now, they were covered in blood-stained bed sheets.

I sank onto the sofa next to Isaac and Karen. He gave my shoulder a squeeze. The Russian, who avoided eye contact, was across from us. Peter stood by the fireplace, staring at his shoes. Olga must've retreated to her room.

"I'm sorry, Vlad," I said.

Lifting his head, his tired eyes met mine. "I vanted to kill you. But vhen you brought down the drone, I knew. You did nothing wrong."

"I don't know about the rest of you," the researcher said, "but I'd like to get these bloody corpses out of my house."

Saying it the way she did, with that imperious New York accent, made us laugh. Wearily, I got to my feet and signaled the scientist.

"Peter and I can handle it."

"Happy to," he said. "But I need someone to explain. The only people who showed up here were Trower and his gang. Where were the cops all this time?"

He had a point. I remembered seeing the other houses when I went after the drone. All were dark. Not even their Christmas lights were on.

"Someone warned the neighbors."

"But how could they without tipping off Karen?"

"Maybe they threatened them. The point is we're the only ones on this street right now."

"Any idea where they might've taken Sasha?" my friend said. "Should we pay a visit to—what did you call it—Hellborn?"

"They won't go there." I recalled something the Russian girl had said. "After I rescued her, she told me they were planning to move her to the desert."

"Great, but where?" the scientist said.

"I don't think she knew."

Painfully, Vlad sat up and gave me a hard look. "Ve are vasting time."

I began pacing. Maybe we should return to Hellborn. If I could make someone tell us where the other facility was, we could attempt a rescue. But the place would be heavily guarded. And with Vlad's injury, there weren't enough of us to be effective. I concentrated on the people I knew who worked there. Walt Freeman. Trower—and Becky. I recalled going through her purse and seeing her home address. Maybe I could force her to reveal Sasha's location.

"We're going back to Glendale," I said to Vlad.

"You vant the Tahoe?"

Isaac looked uncomfortable. "What exactly are you planning to do?"

"Do you remember Walt Freeman's assistant Becky? I know where she lives."

"Isn't that the woman you beat up?" the researcher said.

"I didn't—"

"You hit her with your gun."

"What's your point?"

She side-eyed Maritza. "I was just wondering how far you'll go this time."

Ignoring her, I turned to my friend. "I appreciate everything you've done. But I think you should return to Tres Marias. After we rescue Sasha, we'll join you there. Peter, if you're up to it, I'd like you to go with him."

"Absolutely. But how will we get there? Lewis's Explorer?"

"You can take my Mercedes," Karen said.

Isaac touched her arm. "Are you sure?"

"Yes, Doctor."

"What am I supposed to do?" Maritza said.

Reaching over, I took her hand. "All of you should leave."

I caught a flash of defiance in her eyes and braced myself. When she looked at her mentor, something passed between them.

"I'm coming with you," she said.

The researcher shrugged. "I hate to disappoint you, David, but I'm not going anywhere. This is my house."

Exasperated, I looked at the Russian. "Why don't women ever listen?"

"Because most of what comes out of men's mouths is bullshit," Karen said. "And that's when you're not gaslighting us."

I was starting to lose it and needed a distraction. So I took the scientist by the arm and headed for the front door.

"Where are you going?"

"I'd love to stay and debate this," I said, "but we have bodies to bury."

Peter and I loaded the dead gray-suits into the back of the Escalade. I drove to a remote forested area near Rattlesnake Canyon Park, with my accomplice following in the Explorer. Leaving the bodies, I wiped down the Escalade for prints, and we returned to the house in the second vehicle.

It was still dark when we walked in. Karen and Olga were

on their hands and knees with buckets and sponges. My heart broke as they tried to scrub away the blood and gore. Maritza did the same with the wall, but it was no use.

"This is never coming out," the researcher said, on the verge of tears.

My friend had fallen asleep on the living room sofa, his bags next to him. Sipping a glass of vodka, Vlad watched the women with a blank expression and shook his head. He pulled out his burner and made a call. For several minutes, he conversed with someone in Russian. Apparently, his friends never slept.

When I realized what he was up to, I walked over. "I want someone to stay here and protect them."

He relayed my message, and after disconnecting, signaled Karen. "Someone vill come by morning."

"I don't understand," she said.

He pointed at the bloodstains. "Vhen they finish, you vill not know it happened. Also, two more men vill stay here."

"For how long?"

"Long as you need them."

She thought it over and sighed. "Thank you. Never in my wildest dreams did I ever imagine I'd require Russian body-guards. Are they good-looking, at least?"

"They have guns."

"My standards have really gone to hell since you people showed up."

"Don't get me started," Isaac said.

The scientist grabbed the bags and headed for the front door. I took one and followed him to the garage. Inside were two vehicles—a late-model Lexus sedan and an immaculate 1965 Mercedes Benz 220SE silver convertible. He walked up to the vintage car and unlocked the trunk.

"Okay, so this is a classic," I said. "No putting the top

down." After helping him load the bags, I shook his hand. "Look after Isaac for me."

"I will. And you can do me a favor. Trower injected Sasha with something that appears to control her symptoms."

"And you need a sample. Done."

"Thank you. Good luck, Dave."

He climbed into the driver's seat, and starting the engine, put the top up. This guy had more grit than I'd given him credit for.

My friend walked in with Maritza and took me aside. "I want to apologize."

"For what?"

"Getting us mixed up with Zeles."

"Some good came out of it. You have Peter now."

"Look, I think I should come with you."

I gave him a warm handshake. "These people almost killed you once in Tres Marias. You're lucky to be alive. I want to keep it that way."

"Funny. Almost exactly what I was going to say to you."

"I seem to lead a semi-charmed life."

"Luck can run out."

"When you get home, tell Warnick everything. Maybe he can help."

"I will. Stay safe, my friend."

He embraced me. Then Maritza hugged him and kissed his cheek.

"What was that for?" he said.

She gave him her perfect on-air smile. "Just because."

As they drove off, she held my hand. "By the way, I'm coming with you."

"No, you're not."

"We'll see," she said and, pecking me on the cheek, returned to the house.

SIXTY-TWO

With the rear window blown out, it was cold in the Explorer, even with the heat cranked all the way up. Vlad dozed in the backseat. Maritza did the same next to me as we headed down the 101 towards LA. I had tried convincing her to stay behind, but in the end, it was no good. And though I would never admit it to her, I was actually glad she was there.

I worried the drones would spot the Explorer. But as we got closer to the city, I came to believe that Walt Freeman had lost all interest—because he had Sasha. I also knew that with every passing minute, the odds of saving her dwindled. Chances were she was lost to us forever.

The sky looked threatening, but the road was dry. Even with an acute lack of sleep, I was nowhere near tired. So many times, I'd come to what I thought was the end. I felt that way now. Only this time, it was a dead end. Once we learned where Trower had taken the Russian girl, did I actually believe our little group of amateurs could pull off a rescue?

There was no escaping the answer—we needed more

people. I wished the angel would tell me what to do. She'd warned me to protect Sasha. And God must've meant for me to stay alive, if only for that reason. But I had failed. How many more chances would He give me before deciding I was useless?

We arrived in Glendale well before dawn. Driving past an endless row of cars, I found the house and double-parked on the street. Vlad's friends hadn't yet returned, and the place was conveniently empty.

While the Russian took the wheel, I entered through the kitchen and used a side door to access the garage. My Tahoe was still parked there, undisturbed. I backed it into the street. After Vlad pulled the Explorer into the garage, I parked in the driveway. Like a good criminal, he'd already contacted one of the Armenians and instructed him to dispose of Lewis's vehicle.

Maritza carried in a soft brown leather bag filled with clothes and shoes. I was anxious to see Becky before she left for work. But showing up at her apartment at all hours might attract the police. We decided to rest awhile.

"I'm hungry," Maritza said. She rummaged through the kitchen cabinets and waved a box of Pop-Tarts at us. "I practically lived on these when I was a kid."

She found the toaster and made some for everyone. The lack of sleep was getting to me, and I craved coffee. After we ate, the Russian took the smaller bedroom. I walked her to the larger one.

"You'll be safe in here," I said.

Taking my hand, she yanked me inside. "I'll be even safer with you."

"Are you sure this is a good idea? What if Vlad—"

"Let him find his own fun."

Outside, a blanket of quiet fell over the neighborhood,

broken only by the hooting of an owl. In the shadows of the darkened room, she gazed at me with those incredible hazel eyes. Our clothes came off, and soon we were in bed. She grabbed her purse off the floor and pulled out a condom.

"I know," I said, kissing her hands. "For emergencies."

Losing myself in her, I didn't remember falling asleep. We'd set an alarm, and after two hours, I woke up alone to early morning light streaming in through the sheer curtains. Dressing quickly, I walked into the kitchen. Maritza and the Russian were eating McDonald's. She'd already showered and changed clothes. I grabbed some coffee and joined them.

"Where does this woman live?" she said to me.

"Park La Brea Apartments."

"That's next to The Grove."

"Is that a problem?"

"Ve must get there early," Vlad said. "Later, there vill be a lot of parents vith children vaiting to see Santa."

"Good to know. How's your leg?"

"Hurts like hell. Let's go."

"Are you kidding me right now?" Maritza said. "You can't go like that."

I looked at the Russian, trying to see the problem. "Like what?"

She rolled her eyes. "You two look like Jason Statham after a serious ass-kicking." Then to Vlad, "There's dried blood on your pants. How far do you think you'll get?"

I knew she was right, but we were running out of time. "What do you suggest?"

"You'd better shower and put on fresh clothes. And for God's sake, shave."

"Fine," I said. "I'll go first. Let's hope I can find something that fits."

· · ·

Vlad joined us wearing pressed blue jeans and a long-sleeve shirt, which he wore under a leather jacket. I managed to dig up a black suit, gray cotton shirt, and dress shoes that were too tight.

"You both look nice," Maritza said, kissing my cheek. "You're so young without the beard."

"I feel old." Then to the Russian, "There's no way we can stay dressed like this. Let's take a change of clothes for the road. Do we need gas?"

"Taken care of."

In many ways, Vlad was like me. No matter how broken or bleeding, he did what needed to be done. As we headed to the front door, Maritza followed, carrying her purse.

"Where do you think you're going?" I said.

"What do you mean? I'm coming with you."

I might have groaned. "This again. Stay here till we return."

"Like hell. You came back for me, remember? You said it was because you didn't want to leave me. Besides, two guys who look like Whitey Bulger's bagmen interrogating a woman? Please."

"You said we looked nice."

"I lied to save time. But seriously, I should be the one to talk to her."

When I looked at the Russian, he could only give me a shrug. "Okay, but you're not getting a weapon."

"Baby steps," she said and bounced out the front door ahead of us.

SIXTY-THREE

The Park La Brea Apartments was a sprawling complex next to a massive outdoor shopping mall called The Grove. Vlad was right about the traffic—it was already backing up on West 3rd Street. We circled twice, looking for a spot.

"If we park at The Grove, we can walk over," Maritza said.

The Russian concurred. "Ve can hide the Tahoe in the parking structure."

"Whatever you guys say. I'm only the driver."

As we made our way through the streets inside the mall, I was impressed by the high-end shops and restaurants. There was nothing like this in Tres Marias. They'd cordoned off an area next to the fountain for Santa Claus. Eventually, I found a parking structure, and taking a ticket, continued to the lowest floor.

Long guns were out, so I selected two Glocks and extra mags from my stash. I handed a set to Vlad. We tucked our weapons in our belts and appraised each other to make sure they didn't show under our jackets. Maritza pouted.

"I already told you," I said. "You're not getting a gun."

"Meanie."

We headed towards 3rd Street to our destination. Referring to a glass-covered map, we located Becky's apartment. There were people out jogging or walking little white dogs. The gardeners had gotten an early start, trimming hedges and tending flower beds. If the Russian's leg hurt, he didn't show it. Walking briskly to the building, he and I did our best to look nonthreatening.

Walt's assistant lived on the top floor. As we approached the elevators, an elderly woman came out her front door and instantly judged us. Maritza took my hand. Seeing we were a couple, the old lady relaxed. We waited for her to walk off and rode the elevator up.

The unit was on a corner, and we approached cautiously. Smoothing her hair and slipping on her sunglasses, Maritza walked up to the door and rang the bell, positioning herself in front of the peephole viewer. Vlad and I stood on either side, out of range. At first, there was no answer. Shit, we were too late.

She was about to ring again when a familiar voice said, "Who is it?"

"I don't mean to bother you," Maritza said. "I just moved in and was wondering if you might've seen who's been stealing my newspaper."

In another beat, there was a click, and the door opened a crack. I pushed hard, knocking Becky on her butt, and slipped inside. Maritza went in next, followed by the Russian, who locked the door. The woman screamed. Grabbing her arm, I pointed my weapon at her face.

"Surprised?" I said. Then to Vlad, "Check the other rooms."

Drawing his gun, he searched the place. Maritza knelt,

and pushing aside my hand, looked the other woman in the eye.

"We're not here to harm you. But you have information we need."

Standing, I extended my hand. Reluctantly, the assistant took it and got to her feet. Seeing the bruise from when I'd hit her made me think of Karen's words. *I was just wondering how far you'll go this time.*

The apartment seemed large for a single person, I felt. It was decorated simply but elegantly, with expensive furniture and fine art. I marched her into the modern kitchen and signaled her to sit at the glass table. Soon, the Russian returned, carrying a purring long-haired gray cat.

"I found this cat only."

He set the animal down. It continued purring as it rubbed against his leg. The three of us sat facing the traitorous woman, who gave Maritza a sly smile.

"Do you always wear sunglasses indoors, Ms. Lopez?" she said.

Maritza took them off. "So you recognized me. Why did you open the door?"

"I thought you were here for a story. Reporters have been bothering us for weeks since the IPO announcement."

"Where is Sasha?" I said.

She pretended to be confused. "I really have no idea."

Sighing, I side-eyed Maritza. "I've heard women have a higher pain threshold than men. You need to understand I'll go as far as necessary." I pointed at Vlad. "This is her brother. And he's prepared to go even farther."

Maritza took her hand. "I know you don't want this. And whatever loyalty you might have to these people, they don't deserve it. Think about all those girls who died."

"That... It wasn't my fault."

"Maybe not. But there's another girl out there who's alive. And it's not too late to save her. We both know how much danger she's in. Becky, she's only nineteen. Will you help us?"

She chewed her lip. "I can't."

Maritza's good cop act was wearing thin, and I'd had enough. I spotted a wood block filled with expensive knives on the kitchen counter. Selecting the largest one, I tested the blade with my thumb. Then I grabbed a roll of paper towels and gave the Russian a dead-eyed look.

"Hold her."

Vlad forced the victim's arms behind her with one hand and used his other to cover her mouth. I didn't care that we were hurting her. Squirming, she screamed through his fingers.

"Don't do this!" Maritza said. "There must be another way!"

Ignoring her, I stared into Becky's eyes till she could feel the hate. "It was because of you those girls are dead. You recruited them. It's time to pay for your sins."

I pulled up a chair and reached for her right hand. Laying it flat on the table, I splayed her fingers. While the Russian kept her immobile, I pressed my hand down on top of hers and brought the knife very close. She tried screaming again, her eyes rolling up into her head. I thought she might pass out—I didn't want that.

"I'll take one finger at a time till you tell us. When I'm done with this hand, I'll start on the other." Then to Maritza, "You'd better leave."

She stormed out of the room in tears, her face distorted by anger and shock. "You bastard."

Whimpering, the assistant wriggled her plump body, trying to get away. Mascara ran down her cheeks as she shot glances between the Russian and me. Both of us wore expressions devoid of sympathy. I pressed the knife blade against her pinky at the first joint and nicked the skin. Seeing blood, she wailed.

"I'll ask you again," I said. "Where is Sasha?"

Sucking in air through her nose, she said something in a muffled voice. Vlad looked at me, and noting my expression, removed his hand.

"There's another facility," she said, delirious. "In-in the desert."

"Where?"

"Could I have some water?"

I laid down the knife and went to fill a glass. She drank it gratefully.

"Outside of Rosamond," she said. "It was an abandoned aerospace complex. The buildings are unmarked. The largest one—that's where they're holding her."

The Russian pointed his Glock at her head. "She might be lying."

Maritza stood in the doorway, composed now, and pulled out her burner. "I'll make a call."

Becky sat straight up, not looking at us. Eventually, Maritza handed me the phone.

It was Karen. "She's telling the truth. Baseborn Identity Research purchased the property from Northrop Grumman last year."

"Okay, thanks." I disconnected. Then to the assistant, "You were smart to tell us."

"You'll never get in there. The place is locked down way worse than the LA facility."

"Let me worry about that."

I put away the knife. Relieved, Maritza stood beside me.

"How did the cutters escape?" I said to Becky.

"Cutters?"

"The test subjects who are skinning people alive." She looked as if she were about to lie again. "And don't bother making up a story. I've seen them before in Tres Marias."

She stared at the floor. "We didn't expect them to organize."

"And you have no clue how to stop them?"

"We're looking for them now." She meant the gray-suits. "The police were instructed to kill them on sight."

"That's a shame." I turned to Maritza. "The cops knew the truth all along."

"The Skeleton Murders story was a cover," the assistant said. "When the cops find them, they'll make it look like a shootout with Satanic cult members."

"Who came up with that plan?"

"Eamon Trower."

"Why are the test subjects hunting out in the open?"

"They're incapable of experiencing fear."

Becky had confirmed everything I suspected, and I was grateful. But now she was a liability. When I caught Vlad's expression, I knew he felt the same.

"The moment we leave, she'll warn Trower," I said. "We need to make sure she can't tell anyone."

Maritza panicked. "David, no!"

"I meant we'll take her with us."

The assistant shook her head. "I'm not going anywhere with you people."

Disgusted, I turned to the Russian. "We're on the thirteenth floor. How far can a cat fall without breaking its legs?"

I kept my Glock pointed at Becky while Vlad picked up the purring gray animal. Cradling it, he stroked its head as it kneaded his arm with its paws.

Glaring at me, she got to her feet. "I hate you so much."

"The feeling is mutual."

"I need my purse."

She picked up her bag sitting on a side table in the foyer. Taking it from her, I dug around till I found her phone and set it aside. The Russian led her out of the apartment by the arm. I was about to follow when Maritza stopped me.

"Would you have gone through with it?" she said.

"What, cut off her fingers? I was only trying to scare her."

"I hope I never see that side of you again."

As I looked into her eyes, the memories of my dead wife throbbed like scar tissue in my heart. "You might see worse before this is over."

"I pray that I don't," she said and walked out alone.

SIXTY-FOUR

My plan was simple—return to our vehicle without anyone noticing. Later, we'd decide what to do with our prisoner. When we got to The Grove, there was a large crowd assembled near the fountain. Mariah Carey's "All I Want for Christmas Is You" blasted from speakers that seemed to be everywhere.

A red-and-gold throne sat on the stage. Security guards and LAPD officers kept watch, with constant police chatter coming over their two-way radios. Vlad gripped Becky's arm as we maneuvered past throngs of parents, grandparents, and small children. Fortunately, the parking structure wasn't far.

The crowd erupted into wild applause and cheering. Santa approached the stage, where teenage girls dressed as elves waited. Suddenly, something flashed in front of him. He clutched his throat, bright blood spurting through his fingers. No one knew what had happened—except me. The music stopped, and people veered as the cops tried to contain them.

Another flash, and someone screamed. Santa fell to his knees and collapsed face-first on the ground. As the crowd parted, I saw his costume slit down the middle. The flesh and sinewy muscles were cut away, exposing slate gray lungs that swelled with his last breaths.

Three sides were cordoned off with velvet ropes. The water in the fountain ran red with the slimy bodies of dead security guards. Drunk with panic, everyone tried getting away as cops shouted commands. Mothers and fathers lifted wailing children, desperate to escape the horror.

Two tiny, crying kids were almost trampled as people mad with fear shoved and fought like animals to get away. I scooped up the bawling toddlers and held them as high as I could. A young woman propelled herself towards me, calling their names. When they saw her, they reached out, and I placed them in her arms.

With weapons up, the cops moved in as the frightened onlookers struggled to get past them. The few remaining guards tried calming the crowd, but no one listened. Maritza clung to me as we continued to the parking structure. Then another scream. Turning, I saw a hand with a knife as it came down. In the confusion, Becky slipped away.

The Russian tried grabbing her as she melted into the human river. I reached for my gun, but he stopped me and pointed. We were surrounded by cops. By now, most of the people had fled, leaving only the LAPD, security guards, and us. And that's when I saw them—eight shirtless cutters circling like predators on the stage, their butterfly knives glinting in the morning light.

Roy Batty strode across like a rock star, dragging a blood-soaked woman by her collar. They'd sheared off the skin of her arms and chest and severed her hamstring. All she could do was limp helplessly. Blood ran from her head where they'd made a rushed attempt to scalp her. I recognized her clothes, and as she groaned, my stomach lurched.

It was Becky.

Aiming their weapons, the cops moved in formation towards the stage. Guards tried pushing us back, but I refused to move. Roy gave the cops a triumphant smile, his face shiny with fresh blood. Glancing from side to side, he admired the show he and his friends had put on.

"Look what happens when there are questions with no answers," he said.

Lifting the knife, his eyes found mine, and he smiled with kindness. Then, in one blurred motion, he slit Becky's throat. A stream of crimson blood gushed from her arteries. She slid to the ground as her life drained away towards a tuneless death.

The police opened fire, but the cutters never moved. Instead, they stood in a line across the stage, their arms spread wide as if welcoming the onslaught. Cops with shotguns marched forward. A hail of buckshot tore into the hostiles' arms, legs, and torsos. One by one, kill shots ripped open their heads. As if choreographed, they fell onto the forest-green carpet. Roy Batty was the last to die, swooning in slo-mo and still clutching his butterfly knife.

When it was over, the officers moved in and examined the bodies. Someone radioed for ambulances. I turned to find Maritza using her phone to record the last act in the hostiles' death ballet. And though a part of me felt disgusted, I knew she was right. Someone had to provide proof of Walt Freeman's guilt.

I took her by the hand, and the three of us hurried to the parking structure. SWAT officers had arrived, heavily armed and wearing helmets and body armor. The sound of beating blades now as a police helicopter hovered over the carnage. Then another aircraft—an ABC7 Eyewitness News helicopter—swooped in. An angry voice over a PA system ordered them to leave the area immediately.

We had to maneuver around the maimed bodies of maintenance workers lying scattered across the parking structure floor. Maritza looked at me with a pained expression. Tearing herself away, she dropped to her knees. I held her hair as she vomited.

When she'd finished, she spat and wiped her mouth. Gently, I rubbed her back and helped her up. We continued down a series of concrete stairs to the lowest floor. The Tahoe was the only vehicle down there. Inside, she found a half-empty water bottle and drank all of it.

Minutes passed as I sat behind the wheel with the unholy scene playing in my head. Becky dying, and Roy Batty giving me a devil's grin. And all those cutters, like marble angels in a cemetery, while a black rain of bullets stole away their corrupt lives.

Why didn't they run? They were smart and fast and could've easily eluded the lumbering cops. And even if they had caught a bullet or two, they would've recovered because they were nearly invincible. One question—the only question—continued to plague me. *Why didn't they run?*

I imagined Vlad was thinking about his sister. Was she destined to turn into one of these monsters? Maritza's head rested on her chest. Reaching over, I wiped away a tear with my thumb. I started the engine and wound my way up the parking structure to the street level, which was clogged with police and SWAT vehicles, fire trucks, and ambulances.

I'd seen hell again. And now it was time to proceed to the next circle.

SIXTY-FIVE

I needed time to think and stopped at a place on North Fairfax called Coffee Commissary. Luckily, there was one parking spot on the street. I was never one for hipster hangouts, but this would have to do. Of course, Maritza, the LA native, had been here many times. We grabbed seats outside under an off-white umbrella.

"Poor Becky," she said, sipping her Cubano.

Vlad finished his triple espresso in one go. "I do not have sympathy for her."

"She didn't deserve that, and you know it. No one does."

He squeezed and released his cup without looking at it. "My sister…"

"We'll find her," I said.

"And vhat vill she be?"

His eyes glistened with remorse. It was as if part of him had already let her go, knowing that eventually she would become murderous. I'd seen it before in Tres Marias—all those unfortunates Isaac had tried to save. But he always ended up putting them down. I wondered if, in the end, I would be the one to kill Sasha.

But was her death inevitable? It was a question eating at me ever since I learned what happened to her. And if that was true, why did the angel insist I protect her? What was God's plan?

I recalled a blessing a priest had given me once. *May the Holy Spirit descend upon you. And may He help you accept what must be.* I didn't know it then, but he was talking about Holly. After she died, revenge was the driving force that kept me alive. I wanted to make Walt Freeman pay the price. And now? I needed him to suffer for Sasha and the other girls.

"We *are* going to find her," I said. "I promise."

Gripping my shoulders, he hugged me. "Thank you, my brother."

Maritza held my arm with both hands and rested her head on my shoulder. "I was right. You're a bad boy."

We sat there, saying nothing. Inside, people ordered coffee to go. A few sat at indoor tables, staring at their smartphones. I guessed they were watching live news coverage of the gorefest at The Grove. Others wearing headphones typed furiously into MacBooks. Screenwriters, probably.

These were the ones I envied—people living their lives, unaware of the evil all around them. I was like them once. But now, instead of sleeping peacefully, I got through endless nights of cold sweats and nightmares through sheer will, a gun cradled at my side. I was a death hunter, driven by a maniacal sense of retribution. And if my wife were alive, I wasn't sure I could make my way back to her.

Maritza stood and stretched. "I smell like gunpowder. Going to the restroom. I'll call Karen to see how she's doing."

More customers had joined us outside. Some spoke intensely about the violence they'd seen on the news. A police cruiser sped past, its siren blaring. That was our soundtrack now. I felt the keening in my head would never stop. When I spoke to the Russian again, my voice was quiet.

"There's a good chance we'll die up there," I said.

"I know this."

"I wish…" My burner vibrated, and I checked the number. It was Isaac. "Hey, are you back?"

"We got in a few hours ago. Peter's catching up on some sleep. I explained the situation to Warnick, and he wasn't too happy."

"He never is."

"In fact, he told me to give you a message, and I quote—*You're an asshat.*"

"Tell him I love him too."

"You can tell him yourself." After a pause, a familiar voice came on. "Dave? What the hell, man?"

"Hello, Warnick. Nice to hear your voice. Hang on a sec."

Maritza had returned. There were too many people around us, so I took the stairs down to the street.

"Isaac told you what happened," I said. "The Russian girl is the only survivor of those experiments."

"I know about Sasha. After you left, we conducted an investigation into Walt Freeman and Baseborn Identity Research."

"Then you also know we need to stop them."

A long pause. "Agreed. Look, I can help you, but this is strictly off the books. I'm a supervisor now, and we're getting into some very weird territory. Understand?"

"How many people can you spare?"

"Not sure yet."

"I'll text you the location where she's being held. And we'll need firepower. The facility is heavily guarded."

"It'll take me a few hours to assemble the team. Try not to kill anybody before we arrive."

"Not making any promises. I can't thank you enough—I mean it."

"When you disappeared, you let your friends down. You know that, right? Griffin was so upset. We didn't even know if you were alive."

"It wasn't fair to you guys, but I was in a really bad place after Holly died. I felt like coming to LA was my only option."

"I get it. See you in a few hours."

"Hey, Warnick. Did you find your Bible?"

"I did. Later."

Exhilarated, I put away my phone. Nothing was guaranteed. But at least with my friend's help, we might have a chance to save the Russian girl. I waved to the others, and they came trotting down the steps.

"Good news?" Maritza said.

"The best. We're getting some serious backup."

Vlad was skeptical. "Vhat kind?"

"Don't worry," I said. "They have guns."

SIXTY-SIX

We changed clothes before hitting the road. I got on the 5 going north, which would lead us to the 14 and eventually the 138 to Perro Negro. That was where Warnick had instructed us to wait. Depending on traffic, the trip would take between ninety minutes and two hours.

After twenty miles, the lack of conversation bored me, and I flicked on the stereo. "Something from Nothing" by Foo Fighters came on loud. When the song was over, Maritza turned down the volume.

"Maybe if you listened to different music once in a while, you wouldn't be in such a dark place all the time." Her voice was instructional, as if addressing a bedwetter.

"I tried Taylor Swift once. Didn't take."

"Just sayin'."

Not wanting to get on this woman's wrong side, I made an effort. "Find something better."

She scanned till she found a Spanish station.

"What is this?" I said.

"Lila Downs. It's called 'La Cumbia del Mole'."

"I like it." Then to Vlad, "What are your thoughts?"

"I have no musical opinion," he said.

It was almost noon when we arrived in Perro Negro. Flat and arid, this was an agricultural community of fewer than five thousand people. Fields were dotted with nondescript one-story houses with dirt lawns and trucks parked out front.

"Why did your friend want us to come here?" Maritza said.

"So we wouldn't tip off the gray-suits."

My stomach growled. We should've eaten while we were in civilization. Eventually, I spotted a coffee shop that looked like something out of *Tremors*. A tall rusted pole rose above the highway, crowned with a faded white sign that read CAFÉ in rust-colored letters.

"Anyone else hungry?" I said.

She made a face. "You're not serious."

Vlad leaned forward and gazed at the sign. "I am fine vith it."

I pulled into the small, dusty parking lot. As we approached the entrance, I laughed at a sign in the window— NO HIPSTERS. Maritza gave me the stink eye and slipped on her sunglasses, fearing someone might recognize her way out here in Green Acres. An old screen door was the only thing keeping the blackflies out. And like a movie, it squealed soulfully as I pulled it open.

"After you," I said.

The inside looked decades old—frozen in time. Apparently, we were the only customers. An old dog with a boil lay snoozing in a patch of sunlight. There wasn't anyone behind the counter.

"Hello?"

A grizzled old man appeared in a doorway leading to the kitchen. He had cropped white hair, a nose that looked like it had been in too many bar fights, and tattoos up and down his forearms.

"You can sit anywhere." He sounded German.

I'd eaten at my share of dives, but this place took the prize. I imagined coming down with food poisoning and regretted having stopped. We sat at a table that allowed us to face the front window, which had been recently washed.

Though I expected to see cockroaches crawling up the walls, the place was clean, with a blue A-grade from the health department. The old man, who I assumed was the owner, brought three plastic-covered menus.

"You're in luck. We got carnitas today." He'd said *we* as if this were a thriving enterprise employing armies of kitchen and wait staff.

"Thanks," Maritza said, warming to the environment.

Their selection surprised me. You could get everything from a traditional cheeseburger and fries to shredded beef tacos with rice and beans. They even had ceviche. I flipped over the menu and scanned the back. It featured a forty-year-old black-and-white photo showing a much younger man posing stoically in front of the café. Standing next to him was a small, dark woman. His wife? Above them, a sign read ZWICKIE'S. And under the photo, a caption—*John and Consuelo Zwick*. Looking closer, I spotted a sign that read NO HIPPIES.

The old man reappeared with three glasses of water. "Ready to order?"

"*Zwickie's*?" I said.

"My wife's idea. What'll you have?"

"I'd like to try the beef tacos," Maritza said.

"Comes with black beans and rice."

"Do you have lemonade?"

"Fresh-squeezed."

Vlad and I decided to go with the carnitas special and coffee. I didn't know what to expect, but what the hell—I was starving. Instead of writing down the order, Zwick called to the kitchen in serviceable Spanish. The woman from the photo—much older now—appeared in the pass-through window, mixing something in a stainless-steel bowl.

Soon, the old man returned with our drinks, chips, and delicious-looking, chunky homemade salsa. The food came shortly after, along with a plastic container of steaming hand-made corn tortillas. Incredibly, we'd stumbled across a Mexican food paradise.

"How do you think a place like this can exist way out here?" I said.

Maritza added more salsa to her tacos. "Most of the locals are farmworkers."

The Russian held up a dark red pepper. "Is this hot?"

I gave him a menacing look. "Try it and find out."

She laughed. "That's mean. Don't make him…"

Too late—he'd already taken an enormous bite. Immediately, his eyes watered. He tried ignoring the problem, but it was no good. Grabbing his water glass, he gulped it dry, then drank ours. When he was himself again, he pretended nothing had happened and continued to eat.

"Tell me about Warnick," Maritza said, eyeing me over her lemonade.

"Where do I even begin? He was a good friend in Tres Marias—the best. Saved my life more than once."

I wasn't prepared to go down memory lane. But once I began talking about him, I couldn't stop. I explained how we'd met while holed up in a fortress on a hill built by an insane Indian national named Ram Chakravarthy. One day,

Warnick arrived with a contingent from Black Dragon Security.

Things went sideways when some of the other guards aligned themselves with the Black Dragon supervisor, Chavez, who was certifiable. But the guards who were with us remained faithful to the mission, and we stuck together. Soon, we were hunting draggers, the first-generation victims of the plague.

We survived long enough to see a new Black Dragon supervisor take charge. After he rescued us in a forest overrun by draggers, my wife and I signed on. Once again, we fought alongside my friend and others to exterminate any remaining draggers while trying to rebuild the town. But the corrupt mayor, influenced by Walt Freeman, had other ideas.

It wasn't long before Holly lost her life. During that time, Warnick had been like a big brother to me. A Weezer-loving, granite-faced superhero whose constant companion was the little black Bible he carried in his back pocket.

When I reached the end of my story, I realized for the first time since leaving Tres Marias how much I missed him. And I prayed we'd make it through the nightmare that was still to come.

"I think maybe you love him," Maritza said. "It's a regular bromance."

"Maybe. Jealous?"

"I envy friendships like that."

"Come on. You must have tons of friends."

"Once I left the barrio, everything changed. The people I used to hang out with didn't want me around anymore. And aside from Karen and Nate, I've never really gotten close to anyone at work. Life in LA, right?"

Zwick reappeared to refill our cups.

"This coffee is incredible," I said.

"We get it from Oaxaca. You folks don't look like fertilizer salesmen. Passing through?"

"Something like that."

He gazed out the window at the Tahoe sitting in the parking lot and quirked his eyebrows at me. That made me nervous.

"Anything the matter?"

"I noticed your rear springs look compressed. Must be carrying something awfully heavy. Like guns, maybe?"

Caught off guard, I stared at him. Vlad shifted uncomfortably in his chair. I side-eyed Maritza, who looked scared.

"I overheard you earlier," the old man said. "We need to talk."

SIXTY-SEVEN

Watching Zwick lock the front door and lower the shades made me regret leaving our guns in the Tahoe. Was this guy a cop? Or one of Trower's men? No, that was crazy. As he sat with us, I told myself to accept whatever was coming. So far, he'd done nothing even remotely threatening.

"What do you want?" I said.

"Me? Nothing. But I'm worried about you three."

"Oh?"

"You're fixin' to do something dangerous. And out here, dangerous gets you dead."

Zwick's wife emerged from the kitchen, carrying a tray with a bottle of El Señorio Joven con Gusano and five shot glasses. As she set everything down, Maritza complimented her on the food in Spanish.

"I don't drink," I said.

The old woman poured four shots. Thirsty, I watched the little worm at the bottom of the bottle drifting lazily in the mezcal.

"Here's to truth," the old man said, raising his glass.

No one joined him. He drained the contents and addressed Vlad in Russian, making my friend laugh. Then he turned his attention to me.

"I've spent a fair amount of time in St. Petersburg. You want to know what this is about. I think maybe we should get to know each other first. I'm John Zwick. This is my wife, Consuelo."

Reluctantly, we introduced ourselves—first names only. That seemed to satisfy our host.

"I hope this isn't about the research facility," he said.

My stomach was in knots, and I sensed a trap. "Never heard of it."

"Sure, you have. Why else would you drive all this way? But I feel I must warn you. Whatever you're planning, they'll kill you just as sure as I'm sitting here."

Maritza stood awkwardly. "We should go."

I motioned for her to sit. "Hang on a sec." Then to the old man, "What makes you think you know why we're here?"

He toyed with his empty glass. "Guess you thought I was a rube."

"Vhat is *rube*?" the Russian said.

"Durak. When my wife and I moved here, there wasn't much except farmland and a couple of military bases. You three don't look like the type who would attack the US government. That leaves one other possibility—Baseborn Identity Research."

Though I didn't know what to make of Zwick, I had to know what this was about. "Which brings me to my original question. What do you want?"

"And like I told you, nothing."

I looked into his rheumy eyes. His hands were rock-steady. We could've done what Maritza suggested and gotten the hell out. But this guy knew things—I could feel it. And what I needed now was information.

"They took a friend of ours," I said. "Vlad's sister."

The Russian's expression darkened. "Dave."

I ignored him. "We came here to rescue her. And if you try to warn anyone…"

The old man poured himself another drink. He warmed the glass in his hands and looked at his wife. Touching his arm, Consuelo whispered something in Spanish. When she turned to me, her eyes were shiny. Maritza understood what she'd said and reached for her hand.

I was confused. "What's going on?"

"These people you're after—they killed our son."

"When?" Maritza said.

"Last year."

"What did the police say?"

"Around here, you don't go to the cops." Then to me, "I'm sure you know this. The people you're looking for are powerful. And they have friends on the police force. Our son wasn't the only one. There have been others. Some were curious, like my boy. Others were unlucky. Now they're all dead."

Maritza's drink had gone untouched. She tossed it back, her eyes bright with anger. "What was your son's name?"

"Rudy," Consuelo said. She rubbed her hands, which were scarred from years of cooking. "He was a good boy. Married a local girl. He left two children behind."

The old man ran his wrinkled hands through his hair. "We gave her money and sent her and the boys away. To this day, she believes Rudy died in a traffic accident. We never told her the truth. I'm afraid for her."

"What really happened?" I said.

"He was a reporter at the local newspaper. Dreamed of moving to a big city like LA or San Francisco. He thought if he could write one great story and get noticed, he'd be on his way. Since those devils moved here, people have gone missing —especially girls. When he told me he wanted to investigate, I begged him to leave it alone—like I'm telling you. He didn't listen."

Zwick explained that over several weeks, his son had pieced together a story. When he turned it in, the editor in Lancaster killed it and told the reporter to forget about Hellborn. But Rudy continued to investigate on his own. He even went to the facility and took pictures.

One night, he called his wife to tell her he was working late. That was the last time anyone heard from him. The next morning, the cops found his mangled car flipped over on a desert road, his bloody body lying nearby in the sand. They wrote it up as a hit-and-run and closed the case.

"How do you know it was Hellborn?" I said.

"Is that what you call it? A good friend of ours told us. He likes walking in the desert at night."

"Sounds like a drunk."

"The opposite. It's how he stays sober when the cravings hit. Anyway, he saw it happen. Men in black Escalades. And a tall man with a disfigured face."

I turned to my friends. "Trower."

"They killed my son and destroyed his car to make it look like an accident."

Vlad had finished his drink a while ago and reached for the bottle. "My sister is alive."

The old man leaned back and rubbed the white stubble on his face. "That might be true. But it'll take more than you three to save her."

I wasn't ready to tell him our plan. So instead, I said we were waiting for a friend.

"Where are you meeting him?" he said.

"Not far from here. In fact, we need to get going."

After thanking our hosts, I laid down some cash and prepared to walk out when the Russian stopped me.

"Vhat if he tells someone?"

He'd said it loud enough for the old couple to hear. Embarrassed, I wheeled around. Giving me a grim smile, Zwick got to his feet.

"You're careful—that's good. I could've been lying. No need to worry 'bout me."

"And why is that?"

"Because I'm coming with you," he said.

SIXTY-EIGHT

The cold air cut through me like a dull knife. The sun was setting, turning the landscape blood red. Dust devils tore across the sand like demented genies. The approaching sound of vehicles caught my attention as a dust cloud engulfed us. Squinting through the icy wind, I could make out two Humvees. As they rumbled on steadily, I wondered whether the rest of the reinforcements were en route. I couldn't imagine Warnick planning an attack with only one squad. Anxious, I scanned the landscape. There were no other vehicles.

The Humvees stopped when they reached the place where we'd parked. Now, the only sounds were the wind and the mournful cry of a coyote. Three people climbed out of the first vehicle—my friend, who'd been driving, and two other men. One was blond and athletic-looking, and the other short, stocky, and bald. An African American man and a Latina with buzzed hair climbed out of the second one. Everyone stretched and walked towards us as I ran to meet Warnick.

"So good to see you," I said, grasping his hand.

"Almost didn't recognize you—you shaved."

I side-eyed Maritza. "Didn't have a choice."

As always, his face was a cipher. His hair was shorter, and he looked around ten pounds heavier. Now that he was a Black Dragon supervisor, I pictured a lot more paperwork and not enough exercise. I pointed at our party.

"This is Maritza," I said. "Maritza, Warnick."

He took her hand. "Good to meet you. What do you do?"

"I'm a reporter."

"That'll come in handy," the Latina guard said, unconcerned about being overheard.

Ignoring the comment, I continued. "This is Vlad, Sasha's brother."

"You vere in Iraq?" he said.

"Afghanistan."

"I vas in the army."

"Good fighters, the Russians."

"And this is John Zwick," I said. "The people we're after murdered his son."

Warnick extended his hand and pointed at the blond guard. "That's Ryan."

"Pleased ta meetcha," he said in a noticeable Irish accent.

The short, fat guard waved awkwardly. "Hi, I'm Ziggy."

My friend indicated the remaining two. "That's Hen." The African American saluted playfully. "And Berta."

The Latina stepped forward and fist-bumped me. When she got to Vlad, she averted her eyes. Moving on, she sized up Maritza the way women always do at a first meeting and gave her hand a quick pump.

"Um, about that comment earlier," Berta said. "I run off at the mouth sometimes."

Hen laughed. "Always."

"Shut up, Henrietta."

"Okay," Warnick said to the squad. "The temperature's dropping, so we need a fire."

As he returned to his vehicle, I noticed the worn Bible sticking out of his back pocket. The others split up and began gathering rocks and deadwood. In no time, they'd dug a shallow pit. Soon, we had a blaze going and eagerly huddled around it. Maritza and I sat on the cold ground. The African American slid in next to me.

"What's Hen short for?" I said.

He made sure he was out of earshot of the Latina guard, who, looking flushed, had sidled up to the Russian.

"Hendrix. My parents were huge fans of his music."

"And what's her story?" Maritza said, eyeing the only other woman.

"Berta? Don't mind her, she's cool. Grew up with five older brothers. Guess she had to learn to get tough."

"I can relate. It's not much different with sisters."

My friend sat across from us and spoke to the Irishman.

"So, Warnick. What's the plan?" I said and gazed around the fire at the others.

"Look, I know what you were hoping for. But there was no way I was getting authorization for a full-on assault. We'd incur too many casualties. As it is, I had to make up some crazy story. Why are you laughing?"

"Sounds like some shit I would've pulled."

"Yeah, well." Becoming serious, he addressed the group. "This is a covert operation."

I was intrigued. "That means you must have intel. But how…"

I looked at Ziggy, who was sitting by himself, sketching in the sand with a twig. Perfect. They'd gotten themselves a nerd. This guy probably spent all of high school locked in his mom's basement, playing COD and hacking the power grid.

"That's where Ryan comes in," Warnick said.

"Wait, he's your guy?"

Hen nudged me. "Bet you thought it was Ziggy."

Berta pointed at the rotund guard. "There's a reason they call him Ziggy."

As the others laughed, he looked up. "What?"

"Here's the t'ing," the Irishman said. "My brother works in our security operations center in Dublin. And he's a first-rate hacker. They haven't invented a system he can't crack."

Vlad looked at him, irritated. "Russians are pretty good."

"Erm, when the Russkis get tired o' pullin' their wires, they go to Michael."

"How is he not in prison?" I said.

"Too valuable to Black Dragon. When we learned what youse are tryin' to do out there, I asked Michael to send us everything he could find on Baseborn Identity Research. I've got schematics, codes, the lot."

"Wait, so we walk in through the front door?"

"We've got someone on the inside," my friend said. "Security guard."

"What, did you offer him an obscene amount of money?"

Ryan gave us a cryptic smile. "My brother did a thorough background check on every guard in the place."

Warnick rolled his eyes. "Tell them already."

"Turns out this one likes little boys," the Irishman said.

SIXTY-NINE

Disgusted, Maritza and Berta looked at each other with their mouths open. I'd met my share of scum, but this kind was the worst. The vigilante in me was already thinking of ways to take care of the security guard once he had served his purpose.

"Michael found his username and password on Tor," Ryan said. "We've got pictures, videos... We own him."

Vlad shook his head. "Does he know vhere they are keeping my sister?"

"He confirmed it wit' us. She's being held in a private suite in the medical wing."

The Russian got to his feet and pulled out his Glock. "Let's go."

Warnick side-eyed me. "Not so fast." He glanced at his watch. "It's 1900 hours. We're due to meet Erck at 0200."

"Erck," John said. "He's German."

"The facility is located ten klicks due east. At 0000, we'll drive to the halfway point and hike in from there. It should take us a little over ninety minutes with full gear."

"That means no heavy weapons," I said.

"Affirmative."

Vlad scoffed. "And vhat happens inside?"

"Erck will take us to your sister," the Irishman said. "Security should be light. Most of the guards end up sleepin' when they should be workin'."

"What about the gray-suits?" I'd confused him. "Hellborn's plainclothes security."

"*Hellborn*—I like it. Erck warned us about them wankers. He said that if we see any—what did you call 'em? Gray-suits? —we should kill 'em. Feck!" Using his rifle butt, he smashed a scorpion, then tossed it into the fire. "I hate those little buggers."

I laid a hand on the Russian's shoulder. "Five kilometers is a long way. Are you okay to—"

"I am fine."

Despite the pain, he'd do whatever was necessary to save his sister. When he made eye contact with the Latina guard, she looked away. For a second, I wondered why she was acting like a schoolgirl. Right. She was into Russians.

"I'm going too," Zwick said.

Pursing his lips, my friend gave me a *here we go* look. "I can't allow it."

"These people killed my son. I don't care what happens to me. I have to help."

"And Consuelo?" Maritza said.

"She knows what I came here to do, and it's what we both want. I won't be in the way. All I need is a gun."

Warnick rubbed the back of his neck. "I can't let you have one of ours. That would make us responsible for your safety."

The old man was growing on me. "I got you, John."

"What about me?" Maritza said.

I'd expected this. There was no way my friend would put

this woman in danger, and I waited for the inevitable objection.

"Are you saying you want to be part of this too?" he said.

"I'm saying that I'm not going to sit around here with Gila monsters and scorpions while you guys play *Ghost Recon*."

"This ain't no game, manita," Berta said.

Before I knew it, Maritza was on her feet, wagging her finger at the guard. "¡No me jodas, perra! I come from East Los!" Then she stormed off.

My Spanish wasn't the best, but I was sure she'd meant *Back off, bitch*. I decided it was best to let her cool off. For a few seconds, it was quiet, with the only sound the crackling of the fire. Berta tried shrugging it off, though everyone else knew she'd been called out.

"What got up in her culo?" she said.

Annoyed, Hen shook his head. "Shut up, Berta."

Warnick took me aside. "I'm guessing she's with you."

"For better or worse."

"Well, you know the drill. You're responsible for her—and the other two. They'd better not get in the way."

"They won't," I said.

I found Maritza lingering near a pile of massive, eroded boulders and gazing at an endless blanket of stars. She didn't turn around as I came up beside her. When I placed a tentative arm around her, she rested her head on my shoulder.

"Berta's right," she said. "I don't belong here. Those anxiety attacks I told you about? You saw how I fainted at Karen's when the gray-suits showed up."

"I won't lie to you. This is an incredibly dangerous mission. No one would hold it against you if you stayed behind."

"All my life, I've had to work hard for everything. I was always the smartest kid in my class. But I have this debilitating shyness that... I remember I took a speech class in high school. And when I got up there, my knees were shaking so badly. My hands, they... I dropped my note cards, and everyone laughed."

"But look what you've accomplished. You're a television reporter. People respect you."

She pulled away and held onto my shoulders, her eyes boring into mine. "And you?"

"Holly was stubborn too. But she was also strong—centered. And she never backed down from a fight. It's what I loved most about her."

I recalled when I first handed my wife a gun. She was inexperienced, and we were about to face a dragger pack. But she turned out to be awesome.

I held Maritza close. "I want you with me, whatever happens."

"I promise I won't let you down," she said and kissed me.

A line of torches illuminated a clearing next to an outcrop of boulders. Hen and I had set up a makeshift shooting range using empty water bottles, snack bags on sticks, and other random objects. Maritza and Zwick stood ten yards away, facing the targets. John had an assault rifle. I handed Maritza a Glock.

Taking it, she admired it in her hand. "Is it loaded?"

"Not yet. This is the magazine." I inserted it. "It holds fifteen rounds, plus one in the chamber. You need to carry extra ammo."

"How?"

"Use your pockets. It's more important to wear body armor. A tactical vest won't stop a bullet."

I helped her with her stance while Hen worked with the

old man. Fortunately, these guys had brought ear protection. Meanwhile, Warnick and Ryan reviewed floor plans on a laptop, and Berta and Ziggy did a weapons inventory.

"You need to relax," I said. "And hold the gun with both hands, like this. It will steady you and give you a better chance of hitting something."

"Hijo, I can't believe I'm doing this."

"These targets are small, so don't worry if you miss the first few times. When you fire at a person, aim for the chest."

Maritza and Zwick spent the next half-hour firing rounds at the tiny targets. He was an excellent shot and hit every-thing he aimed at while she kept missing, which frustrated her. Hen got the bright idea to set up a backpack against the rocks. He pinned a Doritos bag in the center. Taking her time, she aimed and fired, hitting it every time.

"Outstanding," the guard said. "Of course, the actual targets will be moving, and you won't have these earmuffs. But I think you guys are ready."

It was close to nine, and we were freezing. My friend had remembered to pack sleeping bags and extra coats, which Hen and Berta distributed. We lay around the fire and tried resting for a few hours. Maritza and I were on our sides, facing each other. Closing her eyes, she held my hand in hers.

"Bad boy," she said, her voice heavy with sleep.

SEVENTY

We went off-road at the halfway mark and navigated the dark desert floor. Our destination was a deep ravine off the main highway. It would have been better to travel without headlights, but the loose rocks and depressions in the sand were dangerous. Warnick drove the first vehicle with me next to him—like old times. Vlad and John were in the backseat with Maritza.

My friend caught me up on everything that had happened in Tres Marias since I left. Black Dragon neutralized the last of the draggers and incinerated the bodies. The few cutters who'd remained behind died from the poison gas that was released during Operation Guncotton. Those corpses were also collected and burned.

Funds had begun to flow. Which, if you thought about it, was ironic considering it was government people who were responsible for the outbreak. Hundreds of contractors had descended like blowflies to begin restoration. According to Warnick, the town was nearing the point where displaced families could return. And there was a plan to reopen schools and businesses in the spring.

"Sounds like it might be a nice place to live again," I said.

Though I was being sarcastic, I hoped it was true. Tres Marias was my home, and despite my repeated denials, I cared about it a lot.

"We're getting there. Dr. Fallow has been incredible. He and Dr. Asimov got the hospital in shape. They're working with a team of researchers on RS-6160."

"They call it Surrelis now."

My friend explained his role in all this. When I left, he'd packed and was ready to deploy to Atlanta with Griffin and Fabian. But at the last minute, an urgent message came down from Black Dragon's regional office in San Francisco. Without an active police force, Tres Marias needed a supervisor to maintain order during the reconstruction. Warnick had grown fond of the town and threw his hat in the ring. He had them at *hello*.

"We tried contacting you," he said as we continued through the blackness. "I thought we'd caught up to you in Phoenix when you withdrew all that cash."

"Didn't stay long."

"I assigned someone from the local office to look for you. He's a pretty good tracker and picked up your trail in Quartzite."

"Huh. I thought I'd flown under the radar."

"There was a lot of chatter on his police scanner about a civilian who'd been shot in a parking lot. Our guy checked in with the local PD, who directed him to a hospital. The victim was lucky—they were able to save his leg."

I side-eyed him. "Luck had nothing to do with it."

"He admitted he'd been pretty drunk. But he provided a good description of his assailant. Our guy had a hunch it might've been you." He waited for me to confirm the story.

I gazed at the stars. "The tool attacked me for no reason."

"So you're saying it was self-defense."

"He had a hunting knife."

"Okay. Anyway, after that, the trail went cold. I was pretty sure you'd head to LA, though."

From the look he gave me, I expected him to pull out his Bible and quote from *Proverbs*.

"Then he met me," Maritza said brightly.

My friend gave her an uncharacteristic fist bump. Then to me, "What I can't figure out is how you got mixed up with Vlad's sister."

"Total fluke. I found her the day I went to Hellborn to kill Walt Freeman. She'd escaped."

"Good thing you were there, I guess."

Arriving at the ravine, we drove down and hid our vehicles in the brush. The moon was bright as we prepared to head out. Each of us wore body armor under our coats. Everyone had assault rifles and handguns—except Maritza, who carried only her Glock.

The temperature had dropped to the low thirties, and I was eager to start walking. Berta shone her light on something moving among the rocks. The beam revealed a kit fox crushing the neck of a prairie dog with its teeth. Acknowledging us, it trotted off into the night with the dead prey in its mouth.

"Let's go," Warnick said.

The trail we'd followed ended at the ravine, and we had to make our way using a compass. The landscape was flat, so the hike wasn't taxing. Soon, the Russian took the lead with Warnick. They chatted amiably, trading war stories. I half expected them to compare scars. Maritza, John, and I followed. The rest of the squad brought up the rear.

"Everything that happened before I met you," she said. "It's crazy that you're still alive."

"Not to scare you, but it's about to get worse."

"I know. Are you still going to kill Walt?"

"If the opportunity presents itself."

"And Trower?"

"Vlad can do the honors. Why are you asking?"

"It's just that I wish…"

"What? That we could arrest them?"

"Why not? They should go to prison."

"Here's a little tip for ya. Men like Walt and Trower don't do prison. They drop out of sight and reappear somewhere else where they can gin up a new killing field."

Maybe it was a bad idea bringing her along. I'd hoped she would understand what I had been through. And would want revenge, if not for me, then for almost losing her life at Karen's.

"I would kill everyone responsible if I could," John said.

Maritza scoffed. "Even if it means dying?"

"At least I would have avenged my son."

"Men," she said and stayed quiet for the rest of the trip.

SEVENTY-ONE

We stood at the edge of a rocky ridge overlooking Baseborn Identity Research. The campus comprised a massive rectangular structure surrounded by smaller buildings. A dual-mesh electrified fence enclosed the entire property. A long road led to the entrance, where a fortified guard shack stood like a lone sentinel.

"Welcome to hell," I said.

The lack of visible activity surprised me. The only sound was the whistling of a chill wind that cut through our gear. We'd made good time and still had forty-five minutes to get into position. The plan called for us to meet Erck on the south side. There, we'd scale the fence after he cut the power.

"Why is it so quiet?" Berta said.

Using binoculars, Warnick studied the landscape. "No one's in the guard shack."

Ryan pointed at the sky. "Feck."

At first, I didn't know what he was staring at. Exasperated, he gestured at a dozen dark objects flying in formation over the complex—drones.

"Do y' not see those t'ings? We can't go in through the front without being spotted."

I reached for the binoculars and scanned an area to the north. The fence ended at a massive wall of boulders.

"Looks like we're climbing," I said.

After my friend confirmed the location, he signaled us to head out. I worried about John. We had a steep climb ahead of us, and I wasn't sure he was up to it.

"They've restricted the drones to the main part of the complex," Warnick said. "We'll take the long way around."

I hurried to catch up. "This will set us back. Any way to contact Erck?"

"Negative." Then to the others, "Double-time, people!"

We trotted single file. I kept glancing over my shoulder to make sure John hadn't fallen behind.

"Don't worry about me," he said. "I quit smoking years ago."

It didn't take long for us to make our way to where we'd have to scale the steep rock face. We took a couple minutes to catch our breath.

"Berta," my friend said.

The guard adjusted her rifle strap and began climbing. Petite and lithe, she reached the halfway point in no time. Continuing up, her boot slipped, sending down gravel. Catching herself, she made it to the top in less than two minutes.

I scowled at Warnick. "You expect us to beat her time?"

"Safety is the key," he said. "Not speed."

Hen was next, followed by Ryan and Ziggy. I expected the round guard to wheeze, especially considering the enormous backpack he carried. But he was like a spherical mountain goat and ascended with practically no effort.

"Vlad," my friend said. "Then Maritza, John, and Dave. I'll go last."

The Russian adjusted his body armor and gripped the rocks. As tough as he was, I didn't think he'd ever rock-climbed. He struggled to get a foothold.

Warnick provided encouragement. "Focus on each step and wait until you have a good grip."

Soon, Vlad caught on and continued slowly, grimacing from the pain in his leg. When he got to the top, the others pulled him up.

"Here we go," Maritza said, rubbing her hands together.

I squeezed her shoulder. "No singing Mexican songs."

"Cállate." She punched me in the arm and gazed up. "I knew Pilates would come in handy one day."

When she reached the top, Berta helped her the rest of the way. The old man moved into position.

"Not like hiking in the Black Forest," he said.

Taking his time, he made good progress. Then he slipped and slid down a couple feet, but regained his footing.

"I'm okay."

It was my turn. While surviving with Holly and Warnick in Tres Marias, I'd learned to become physically versatile. I gave myself time to assess the situation, then placed my right foot in a depression in the rock. Gripping a small ledge, I ascended.

It had only occurred to me halfway up just how high I was. I wasn't afraid of heights. But if I fell, I'd break bones and be useless to the team. That was the stark truth. You were an asset till you weren't. And given enough time, everyone becomes a liability.

I looked up at Maritza through the cold sweat dripping from my forehead. Not remembering when or how it happened, I knew in my soul she'd given me something to live for. I'd lost everything and came here to die. But now, I wanted more than anything to save Sasha. And, if we made it out alive, I would make a life with someone I loved. Maybe with God's help, I could. When I paused to catch my breath, she crouched and gave me a devilish smile.

"Move your ass, güerito."

Laughing, Berta joined in. "You heard the lady. Güerito."

I continued till I saw the Irishman, who extended his hand.

"Nice o' you ta join us."

"Not bad," Maritza said.

"For a white boy."

She kissed my cheek. Finally, my friend came up, breathing hard. Though he appeared out of shape, he had little trouble making it to the top. In spite of the cold, his face and neck were shiny with sweat. Below, the facility lay dark and silent before us. The rock face made for a steep drop.

"No way we're going down that," I said.

Warnick signaled Ziggy, who set down his backpack. He removed a climbing rope, a sling, carabiners, screw links, and some tools. With precision, he drilled a hole and blew the rock dust out using a plastic tube. Next, he hammered in a bolt and, tightening it with a crescent wrench, attached the rope. In no time, we had a way down.

We descended one by one, starting with the Latina guard. No one made any jokes. Instead, we focused on not dying. It was nearly two-thirty when the last person hit the ground—a half-hour past our rendezvous time.

"What about the rope?" John said.

My friend glanced at it. "No choice but to leave it. We need to get to the south side. We'll go that way. Stay close to the buildings."

We slid along the wall of the main building. Overhead, the

drones circled darkly. In moments, we'd covered one side. As we rounded the corner, the old man's rifle strap caught on something. When he pulled at it, he inadvertently stepped into the open. Like a shark to blood, a drone swooped in and hovered close.

"Don't move," Warnick said.

The drone flitted away like a frightened bird. In another beat, emergency lights came on, and a high-pitched alarm blared across the compound. We ran towards the south side, where we discovered a set of concrete steps leading to a metal door.

My friend trotted up and gripped the handle. The entrance was unlocked. We followed him into the building. Inside, emergency lights flashed in a dizzying pattern, creating a strobe-like effect that made it hard to see. The Latina guard pointed at something.

A man in a security guard uniform limped out of the shadows with one hand outstretched. He was tall, with jet-black hair and rodent eyes. His arm dripped fresh blood.

"Over here!" he said.

Clearing the room, Berta and Hen made their way to the staggering figure. Warnick ordered the rest of us to follow. Weakening, the injured guard fell to his knees. Setting aside their weapons, our people rolled him onto his back.

Ryan turned to us. "It's Erck."

Our contact was white with shock and babbled something over and over. Vlad pushed through and knelt beside him. Grabbing him by the collar, the Russian lifted his head.

"Vhere is Sasha?"

Pink saliva bubbled from the guard's lips. It wasn't till this moment that I saw the blood pooling on his shirtfront.

"Vhere is she?"

Erck looked from person to person as if trying to recognize a familiar face. The blood kept coming. I tore open his shirt to assess his injury. Maritza covered her mouth.

"Dude..." Berta said, grimacing.

Shivering, the guard raised his hand towards us. His pale intestines seemed to pulsate under the flashing lights. He was bleeding out and had maybe a couple minutes. Ignoring the gore, Vlad persisted.

"You piece of shit—tell me vhere my sister is!"

My friend pulled him away. "Leave him alone."

Lying in blood on the cold cement, Erck breathed rapidly. Then his eyes went glassy. I waited for the death rattle. No matter what the Russian said now, it was too late—the guard could no longer hear us. At the last second, his eyes went wide as he grabbed Vlad's coat. His voice was an urgent, terrified whisper.

"Get out!" he said. "They're everywhere!"

SEVENTY-TWO

Gutted. Bled out. Dead. That was Erck now. As we prepared to move out, we found we weren't alone. The silhouetted figures of a dozen hostiles stood against a harsh light coming from an open set of doors. Berta raised her rifle. A warning shot ricocheted off the floor near her feet.

"Weapons on the ground," the gray-suit in charge said.

We did as we were told. As they swept in, something blurred past my field of vision. Instantly, a hostile fell, clutching his throat. A fountain of blood spurted through his desperate, grasping fingers. The lead gray-suit signaled the others, and they formed a circle. Each aimed at the darkness while the flashing emergency lights and alarm intensified the confusion.

Grabbing our guns, we ran as bullets rained. Holding Maritza's hand, I followed Warnick across the vast space to a storage area. High racks held stacks of wood crates filled with lab equipment. For the moment, we were safe. Wait—John was missing. Peering past a forklift, I saw more hostiles on the ground. The old man stood alone, not watching. What in hell was he waiting for?

"John!"

He turned to us, his face a question. A flash of movement, and another gray-suit went down. The survivors bellowed conflicting commands at each other, trying to target the invisible menace. The old man snapped out of it, and gripping his weapon, ran to safety.

"Senior moment," he said to me. "Whatever's killing 'em, there's more than one."

"They're cutters."

Vlad pushed through, his eyes intense. "I vant to find my sister—*now*."

Warnick gripped his arm. "We will. But we stay together."

When I looked at Maritza, she was shaking. "You okay?"

"At least I didn't faint this time. How are we supposed to make it past the gray-suits?"

"No hay bronca," the Latina guard said and nodded to Hen.

Together, they marched into the open and began firing, killing anything that moved. When the last gray-suit was dead, my friend signaled us to get going. We made our way to the lighted hallway. Midway, I noticed a line of thick iron chains with grab hooks dangling from the ceiling. Up ahead, Berta and Hen waved us on.

From out of nowhere, a lone gray-suit fired at me. The bullet struck me in the chest, making me stumble. Furious, Maritza shoved me aside. With both hands, she aimed at the hostile. He grinned at her, his eyes like twin black pools.

"Pinche güey," she said. "What's so damn funny?"

"You."

Screaming, she mag-dumped him. He stayed standing for

a beat, then melted to the floor. The Latina guard's mouth fell open.

"Dang, girl."

I took Maritza's hand. "I owe you."

"Yeah, you do. Are you injured?"

"Hurts like hell, but I'm okay."

When all of us were in the elevator bay, Berta used a zip tie to secure the doors.

"Ryan, see if you can kill the alarm system," Warnick said.

Gathering equipment from Ziggy's backpack, the Irishman trotted towards a far wall. He tripped on an empty glass soda bottle and fell. A grenade rolled out from his pocket.

"Feck!"

Putting away the explosive, he got up and moved along the wall till he found a panel. After drilling out the bolts and removing the cover, he tested the wires with a probe. He attached a black device the size of a cigarette pack. A series of lights flashed in sequence. In seconds, they turned green, and the alarm stopped.

It was warm inside, so we ditched our coats. Warnick and Ryan huddled over the laptop, examining the floor plans. The rest of us stood behind them in a half circle. The Russian was next to me, ready to explode.

"The medical wing is here," the Irishman said.

I approached the elevator doors. Apparently, no one else had noticed the card reader. Ryan may have disabled the alarm, but the security system was still operational. I headed to the doors leading to the outer area.

"Ziggy, I need you to cut this tie," I said.

Maritza held onto me. "You're not going out there."

"We need an ID badge to access the elevators. One of those gray-suits must have one."

Anxious, she turned to the Irishman. "Can't you disable the security like you did the alarm?"

"Not from here, I'm afraid."

John moved to the front. "I'll go."

"It's fine," I said. "I can do this."

He laid a hand on my shoulder. "You have your whole life ahead of you. Don't be an asshole."

I felt guilty, but I could see he was determined. Ziggy cut the tie with a pair of clippers. Giving me a sad smile, the old man opened a door and went out. I watched through the glass. He moved forward cautiously, aiming his assault rifle at the darkness. Bloody bodies lay everywhere. He made his way to the closest one and knelt.

I slipped out. "I'll cover him."

John went through the gray-suit's clothes and, finding the badge, put it in his pocket. As he got to his feet, something blurred past him.

"Get back here!" I said.

He double-timed it, clutching his bleeding arm. A cutter with straight black hair and iridescent purple eyes came after him, carrying a postmortem knife. I fired at the hostile, but he was quick. A bullet struck him in the chest. Stopping cold, he looked at the wound, then at me.

The old man returned and went in. As the cutter grinned viciously, I fired again. His face blossomed into a dirty red flower of flesh and bone. Dropping to his knees, he continued breathing, his one good eye staring defiantly.

"Get inside!" It was Warnick's voice.

I retreated and slammed the door behind me while Ziggy secured it. There was a sudden thump on the glass, and the bloody, faceless cutter appeared.

"He should be dead," Vlad said.

The hostile shrieked. Unfazed, Berta walked up to the

glass and glowered at him. She cussed him out in a Mexican stew of pure vitriol.

Hen laughed. "You about done?"

"Yeah. I feel pretty good right now."

"Remind me later why I hired you clowns," Warnick said. Grabbing the badge, he marched to the elevators and pointed at John. "Somebody patch him up. We have work to do."

My friend had changed.

SEVENTY-THREE

We found ourselves in a shadowy corridor. There was a set of glass doors opposite us. And beyond that, a laboratory. Rows of tall tables with microscopes, centrifuges, and other electronic equipment filled the room. Along the walls, there were conference rooms and offices. I'd expected to see security personnel, but the place was deserted.

"Where is everyone?" Maritza said.

The doors were unlocked. Once inside, Warnick ordered us to fan out. Maritza and I stayed with my friend. It took us only a few minutes to clear the area. We didn't find anyone.

"The medical wing is this way," Ryan said.

Regrouping, we followed him into the next room, which was even darker than the first except for an eerie bluish luminescence. As we entered, Berta and Hen stared at something. Identical tanks the size of coffins blanketed the floor. Curious, I moved closer. Naked men and women lay motionless in clear liquid. All appeared to be asleep. Sensors attached to wires covered their bodies. The glow came from submerged LED lights.

"Any ideas?" Warnick said.

Ziggy dipped his hand in and sniffed his fingers. "Targeted temperature management."

"Care to elaborate?"

"It's used to reduce the risk of tissue injury from lack of blood flow. Myocardial infarction, stuff like that."

"And you know this how?" Berta said.

"Discovery Channel."

I dipped my hand into the cold liquid. It was water. "And what about the brain?"

"Protects that too."

"It might have something to do with the virus. Maybe they're trying to control the negative effects."

"I don't understand," Maritza said. "Are they asleep?"

"Induced coma. Look. Each one has an IV."

We made our way from tank to tank. I stopped at a woman with raven hair and flawless skin. She looked to be around my age. As I leaned closer, her eyes flew open. Letting out a yip, Maritza tottered back. When I checked the woman again, her eyes were closed.

"We need to keep moving," my friend said.

"What about them?"

"Not our problem."

The doors leading to the next room were closed. When we opened them, hundreds of lab animals greeted us—rhesus monkeys, dogs, cats, and mice. Their eyes gleamed in the darkness, their cries pitiful. Some cowered while others attacked their cages. My instinct was to put them down, but there were so many. And Sasha was our priority. I caught Maritza approaching a small mixed-breed dog and yanked her hand away.

"Careful," I said.

Warnick pulled the Irishman aside. "How much farther?"

"We're nearly there."

The next set of doors was reinforced steel. Ziggy and Hen trotted over and waited for my friend to swipe the ID badge. Each grabbed a handle. Grunting, they pulled open the heavy doors. Inside was a vast soundproof room made of concrete. It looked like an indoor target range. The rest of the squad ventured in first and began clearing the area.

Assault rifles, shotguns, and handguns were bolted to a long table. Next to that, video cameras mounted on tripods. Opposite us, there was a bullet-scarred wall coated in a pastiche of dried blood. And anchored to the floor, six-foot steel stands with shiny metal cuffs for hands and ankles.

"What is this place?" Maritza said. "An execution chamber?"

Vlad strode across the room, passing a large metal panel on the floor. He examined the cuffs on the stands. "They do not kill them here."

Berta scoffed. "What kind of pinche..."

Warnick shushed her and listened. There was a faint moan, followed by another.

"Where's it coming from?" John said.

I crossed to the metal panel and stared at it. Kneeling, I ran my hand over the surface. It was warm. "It's coming from underneath."

Ryan headed for a control booth next to the video cameras. "Found it. Dave, get off o' there."

In another beat, unseen machinery whined, and the panel descended. Now, a soft beeping, followed by a creepy synthetic female voice.

"Elimination pit door opening."

The panel disappeared under the concrete, revealing an abattoir reeking of blood, urine, and feces. Grabbing our weapons, we lined up at the edge and peered into the darkness. At first, there wasn't any movement. Then, a bloodcurdling howl. My friend shone his flashlight.

"Oh no!" Maritza said, turning away in disgust.

Hundreds of mutilated human bodies lay piled on top of each other. Most were dead, but a few moved, raising their skinless arms towards us. Many had no faces—only the eyes and the tongues. It was hard to tell who they were because of all the blood. Some wore medical lab coats. Others had on security guard uniforms. And the rest were dressed in gray suits.

A woman lifted her disfigured hand. "Help us!"

The beeping got louder—more urgent. Then, "Waste compression beginning."

Now, the sounds of machinery again. Only this time, it made the room vibrate. The mass of bodies began moving as the walls closed in.

"Ryan, turn it off!" Warnick said.

"I'm tryin'…"

As the walls continued to compress the bodies, heads burst open like rotting melons, spewing brains everywhere. Eyes popped out of their sockets and shot across the pit like bullets in a bonfire. Maritza became faint.

Before I could catch her, she fell in.

SEVENTY-FOUR

Maritza lay unconscious on the moving mass of human carnage. My instinct told me to jump in, but I'd end up dead too. I reminded myself of the mission—save Sasha.

"Somebody do something!"

Ryan labored at the control panel, trying to prevent the horrifying meat grinder from finishing its work. Nearby, Warnick signaled the others to join him as he disconnected the video camera cables. I remained near the pit, my heart thudding as the walls closed in.

"String them together," my friend said.

In seconds, we had a safety line. Warnick and Ziggy secured it around my waist. Forming a line, the others lowered me. Maritza had drifted farther away. As I moved towards her, she regained consciousness and screamed.

"David!"

"It's okay, I've almost got you. Give me your hand."

Whimpering, she struggled to reach me. As I grasped her forearm and drew her close, she threw her arms around my neck. The others dragged us towards the edge as desperate, bloody hands grabbed at our feet. Warnick and Vlad lifted Maritza out first.

Before I could follow, a faceless gray-suit pulled me under. I couldn't see anything. The pressure from the walls increased, and distant voices cried out. I heard a gunshot and felt myself rising. Thank God I had the cable. Soon, the others brought me to safety.

The screams faded as more bodies were crushed. I helped Maritza over to the Latina guard, who embraced her. Delirious, I joined the Irishman at the control booth. He was drenched in sweat, searching for a cutoff switch.

"It's an automated sequence," he said. "I can't stop it."

"Warning. Incineration will begin in fifteen seconds," the demonic voice said. "Elimination pit door closing. Please stand back."

We watched helplessly as lights flashed and a computer monitor lit up with a rotating 3-D animation of what was taking place below the floor.

"There's nothing more we can do," I said as the metal panel closed completely.

"Commencing incineration."

As we exited the room, I heard the sound of gas jets. All those people were being reduced to ash and cinder. Examining her soiled clothes and hair, Maritza took my hand.

"Guess I owe you now." Then to the others, "And everyone. God bless you."

"It's what we do," my friend said.

We continued down a long, dark hallway. Consulting his laptop, Ryan pointed straight ahead. Eventually, we reached an intersection and began looking for signs. Soon, we found one that read MEDICAL WING. Leading the way, he directed us to the right. Something moved up ahead. I positioned Maritza behind me. Slowly, we advanced.

In the dim light, three cutters crouched like Neanderthals around a campfire. Using postmortem knives, they carved off strips of flesh from the six or seven bodies lying on the cold tile floor. An arm moved—the victim was still alive. Warnick signaled Berta and Hen, who began shooting. Angry, the cutters took off running into the darkness. We approached the gored bodies.

All were dead except one. The survivor was a frightened scientist covered in blood. Most of the skin from her torso was cut away. Without hesitating, Vlad shot her in the forehead. She never made a sound.

"Time to get Sasha," he said.

Up ahead, double steel doors protected the medical wing. My friend tried the ID badge, but the card reader continued to glow red. The Russian dug through the dead scientist's pockets and found a badge that looked different from ours.

Something blurred across the hallway. As I turned to see, Ziggy fell to his knees, clutching his throat. He made a gurgling noise as blood leaked through his fingers.

"Stay together!" Warnick said.

Another blur, and a horizontal line of blood appeared across the guard's waist. He convulsed, one hand on his throat, as my friend eased him onto the floor. Surrounding the two, we faced outward with our weapons pointed. Now, two blurs. Berta and Hen began firing. The rest of us joined in.

"Can't even see 'em," the Irishman said to me.

"When you do, go for the head."

Crying out, Maritza held up a bloody hand. Filled with rage, I scanned the darkness. I spotted a cutter and fired. The hostile crawled out of the shadows, brandishing his post-mortem knife. I sent him to hell.

"Get inside the circle," I said to her.

There were two left. One raced past, trying to attack John. Vlad saw him in time and unleashed a barrage of bullets that sent the cutter backwards against the wall. As he sank to his knees, he left behind a blood smear. The Russian finished him.

Only one left. The Latina guard was the first to spot him and shot his legs out from under him. Hitting the floor, he army-crawled into the darkness. She and Hen gave each other a nod and went after him. Far off, shots echoed. In seconds, the guards reappeared unscathed. Berta knelt next to Ziggy and felt for a pulse. She looked up at us and shook her head.

Ryan treated Maritza's injury. At the steel doors, Warnick swiped the new ID badge. It worked. Inside, we found ourselves in a brightly lit lobby. After clearing the area, we gathered at the nurses' station, where the Irishman consulted his laptop. He pointed at a side corridor.

I'd expected to encounter more hostiles, but we were alone. We arrived at a long glass wall with a set of doors in the middle. Beyond it was a white room with a hospital bed surrounded by medical equipment. Sasha sat there, looking tired. Dressed in a patient gown, she appeared much the way she had when I'd first found her.

Walking into view, Trower sat next to her, holding a gun to her head. He stared at us, his pale blue eye shining like a cursed gem. The glow from the ceiling lights made his scar look even darker.

"I'm going in," I said.

My friend glared at me. "Negative. I need you and Vlad to come with me. The rest of you, fall back."

Ignoring the order, the Russian charged in. As Warnick

and I followed, the doors snapped shut behind us. Maritza and the others banged on the glass, trying to get in. My friend signaled them to go around.

Though Trower appeared calm, I could see the nervous sweat on his forehead. As we moved in, he pressed the barrel of his weapon against the prisoner's head.

"That's far enough," he said. "So it's come to this."

SEVENTY-FIVE

Gripping his Glock, Vlad glared at the pale-eyed psycho, with Warnick and me on either side. Two gray-suits appeared from out of nowhere. Aiming their weapons at our heads, they disarmed us. Trower seemed to enjoy the moment. Once again, he'd gotten the better of me.

He took Sasha by the arm and forced her to her feet. Glowering, she spat at him. He ignored the insult and wiped his cheek. I braced myself for the inevitable monologue.

"Is there going to be another long speech?" I said. "I was thinking maybe we should sit down."

He chuckled, then turned serious. Walt Freeman stepped out of the shadows. Seeing his sloppy, oversize frame sent a bolt of adrenalin coursing through my body. My hands sweating, I came closer.

Trower tick-tocked his finger. "Ah-ah-ah."

One of the gray-suits gave it to me in the gut while the other waved us back with his gun. Hellborn's CEO frowned like he was sorry for me. The last thing I wanted was sympathy from a madman.

"You should've left it alone, Dave," he said. "We had it under control."

"This was all about the money."

"The IPO is nothing more than a financial vehicle to position our firm for the future. Our young men and women fighting overseas need an edge. I plan to give it to them."

"It's no good, Walt. None of it works. Those freaks you created? They actually believe they're immortal."

"I've put my faith in science."

"So did Mengele."

"I don't expect you to understand."

My friend scoffed. "Don't patronize us. How many more thousands have to die before you stop?"

"It's called 'acceptable risk.' Having been on the battlefield, you should know that better than anyone."

"D'yavol!" the Russian said.

Lunging, he locked his hands around the CEO's fat neck and squeezed with his thumbs. The gray-suits tried tearing him away. One drew his weapon and fired point-blank at his back. Groaning, he sank to his knees. Then the blood came.

His sister struggled to free herself. "Vlad!"

As the gray-suit aimed at her brother's head, she let out an ear-piercing shriek. Warnick and I tried helping our comrade, but the other gray-suit kept his gun trained on us.

The CEO coughed violently, his face bright red. After catching his breath, he glared at us like a kid who'd gotten his ass kicked on the playground.

"I pity you," he said, barely getting the words out. Then to Trower, "End this now."

Walt faded into the shadows and was gone, his rasping cough echoing. Trower hadn't noticed, but I did—Sasha's irises had gone purple. Mewling, she freed one hand and clawed violently at her captor's face.

"Get the drug!" he said, fighting to keep her under control.

While one gray-suit covered us, the other hurried to a locked cabinet. His hand shaking, he got out a set of keys and tried each one till he could open the top drawer.

"Hurry, dammit!"

The Russian girl thrashed like a wild animal, her shrieking voice filling the room. With her hair obscuring her face, she viciously tore at Trower's head and neck. Slick blood dribbled onto his shirt collar as he fought to resist. In seconds, the other gray-suit joined him, clutching a glass syringe filled with iridescent purple liquid.

Sasha grabbed Trower's wrist, and with superhuman strength, snapped it. His weapon fell to the floor. As he cried out, she sent him reeling across the room like a ventriloquist's dummy. Out of instinct or fear, the gray-suit aimed at her chest.

"No!" Trower said, scrambling to regain his footing.

The hostile shot her anyway. A wave of loss and dread washed over me. God, I'd done everything You asked to save the Russian girl and her baby. You saw! But it wasn't enough. I'd failed—just like I failed Holly. Nothing left to do now except kill Trower.

The bullet had passed through Sasha into the wall. The room went quiet as she stared at the hole in her chest. There wasn't any blood. Fascinated, she touched the wound. Then, growling like an animal, she lunged at the gray-suit, who was too frightened to move. In a blind rage, she drove her fist into his chest and squeezed his heart till it stopped beating. Shuddering, he sank to the ground in a dead heap. She withdrew her bloody hand, which was still clutching the organ.

Seeing my chance, I struck the last gray-suit in the head

and took his gun. I locked my arm around his neck, and with my other hand, delivered a powerful jerk. Only it didn't kill him. Waving his arms and gagging, he lay on the floor, his head forever twisted to one side. I wanted to leave him that way, but my friend stepped in and shot him.

By now, the Russian girl was on Trower again. She gouged out his eyes with her thumbs as he tore at her arms. With fresh blood gushing from the sockets, he tried getting away. Unlike him, she was serene. Glancing at us with cold determination, she glowered at the object of her hatred and reached out her hand.

"Burn in hell," she said and tore out his throat.

Gurgling, he fell sideways as the blood spurted to the beat of his dying heart. Warnick pointed his weapon at her. This was Ariel all over again. I grabbed his arm. The Russian stood between his sister and us. Then he took her hand, and they fled. In the distance, voices erupted. Soon, Maritza and the others were in the room. She crossed to me.

"Where's Sasha?"

"Gone. With her brother."

Warnick holstered his gun. "Let's go."

I was the last to leave when I remembered Peter Asimov's request. In the cabinet drawer, I found a black leather case. It contained dozens of glass syringes filled with the serum. Each was labeled SURRELIS DRUG TRIAL 6160. I picked up the undamaged syringe from the floor and replaced it. Slinging the case strap over my shoulder, I headed out.

Outside in the hallway, I caught up with my friend. "What about Walt?"

"Forget about him."

"But he needs to die."

He grabbed my shoulders. I'd never seen such a look of

anger and disgust, and I thought he might hit me. His eyes never leaving mine, he spoke in a low, clipped voice.

"I won't tell you again," he said. "Let it go."

SEVENTY-SIX

The Russians could be anywhere. I worried that if they weren't careful, they'd end up like Ziggy. Warnick and Ryan took the lead, with Berta and Hen bringing up the rear. Maritza clung to my arm while gripping her Glock. John carried his AR-15 and stayed glued to my other side.

"This will never work," I said. "Too much ground to cover. Maybe we should split up."

My friend shook his head. "Too risky."

I was grateful he'd decided not to kill Sasha. Berta and Hen pushed past us to the front of the line. Everyone stopped.

"At least let us go," she said. "We can cover the other side of the building and be back in no time."

Warnick considered it. Then, "Radio silence unless there's a problem."

"Copy," Hen said.

The guards checked their weapons and radios. Then they trotted off into the darkness of the vast facility. I said a silent prayer.

Random skittering noises heightened my fear as we

searched room by room. Our only objective was to find the Russians and get them out safely. Still, I kept hoping Walt was in the building. Because when I found him, I'd end his fruitless life. Then I'd leave his bloated carcass to rot in this twisted tomb of science. I realized my fantasy was a waste of energy, though. He was miles from here—on his way to Washington, probably. There, he'd continue the vital work of schmoozing powerful congressional committees and starry-eyed military brass.

"What happens when we find her?" Maritza said. "From what you described, she's dangerous."

I didn't want to think about that. "She could control the virus before. Maybe if she stays calm—"

"She'll calmly kill us all," the Irishman said.

We passed the unfortunate lab animals and arrived at the room with the glowing tanks. A persistent beeping made us pause. Warnick and Ryan hurried ahead to investigate, moving cautiously between the rows of tanks. Suddenly, they stopped.

"What's going on?" I said.

Ryan pointed. "Look."

The nearest tank contained a man with blond hair. His eyes were open as he convulsed in silence. I noticed that the tube feeding him was filled with black liquid. With fear in his eyes, he gripped my hand. Seeing him brought tears to Maritza's eyes. The test subject opened his mouth to speak. Instead of words, water gushed out. Crouching, the Irishman examined the side and found a lighted panel, which displayed life functions.

An indicator glowed red. I looked at the frightened man. The poisonous fluid erupted from his mouth and oozed like crude oil. He stiffened and, staring straight up, relaxed.

Releasing his dead hand, I went to examine several more test subjects. All had died in that same torturous way.

"Someone wanted them dead," Ryan said to me.

"Walt Freeman. He's planning to shut down this site and bury the evidence."

My friend's radio clicked, and Berta's voice came on. "Higher, this is lower. Enemy spotted. Over."

Pressing his mouth to the microphone, he spoke quietly. "How many? Over."

"I count at least six."

"Feeding?"

"Hunting."

"Lower, do not engage. Repeat, do not engage." Side-eyeing the Irishman, he spoke into the radio again. "Get out of there. Do you copy?"

A long silence. Then, "Copy."

He put away his radio. "This place isn't secure. There are cutters in the area. We need to stay together. No one goes off on their own." Then to Maritza, "You okay?"

"I was until you made that speech."

When we'd started out, I wanted her by my side. Now, I regretted it. Though she had shown me she was resilient, she wasn't battle hardened. And then there was the problem of her debilitating anxiety. But it was too late—she was here. And I'd protect her. With guns up, we kept going, knowing that bloodthirsty cutters could overtake us at any moment. As we approached another set of doors, Maritza touched Warnick's shoulder.

"What if we can't locate them?"

"We'll find them," he said and continued without looking back.

SEVENTY-SEVEN

We'd come full circle. I spotted the double doors leading to the elevator bay. Maybe the Russians had found another ID badge and made their escape. A distant clanging noise echoed. It sounded like a crowbar hitting the concrete floor. Warnick signaled us to stop.

Warily, we made our way towards the light. Before we could reach the doors, Hen stepped in front of us, waving his hands. He directed us to an aisle, where Berta was waiting. Her body was tense as she gripped her rifle. Huddling close, we communicated in whispers.

"We heard a woman crying," she said.

John peered at the double doors. "They could be hiding in there. Did you check it out?"

"Negative. There are cutters all over the place. Hen and I took care of a few, but..."

"So, how do we do this?" I said.

Ryan consulted his laptop. "There's another corridor to the right. We might be able to come around the other side without being detected."

My friend checked the floor plan. "That might work."

We advanced single file to our new destination. Up ahead, another set of doors. Warnick waved Berta and Hen forward. With weapons up, they trotted ahead and peered through the windows. Hen grabbed a handle and eased open a door. We followed them into the darkness.

Shadowy wood crates containing machinery and other equipment lined the walls. This was a storage room. My heart jolted as the door slammed shut behind us. A cutter grinned through the glass like a demented child.

I tried the doors, but they were locked. Now the sound of chains clinking as someone rushed past. Something lifted Berta and Hen off the ground. Struggling, they aimed straight up and fired. A rifle fell, followed by another. Pointing his gun, my friend scanned the high ceiling, but it was too dark.

"We're in a kill box," the Irishman said.

Warnick side-eyed him. "Everyone stay together."

We formed a circle around Maritza and John, our rifles pointed outward. If someone was coming for us, we'd see them. Gurgling noises echoed from above, then something rained on us. Maritza felt her shirt and gasped.

My friend pulled out his flashlight. The light beam played off the guards' swinging bodies as their blood ran. The hostiles had slit their throats and taken their eyes and ears as trophies.

Berta shuddered—she was still alive. Using his handgun, Warnick shot each guard through the head. Another noise— they were close. He dropped the flashlight, his hand bleeding. I fired in a half-circle and reloaded.

Something blurred past, and I delivered another burst. Two cutters fell and tried army-crawling to safety. But I found their heads and finished them. More blurs. Ryan's mouth was wide open. Holding his weapon limply, he stared at his leg as blood spurted from an artery.

"Ah, feck!"

Instantly, his body shot straight up. Pushing the others against the wall, my friend peered at the ceiling while I scanned the immediate area. Aiming, he fired. Two more bodies fell—both hostiles. Then a third one dropped—the Irishman. We ran to the opposite doors. Also locked. Warnick glanced over his shoulder and waved us away. He fired at a handle and assessed the damage.

"We need explosives," he said.

I remembered something and felt my way through the dark. When I heard breathing, I knew I wasn't alone. I located the Irishman's body and knelt. Digging through the pockets, I found what I was looking for—two grenades—and got to my feet. Before I could rejoin the others, I was face-to-face with a cutter.

He leered at me, his eyes glowing purple in the darkness. When I saw the grab hook in his hand, I knew it was my turn to die. Dropping the grenades, I inched away. He tried flipping me around, but I crushed his hand against the wall with my rifle butt. Howling, he backed off, and I shot him in the head.

The bullet had entered near the temple. Dropping the grab hook, he wrenched his body to fight off the death spasms overtaking him. I picked up the hook and wound the chain around his neck. Unable to breathe, his eyes glassed up. Before losing consciousness, he grabbed my hand, and with the last of his strength, pulled me close.

"There is only one question," he said. "What am I?"

Wishing I had an answer, I watched him die. I handed a grenade to my friend. Using his knife, he cut the strap guard on a crate. Ordering us to take cover, he tied the grenade to the handle and pulled the pin. We had five seconds.

"Fire in the hole!"

Sprinting, he rejoined us as we crouched behind the crates and covered our ears. A deafening explosion rocked the room. When I looked up, a door was hanging off its hinges. He waved us forward, and one by one, we slipped through. My ears rang. I turned around as more hostiles appeared, all brandishing postmortem knives.

"Warnick!"

I tossed him the last grenade. He pulled the pin and, waiting a beat, rolled it towards the doors as the cutters advanced. We took cover around a corner. Another explosion. My friend and I returned to see what had happened. The doors were coated in blood and flesh. A severed hand lay outside, its fingers wrapped around a knife.

We found Sasha in the elevator bay, surrounded by dead cutters. She was holding her brother's lifeless body. Moved to tears, Maritza embraced her. Like a terrified child, she clung to the woman. Joining them, I extended my hand to the Russian girl.

"Come on," I said. "We're done here."

SEVENTY-EIGHT

It was nearly dawn when we left the facility. Above, the drones circled lazily, recording our movements with no one left to care. The last stars shone brilliantly in a sky tinged with red and gold. I heard music somewhere far away. It was the angel. She was singing "O Holy Night," and her voice was sweet and pure. I knew I was the only one who could hear her.

Rescuing Sasha had cost us five good people. At least Trower was dead. She held me tight as I carried her. Wearing only a patient gown, she was barefoot and felt small in my arms. The air was freezing. Stopping, I removed my coat and wrapped her in it. Then I carried her down the steps.

The angel's voice followed me. How could anything be wrong with the world on a morning like this? I felt my lips moving in prayer. Thanking God that the Russian girl was safe. I didn't know what would happen to her and the baby. But if only for this moment, I allowed myself to believe that everything would be all right.

"It's Christmas," Maritza said, taking my arm.

I remembered how much Holly and I used to look forward to the holidays, like a couple kids with no money and a million wishes. One year, we tried homemade presents—epic fail. But the exercise had us laughing for weeks. The best time was the year we had to work late at Staples. We'd been so busy, we hadn't bought presents. When we got off work, all the stores were closed. So we went home, ate leftover pizza, and gave each other our love under a warm comforter. Best Christmas ever.

Maritza stayed close as we made our way through the parking lot. Though she was covered in dried blood from that hellish death pit, she was happy. I didn't know what I would've done if I'd lost her too. She gave me a curious smile.

"What?" I said.

"Look at you. You saved the girl."

"*We* saved her."

There were rows of black Escalades parked in front of the building. I wondered how long before we found one with the keys in it. Warnick pulled an electronic device from his pocket. He approached the first vehicle and pressed a button. The Escalade not only unlocked itself, but the engine started.

"Are you kidding me right now?" I said.

"Black Dragon tech."

I helped Sasha into the backseat with John and Maritza on either side of her. My friend got behind the wheel, and I climbed into the front passenger seat.

"There's no way we got all the cutters," I said, looking back. "I wish I could blow it all up."

Outside the gate, a coyote trotted across the road. With its head low, it stared at us. Warnick gave the animal a quick horn blast, and it trotted off. We'd gone only a short distance when my friend slowed down. Up ahead, boulders and sand from a recent rockslide covered the road. Beyond that, another black Escalade lay upside down. No one was inside. The driver must not have seen the rocks till it was too late and lost control.

Farther up, a man in a suit limped along in the middle of the road. He was fat and walked slowly, each step a struggle. Warnick pulled over and grabbed my arm. Freeing myself, I got out. With my Glock in my hand, I marched up to the lone figure. He kept going as if I wasn't there.

"Walt!"

In obvious pain, the CEO turned around. There was a gash on his forehead, and his shirt was bloodstained. I considered the situation. Here he was all by himself, with no Trower or gray-suits to protect him. And there were no other drivers to act as witnesses. I knew what I had to do.

As I confronted the loathsome excuse for a man, my friend called after me. I ignored him and pointed my weapon at the object of my hatred. A keening in my ears turned my vision red. Behind me, Warnick and Maritza yelled, but I couldn't make out what they were saying.

"Going to kill me now?" Walt said.

There was a distance of maybe ten feet between us. Though my gun was pointed at his head, he was defiant. I was glad. It would make killing him even more satisfying.

"I have no choice," I said. "This ends with you."

"And you think you're going to be the one to stop this, is that it?"

"A man needs to start somewhere."

Warnick and Maritza stood on either side of me. I didn't care—this was inevitable. She tried reaching for my gun hand. When she realized my finger was on the trigger, she stopped. The moment I'd been waiting for was finally here. Yet somehow, it felt false.

"David, please," she said. "He's not worth it."

"You don't understand—I have to."

"No, you don't. You can let him walk. There are other ways to stop him. We have evidence now. We'll let the whole world know what he's done."

"Listen to her," my friend said. "We'll find another way, I promise."

I glowered at him. "What are we going to do? Arrest him for crimes against humanity?"

Maybe it was out of pity or that he saw me as ridiculous, but the CEO shook his head. Focusing my mind, I prepared to fire.

"Killing me accomplishes nothing, son," he said. "We're in the middle of an arms race."

"What the hell are you talking about?"

"I'm saying we're not the only ones. Our intelligence tells us similar projects are underway in Russia, China, North Korea, and Iran. And those are only the ones we know about. Like-uh-said, it's a race to see who gets there first. It has to be us, or game over."

"But aren't we supposed to be better than them?"

"Grow up, Dave. The world is a dangerous place. There's only one choice. Either we let the enemy win, or we fight. There was never any other option."

"No, there has to be another way."

Sighing, he started to turn away from me. I fired a warning shot. The bullet glanced off the asphalt near his foot. Our eyes locked. For the first time, I saw a tired old man who'd taken on a mission he never wanted. In truth, he was nothing more than a bureaucrat—good at making deals and moving around secret funds. But now, there was blood on his hands—a lot of blood he couldn't ignore.

"And there's really no way to stop this?" I said.

"Not even if I wanted to."

"It doesn't matter." Adjusting my aim, I concentrated on his face. "You need to die now."

"David, no!" Maritza said.

SEVENTY-NINE

Walt's expression was as blank as an unwritten tombstone. Here was a man who was ready to die, as I had been once. I almost squeezed the trigger. But then, a pinpoint of light appeared, rapidly growing in size and intensity. I had to shield my eyes.

It was the angel.

She stood near the rocks, a little girl with blonde hair and hurt green eyes. Wearing shorts and a T-shirt with the words *Li'l Princess*. A replica of the girl I'd put down in Tres Marias. Only now her clothes were clean. In an instant, she was between the CEO and me. She didn't say anything—she didn't have to. Because I was the one who was about to betray her.

A sudden realization hit me like a fist to the gut. It was something she'd tried teaching me all this time. An idea that, till now, I was incapable of understanding because my rage had blinded me. It was a simple truth, shiny and clean, like the angel herself.

I was supposed to be better—me.

Lowering my gun, I wiped my eyes. And when I opened

thcm again, she was gone. Walt stared at me, perplexed. It didn't matter that no one else had seen her. At last, after everything I'd been through, I understood why God had sent her. It was to save me.

"I hope you rot in hell," I said.

With Maritza's arm locked in mine, I returned to our vehicle. Before getting in, she touched my face.

"You saw something," she said. "What was it?"

"My past. And maybe my future."

"In time, you'll see we're right," the CEO said, his voice a distant dirge. "Take good care of the Russian girl."

We drove off, leaving him to fend for himself. I watched him in the side mirror as he became smaller and smaller. Soon, we were at the ravine. I carried Sasha down the steep incline so she wouldn't cut her feet.

"What about the other Humvee?" I said to Warnick.

"I'll send someone to retrieve it. And I need to recover the bodies of my squad. And Vlad." He touched the Russian girl's hand. "Your brother was brave the way he took them on. He loved you very much."

With tears in her eyes, she embraced him. "Thank you."

He pulled me aside. "I want you and Maritza to take Sasha to Tres Marias. I'll drop John and join you."

After helping the Russian girl into the backseat of my Tahoe, I opened the rear of the Humvee and found an RPG among the weapons. What kind of resistance had my friend been expecting? I retrieved a blanket and covered Sasha. Soon, she was asleep. As I was about to get into the SUV, the old man hugged me.

"Thanks," he said. "I would've killed him. But I understand why you didn't."

"Better get going before Consuelo sends out a posse."

Maritza kissed our new friend. "Take care of yourself."

Leaving that place of death, I didn't regret sparing Walt Freeman's life. He was already in hell. With the IPO, he'd secure funding to build a new facility in some other unlucky state. It was up to God to sort him out—I was done. Whatever happened, I was confident he would never again show his face in California.

Maritza and I said little as we navigated the uneven dirt road. The sun was full up, and the air had gotten warmer. I looked forward to returning to Tres Marias. No, it was more than that—I longed to be there. I couldn't help thinking about Maritza and me. What were the chances she would stay? And more than that, why would she? Her life was in LA. She had family and a career. Tres Marias could offer nothing to a bright young woman with a future in broadcasting. Maybe she'd surprise me.

The distant sound of beating helicopter blades cut through the stillness of the desert air. At first, I thought the highway patrol or the sheriff's department had gotten wind of the slaughter at Hellborn. The SUV shuddered as the chopper approached us. Slowing down, I peered through the windshield and saw it—black and unmarked. It was identical to the ones that had attacked us in Tres Marias.

"This isn't over," I said, gripping the wheel.

The helicopter descended in front of us, forcing me to hit the brakes. Turning one hundred eighty degrees to face us, it set down in the middle of the road. The sun glinted harshly off the windshield, but I could still make out Walt in the seat next to the pilot. A gray-suit armed with an AR-15 got out—a woman with short dark hair and wearing a sneer. As she aimed at us, Maritza grabbed my hand. Behind me, I could feel Sasha's warm, broken breath on my neck. Like the voice of God, the CEO spoke to us over a PA system.

"All I want is the Russian girl," he said.

Maritza reached over to calm Sasha, who was holding herself. I stared at Walt. Despite what the angel believed, it was a mistake letting him live. I told the women to stay inside as I exited the vehicle. With a clear line of sight, I pointed my Glock at his head. The hostile glanced back nervously.

"Don't do this. I thought I explained. You can't stop it—no one can. We need that baby."

I was right. It wasn't the Russian girl they were after—it was her child. She was the future, the edge we'd have over those other nation-states.

"You'll have to kill me first," I said.

The gray-suit moved in for a better shot. "No problem."

Before she could fire, an explosion ripped open the rear of the helicopter, driving her to the asphalt. When I looked up, the tail rotor was spiraling into the desert. Smoke and flames now as the cabin tipped forward. Frantic, the hostile reached for her gun. I put her down.

A second explosion ripped apart the chopper's frame, engulfing the interior. I jumped into the Tahoe and threw it into reverse. Carefully, I navigated around the burning hulk. The pilot was dead. Screaming, Walt pounded on the passenger door—his body on fire. Through the smoke, I saw Warnick's Humvee in the middle of the road. John was in the passenger seat. My friend stood there, holding the spent RPG and staring at the flames.

Stopping, I ran to him. "How did you know?"

He didn't answer right away. Then, "It was the way he mentioned Sasha at the end. Didn't feel right."

"You're so predictable," I said.

Maritza flicked on the stereo as we continued north. Jose

Feliciano's "Feliz Navidad" came on, making me smile. She took my hand.

"Dígame," she said. "So is this, like, a normal day for you?"

"Mm...semi-normal."

"Merry Christmas, David."

I kissed her hand. "I love you."

"Ha! I knew it," the Russian girl said from the backseat and buried herself under the blanket.

Stroking my face, Maritza gazed into my eyes. "Say it again."

"I love you."

Holly used to always make me laugh when she said *You butter*. She was the queen of malaprops. When Maritza pressed her smooth hand to my face and spoke, I thought maybe the Big Guy was throwing me a bone.

"Más te vale," she said. "You better."

EIGHTY

Sasha died in the summer giving birth. Isaac and Peter had done everything to keep her healthy and stable throughout the pregnancy. Because of her ability to control the virus, she needed only a minimal amount of the serum I'd brought from Hellborn. The scientist had fallen for the Russian girl, and though he never told her, hoped to marry her one day.

During the initial examination, the doctor looked for evidence of the bullet that had gone through his patient's chest. There was none. And the child she carried was a strong, healthy girl. Peter suggested a cesarean to save his sweetheart from the pain of childbirth. But Isaac overruled him and delivered the baby the old-fashioned way.

I can still remember her lying in the hospital bed, screaming in agony while trying to follow instructions. With coaching from her new boyfriend, she employed the breathing techniques she'd been taught. Maritza and I remained in the background as she struggled to bring forth new life.

"I can see the head!" Maritza said.

Amazed, I watched the tiny pale dome crowning. It was covered in fine blonde hair. I'd looked forward to experiencing this with Holly—the birth of our precious child. As more of the baby emerged, the doctor suctioned off the blood and amniotic fluid from her nostrils and mouth.

"Push!" he said. "Relax. And breathe."

It went on like this for what seemed like forever. Now, the baby's shoulders were visible. Isaac reached down and gently pulled the tiny body out the rest of the way. Peter used surgical scissors to cut the cord. In a last spasm, the afterbirth followed, and Sasha relaxed.

After cleaning up the infant, the nurse wrapped her in a sterile towel and brought the little bundle to her mother, who laughed and cried at the same time. Exhausted, she took her daughter in her arms and kissed her. The nurse placed drops in the baby's eyes and administered a shot of Vitamin K.

"She's perfect," the Russian girl said.

The room was thick with emotion. The scientist stood next to the bed, holding her hand. All of us marveled at this new life. I'd never expected to see this when I first learned the patient I had rescued was pregnant. And I knew one thing. Even though Walt Freeman was dead, Hellborn would never stop searching for this child. That's why we had to prepare.

Later, Maritza would use her media contacts to spread the story that Sasha had given birth to a stillborn baby that was cremated. Isaac had already agreed to support the lie by signing a fake fetal death certificate. Working long distance, Maritza and Karen planned to assemble the evidence we'd uncovered, including files, videos, and the Russian girl's blood sample. When they were ready, Karen would leak everything anonymously to the major news outlets.

"What will you name her?" Peter said.

Sasha didn't hesitate. "She is Alex."

The electronic equipment monitoring the Russian girl indicated that she was fine. Respiration, heart rate, blood pressure, and EKG tracing—everything looked normal. As we made plans for the future, the orderlies prepared to move the patient and her baby to a postpartum room. Then, an alert sounded.

Isaac rushed over to check the readings. Unaware there was a problem, Sasha looked peaceful holding her sleeping child. Without warning, she gasped, and her irises glowed purple. The virus wasn't done with her. He handed the baby to a nurse and ordered her to call a code. The Russian girl never made another sound. As he checked her pulse, he couldn't pinpoint the problem. Exhaling softly, she flat-lined. Immediately, he began CPR.

When the code team arrived, they sent us out of the room and went to work. Outside in the hallway, Maritza held Alex close and rocked her. The team did everything to save the patient. When the defibrillator and injections didn't work, they turned to Isaac. His eyes glistening, he called the time and pronounced Sasha dead. The first thought that came into my head was that the Russian girl was undead and would soon reanimate. Nothing happened—Sasha was gone.

We buried her and her brother's ashes in Redding, in the cemetery where Holly's body lay. As far as I knew, the Russians had not been religious. I lied to the priest, insisting they were Catholic. He sprinkled holy water on the coffins blanketed in flowers. After blessing them and forgiving their sins, he commended their souls to God.

I tossed the bag of worry dolls I'd bought Sasha onto her coffin and waited with Warnick, Isaac, and Maritza, who held Alex. Unable to cope, Peter had already returned to Baltimore. My friend promised to push through the paperwork needed to make me the baby's legal guardian. And Maritza said she would stay with me to help raise Alex, but only if we were married.

After the funeral, I slipped away to visit my late wife. I thought I'd never again set foot in this place—the memories were too painful. But I was glad I came. It was June—almost a year since the nightmare in Tres Marias had begun. A warm breeze wafted through the trees as I stood near her gravestone and read what was carved there. HOLLY MITCHELL PULASKI. WIFE AND MOTHER.

"I'm sorry," I said through my tears. "I tried to save her. But we have Alex now. And I think—I *know*—you would've loved her like she was your own."

The angel stood a few feet away. A brilliant light shone around her, making it hard to see her among the gravestones. But I knew it was her. She raised her child's arms to me as an offering. The light intensified into a blinding whiteness and winked out. When my vision cleared, Holly was standing in her place, wearing the loose-fitting summer dress I loved. She was radiant and seemed at peace. I wanted so much to be with her, but I knew I couldn't. I had a child to look after— that was my new mission.

"I love you so much," I said, dropping to my knees.

"You butter," I thought I heard her say.

I wiped away the tears. When I looked up again, she was gone. I turned to find Maritza standing next to me, cradling the baby. With the diamond in her engagement ring catching the light, she extended her hand.

"It's time to come home," she said.

Dave's not here because I call myself David now. When God made Abram the father of a nation, He gave the old man a new name—Abraham. I don't mean to compare myself to that famous guy. I'm easily one of God's lowliest creatures, with enough flaws to fill a book of sorrow. Still, I believe He has a plan for me. In His way, He's telling me to raise Sasha's child as my own. And for that, I must have a new name.

Alex means "protector of men." I don't know what God has in store for her, but I'm sure of one thing. Till she's old enough to fulfill her own destiny, I'll be there.

Always.

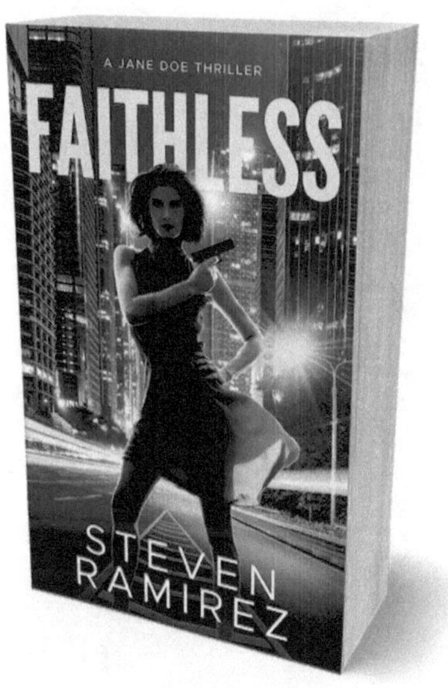

A JANE DOE THRILLER
FAITHLESS
STEVEN
RAMIREZ

YOUR FREE BOOK IS WAITING...

When your boss pulls a gun on you, it might be time to quit.

Get your free copy of *Brandon's Last Words: A Jane Doe Thriller Prequel.*

BOOKS.STEVENRAMIREZ.COM/GET-THRILLER

ABOUT THE AUTHOR

Steven Ramirez is the award-winning American author of thriller, supernatural, and literary fiction. A former screenwriter, he's written about man-made plagues and idyllic towns infested with ghosts and demons. His latest novel is *Let's Get Lost*, a modern fairy tale. Steven lives in Los Angeles.

AUTHOR WEBSITE

stevenramirez.com

instagram.com/byStevenRamirez

goodreads.com/byStevenRamirez

bookbub.com/authors/steven-ramirez